The
Revealing

Books by Suzanne Woods Fisher

Amish Peace: Simple Wisdom for a Complicated World

Amish Proverbs: Words of Wisdom from the Simple Life

Amish Values for Your Family: What We Can Learn from the Simple Life

A Lancaster County Christmas

LANCASTER COUNTY SECRETS

The Choice

The Waiting

The Search

SEASONS OF STONEY RIDGE

The Keeper

The Haven

The Lesson

THE INN AT EAGLE HILL

The Letters

The Calling

The Rescue: An Inn at Eagle Hill Novella (ebook)

The Revealing

THE ADVENTURES OF LILY LAPP (WITH MARY ANN KINSINGER)

Life with Lily

A New Home for Lily

A Big Year for Lily

A Surprise for Lily

The Revealing

A Novel

SUZANNE WOODS FISHER

Revell

a division of Baker Publishing Group
Grand Rapids, Michigan

© 2014 by Suzanne Woods Fisher

Published by Revell
a division of Baker Publishing Group
P.O. Box 6287, Grand Rapids, MI 49516-6287
www.revellbooks.com

Printed in the United States of America

Library of Congress Cataloging-in-Publication Data
Fisher, Suzanne Woods.
    The revealing : a novel / Suzanne Woods Fisher.
        pages cm — (The Inn at Eagle Hill ; 3)
        ISBN 978-0-8007-2095-7 (pbk.)
        1. Amish—Fiction. 2. Mennonites—Fiction. 3. Bed and breakfast accommodations—Fiction. I. Title.
    PS3606.I78R48 2014
    813'.6—dc23   2014007058

Scripture used in this book, whether quoted or paraphrased by the characters, is taken from the New King James Version. Copyright © 1982 by Thomas Nelson, Inc. Used by permission. All rights reserved.

This book is a work of fiction. Names, characters, places, and incidents are the product of the author's imagination or are used fictitiously. Any resemblance to actual events, locales, or persons, living or dead, is coincidental.

Published in association with Joyce Hart of the Hartline Literary Agency, LLC

15 16 17 18 19 20   7 6 5 4

To my son, Gary,
who has a special knack
for encouraging others
to be originals

1

This secret life was doing her in.

At times, Naomi King wondered how in the world she had become so secretive. She used to be the type who would answer any question, talk to anyone about anything. No longer. Maybe years of enduring dreadful migraines that had kept her pinned home so much of the time, waiting for the worst to pass, had made her more reticent and reclusive. Maybe it was because she'd never had a reason to keep a secret of this magnitude. Most likely, it was because she didn't realize what she was missing until now. It was as if she had come out of the shadows and into the real world.

And it all had to do with Tobe Schrock.

Tobe was serving out a sentence at FCI Schuykill in Minersville for withholding evidence about wrongdoings in Schrock Investments, his late father's investment company, from the Securities Exchange Commission. Minersville was a one-hour-and-thirty-one-minute bus ride from Lancaster, plus another twelve-minute bus ride from Lancaster to Stoney Ridge. Naomi had it timed to the second.

Except for today, when the bus to Stoney Ridge had run late.

As she walked down the lane, she unrolled a half-eaten pack of Tums, chewed two tablets, and tried very hard to do nothing but take deep breaths and think about Tobe. It helped a little, but not enough. She found herself nervously twirling the strings of her prayer cap and forced her hands down by her sides. Stubbornly, she wrestled against the anxiety. If Galen were already home and asked where she had been, she wouldn't lie to him. *I will not lie.* She had never once lied to him, though she didn't tell him everything, either.

So what would she tell him? The band around her chest cinched tighter and her pulse picked up speed. She would say that she had gone visiting a friend on a Sunday afternoon, which was true. And yet it wasn't. Tobe wasn't just a friend. He was much, much more than that. But Galen, her dear, intrusive, overprotective brother, could never understand that.

She heard a horse nicker in the darkness and another one answer back, and panic swooped down and seized her from head to toe.

She took another Tums and chewed fast.

She couldn't keep this up. She couldn't keep the secret about Tobe much longer. Today he had promised her that the time was coming soon when everything would be out in the open. He said he would be released from prison soon. Any day now.

But until then? Her hands were trembling and her stomach was churning and her heartbeat thundered. Galen *must* be home by now. The horses would need to be fed soon.

Unease tightened in her stomach. She took three more Tums out of the package and chewed them, fast and hard.

Oh . . . where had she left that bus schedule to Minersville? *Where, where, where?* If her brother found out she had been to see Tobe Schrock . . . at a federal prison . . . She cringed.

Naomi and Tobe were an unlikely pair, she knew that. He had been born Amish but spent his growing up years in a Mennonite church and remained unbaptized. Uncertain. Worldly. She was sheltered, overprotected by her brother. Her life was on the horse farm that her brother managed. Her work was to care for their home and be a part of the Amish church, and she loved her life.

Her brother did not think well of Tobe Schrock. It wasn't just because of the recent troubles the Schrock family had with their investment company imploding—his disdain went farther back. He considered Tobe to be lazy and selfish, an opinion based on Tobe as a young teen. But Naomi saw past that and found so much more in Tobe. She believed the best about him. There was a fine man in there, a diamond in the rough, and she was desperately, hopelessly in love with *that* man.

She took a new pack of Tums out of her dress pocket, chewed two tablets, and swallowed so fast she didn't even taste the chalky cherry flavor, turned down the wooded driveway of the King farm, and stopped short. There, in front of the house, was her brother Galen. He stood with his arms crossed against his chest, deep in conversation with Bishop Elmo and Deacon Abraham.

Lightning split the sky, followed by a great clap of thunder and a torrent of soft raindrops. There was a sweet smell in the air on this gray Monday morning, the mulchy smell of wet earth. Spring was but a promise, but a promise was better than winter.

Rose Schrock crossed the yard to the henhouse with an empty basket in her arms, hardly aware of the rain that was falling, mindful of all she needed to do before the children returned from school. The guest flat needed to be cleaned, aired out, fresh sheets and towels brought in. She just received a message on the machine in the phone shanty from a woman who wanted to reserve the guest flat for an extended stay. The woman said she needed a quiet place to "reinvent herself"—whatever *that* meant.

Rose felt relieved to have someone stay in the guest flat during the off-season. The inn had provided a far more steady stream of guests than she could have imagined, mostly because of the mistaken notion of Eagle Hill as a place where miracles occurred. But the stream of visitors drizzled in December and came to a complete stop in January, February, and March. It was a worry. This was her first year as an innkeeper. She didn't know if it was normal to expect a seasonal dip or if it meant an inevitable decline, but she did know she counted on that income to help make ends meet for her family.

Something on the road caught her eye and she stopped for a moment. It was a truck, following a buggy, and it looked as if they were turning into the vacant property across the road. She'd heard that a new Amish family was moving into the district. Vera, her mother-in-law, who rarely left home but knew the business of everyone, said that the recently widowed father was a minister. He had bought the Bent N' Dent grocery store, looking for a fresh start for his brood, and Rose certainly understood that. A fresh start sounded delightful on days when life's complications seemed to hold her by the ankles.

The chickens fussed and clucked as she entered the rickety henhouse. She let them out into the yard and gathered the eggs in the nest boxes, taking care with Harriet, the old hen who refused to leave her nest and pecked with a vengeance. When the basket was full, Rose hurried outside and latched the door behind her. As she turned, she found Galen King, her particular friend and neighbor, waiting for her with an odd look on his face.

"Rose, there's something I need to talk to you about." His voice was both soft and gruff, very, very bass, like rumbling thunder from the next county. She loved the sound of it.

He paused, shifting from one foot to another as if he had a pebble in his shoe. He coughed, and Rose saw a bead of perspiration trickle down his temple under his black felt hat. She looked at him, wondering if he wasn't coming down with a fever and thinking that standing here in the rain couldn't be good for him if he was. "Come inside for a cup of coffee."

He glanced toward the house. "Vera's inside, isn't she?"

"Yes. In the kitchen."

He cleared his throat and met her eyes at last. "Then, no. I'd rather say what I have to say in private."

"Well, could we at least get out of the rain?" She walked over to the porch and spun around to face him, a tad impatient. He followed behind, glancing nervously at the kitchen windows to see if Vera was peering out them. What did Galen have on his mind? It was cold and her feet were wet. She was in no mood for a mystery. "Is something wrong?"

"No, no, nothing's wrong. Well, actually, maybe there is. Did something happen to trouble Naomi yesterday?"

"Nothing that I know of. Why?"

"Bishop Elmo and Deacon Abraham dropped by yesterday afternoon to ask if I would take on another apprentice, since Jimmy Fisher is busy with the chickens."

That didn't surprise Rose—she knew Galen had more work than he could manage—but she held out a hope that he might wait for Tobe, to apprentice him after his release. Beyond Galen, Rose noticed a porch gutter was clogged with leaves, causing the water to spill over the gutters. The droplets fell to puddles on the ground with uneven *plips*. She looked at him, not sure what an apprentice had to do with Naomi. It wasn't typical of Galen to circle around the block before getting to his point. "So . . . about Naomi . . . ," she urged.

"Naomi walked up the driveway like she'd seen a ghost, then shot past us and into the house. Acted as twitchy as a cow's tail at fly time all evening long."

Rose shivered in the damp air. "I can ask Bethany if she knows something, though I'm not sure she'd tell me." She started to move past him.

He reached out to stop her, his hands on her arms. "But Naomi's not the reason I stopped by." He glanced over her shoulder to the kitchen windows. Satisfied Vera wasn't peering out at them, he looked straight into Rose's eyes, took a deep breath, and said, "I think it's time we moved things along."

She glanced around the farm and saw all the things that needed moving along—a pasture fence that needed repairing, a barn door that kept falling off its track, a sagging clothesline that was threatening to fall over in the next big windstorm. She was surprised it had lasted through the winter. In May, they were due to take a turn hosting church at Eagle Hill. The to-do list was endless. Where to start?

But Galen's face had such a strange look on it, uncomfortable and shy, not like a man who was creating a to-do list. A blush began to creep up his face. Slowly, his meaning began to dawn on her and she was astounded. "Galen!" she exclaimed. "Are you asking me to marry you?"

His eyes flew open wide, and he swallowed hard. "Doesn't it sound like I am?"

"Well. Sort of. Maybe. Not quite." The more she said, the sillier she felt. But at the risk of embarrassing him even further, she knew she'd better make her position clear. She wasn't ready. Her husband Dean hadn't been gone two full years and things were still unsettled, unfinished.

Galen took another deep breath. "Yes. Yes, I am. I am asking you to marry me." He took her two hands in his. "Rose, there will always be obstacles. I want us to face those things together. I want us to get married. Soon."

"I . . . I don't know what to say."

"Just say yes." To Galen, everything was simple.

But it wasn't a simple question. The very thought of getting married was ridiculous. It made no sense. Frankly, their entire relationship made no sense! She was older than Galen by more than a few years. She had a family—two stepchildren, three children, plus a very cranky mother-in-law; he had never married. She was still trying to unravel the mess of her husband's investment company gone awry. Tobe, Dean's son, was serving time in jail. Jake Hertzler, a key player in the downfall of the company, charged with all kinds of terrible crimes, hadn't been found. Getting married was the furthest thing from her mind.

And why now, on a rainy Monday morning, would Galen blurt out something like asking her to marry him? Why not yesterday, when the sun was shining as they had picnicked up at Blue Lake Pond?

Yet such an unrehearsed proposal was so like him. Words were few with Galen, but when he did speak, they were impactful. He was a man of action instead of words, purpose rather than intention. So different from her first husband, who could stir up a dust cloud with his fancy way with words.

Rose remembered the first time she had noticed Galen—truly noticed him. It was a sunny afternoon, sometime after the foggy period when Dean had passed, and Galen had offered to teach her how to drive a buggy. She had been raised Amish but had left the church over a dozen years ago. She hadn't been near a horse in as many years and it was high time she grew comfortable with them again. As she was climbing into the buggy, the horse pranced sideways at a scurrying mouse, and Rose leaped back with a screech, startled. Immediately Galen stepped forward, taking the bridle, rubbing the mare's forehead, and the horse soon quieted. But Rose's reaction must have been so unexpected to Galen that his eyes went wide.

"I take exception to mice," she explained, feeling color rise in her cheeks.

Then Galen broke out in a rich laugh. Never having seen him even smile before, she was unprepared for the impact. The sight was incredible; it completely changed him. She had not known his eyes to sparkle in such a way, his jaw to be so perfect, his throat so tan, his mouth so handsome. It was the first time she saw all that he could be.

An embarrassed laugh left her throat, then a second, and soon her laughter joined his and she suddenly found herself feeling happy. Happier than she had felt in a long, long time.

He had held out both his hands to her to help lift her into the buggy and she felt an unexpected jolt of excitement. As they sat together in the small buggy, she was as close to him as she'd ever been and the thought made her light-headed.

Each time she saw him after that buggy ride, there was a knife-edgy feeling in the pit of her stomach. Galen was so quiet and composed that she had no idea he felt the same way. It was months later that he admitted he had fallen in love with her.

With the rain falling behind him, Rose looked at Galen. He had a rugged, capable face. Firm features, determined jawline, placid eyes. She saw the great kindness in his expression, and she saw his wisdom, which was well beyond his years. She saw compassion in those green, green eyes. She saw love there.

It made no sense to marry now. No sense at all.

But . . . the thing about love was, once started, it couldn't easily be stopped. A voice that she was surprised to realize was hers said, "Yes, Galen. I believe I would like to marry you."

2

Bethany popped up in bed again and stared at the window. For one crazy moment she thought Jimmy Fisher might have come calling. He certainly needed to do something to make amends to her after totally deserting her two nights ago. He had told her that he wanted to take her home after the youth gathering on Sunday night, and so she expected him to be there, but he never showed up.

She ended up going home with Simon Glick, a thoroughly awkward young man. So tall, his elbows and knees seemed to stick out at angles and she felt that if he fell he might break into small pieces. And yet that was a little unfair, because he wasn't all that clumsy—he only looked as if he might be. In fact, he was more talkative than she expected. He even made her laugh once or twice. Nothing like the way Jimmy made her laugh, but it would serve him right if she started going out with Simon Glick.

She shifted on her bed to try to get more comfortable and shut her eyes. She tried to think of nothing, but crazy thoughts kept shooting through her mind.

Bethany picked up her pen and wrote "Mrs. Jimmy Fisher"

on the page of her journal. Not that she wanted Jimmy Fisher to propose, but she wondered if he might. And when.

She must have dozed off because, a short while later, she was startled awake when her room filled with light. A broad beam of light swept the wall and the ceiling, circling again and again. She came up on her elbows, heart pounding, crawled out of bed, and knelt at the window. At first she could see nothing; then Jimmy Fisher removed his hat, waving furiously at her, and the moon bounced off the crown of his hair.

She should ignore him and go back to bed. She knew she should. But of course she didn't. She slipped into her clothes, wrapped a shawl around her shoulders—it was only March and the air was brittle—and hurried out to meet him.

She would scold him, of course, for dragging her out on a night as cold as this one, with off-and-on rain, but then she'd climb in the buggy with him, hidden at the end of the driveway, and they'd go to one of their favorite spots to talk. And hug. And cuddle. And kiss. And when things got a little heated, she would act indignant and insist he take her home again. On the way back, she would let her shoulder bump up against his now and then to know that she didn't mean it.

It was a game they played, and one that Bethany hoped would entice Jimmy to think about how nice it would be not to have to say good night. To get married and live happily ever after. *Shootfire!* Was that too much to ask?

Jimmy was waiting with the flashlight, which he turned off the minute he saw her framed in the doorway. Once Bethany walked outside, he caught her in his arms and tipped his forehead against hers. She could feel his breath, his words, falling onto her. He tilted his face so that their mouths came together.

She wedged her hands up between them to set her distance. "And where were you on Sunday night, Jimmy Fisher? You can't just show up like I'm at your beck and call and think I'm available for kissing."

She looked at him, daring him to say he was sorry. Instead, he said, "My mother was so distraught . . . you know . . . after you dumped her out of the wheelchair—"

"Dumped is a strong word. I prefer to think of it as tipped." Edith Fisher was recuperating from bunion surgery, and Bethany wheeled her outside after the fellowship lunch at church to get some fresh air and a little sunshine. There was a ramp, after all, and the air was unusually warm, almost springlike.

But Bethany had never taken a wheelchair down a ramp. As she guided Edith backward, the wheelchair started to gain momentum. Edith's weight, plus the wheelchair's, surpassed Bethany's. At the bottom of the ten-foot ramp, the wheelchair flipped sideways and dumped Edith out, facedown on the grass.

Naomi, Edith's favorite girl, ran for a wet rag to hold against the scrapes on her forehead and a towel for a pillow. Edith, furious and humiliated, wouldn't accept Bethany's profuse apologies. Jimmy ended up taking his mother home early.

"—after I finally got her settled down, I fell asleep on the couch and when I woke up, it was morning."

"Did you happen to hear that Susie Glick and Tim Riehl have an Understanding? And Elizabeth Mast and Eli Miller do too." She squeezed his hands. "Eli said he'd like to marry before spring planting starts." That's exactly what Bethany would like to have now . . . a formal Understanding. She would like to know where she stood with Jimmy Fisher.

"Hmmm," Jimmy said, nuzzling that tender spot on her neck that he knew she liked.

"It's nice, isn't it, when a couple has an Understanding? When the fellow steps up and makes a decision to move forward."

"Mmm-hmm."

"Folks say that weddings always come in threes."

"Yup."

"You haven't heard a word I've said, have you?"

"Mmm-hmm."

Bethany's temper went up like a March kite. She broke away from him and thrust her hands on her hips. "Ever since you've been taking care of those chickens full-time, you have turned right back into the boy I first met. As immature as can be."

Enjoyment fled Jimmy's face. He sighed and met Bethany's gaze. "I know. You're right. There's something about those birds that makes me feel like I'm thirteen all over again. It's those chickens. They're running me ragged . . ." His voice trailed off. "You know, I've hated chickens for as long as I can remember. They stink, they squawk, they peck at me. They make me stink and squawk and act peckish."

He was always griping about those chickens and she was tired of hearing about it. It wasn't just the chickens. It was living under his mother's thumb. As Galen King always said, Edith Fisher cast a long shadow on her boys. She sucked the joy of life out of them. And when Jimmy was away from his mother, like now, he acted like a silly schoolboy on summer break. Nothing on his mind whatsoever. She walked a few steps away from him and looked up at the clouds gliding past the moon. He followed behind and slipped his arms around her waist.

"Jimmy, the solution is simple. You need to find someone to work for your mother."

"It's not that easy." He sounded a million miles away. Miles from Bethany and from Eagle Hill.

"You'd better figure it out. And you'd better start making noises about our future together, Jimmy Fisher, because if you don't take me more seriously—"

Spinning her around to face him, Jimmy put a finger to her lips, reached for her hand, and pulled her out of the moonlight and into the shadows. "I take you plenty seriously! You're my best girl, Bethany."

Immediately her temper sizzled. "I'd better be your only girl, Jimmy Fisher!" She knew her voice had risen an octave and sounded sharp, and she regretted it. But he was always saying they would get married someday, and someday never seemed to come. Perhaps the rainbows had gone and the glow had dimmed for Jimmy. If so, she'd rather know it now.

He lifted his eyes. "That's what I meant. You're my only girl. My best and only girl." He took his hat off. "Aw, Bethany, what's the rush? We're young. We have our whole lives ahead of us."

"Maybe you do, but I'm not about to waste my life on a fellow who hates chickens and won't do anything about it. I only agreed to go out with you because I thought you were a fellow with some plans for himself."

"I did have plans! I did. Good ones. But without Lodestar as the cornerstone, my entire horse breeding business fell apart."

She rolled her eyes. "There *are* other horses."

He cut a smile in her direction. "None like that horse."

She let out a big sigh. "Have you looked for him?"

"Every chance I've had. That's what I've been doing on Saturday afternoons." So *that's* where he'd been when he was supposed to be stopping by Eagle Hill.

"What about Galen? Have you asked him to look for you?"

"He's no help at all. He told me I needed to let that horse go and stop making excuses for being a man." He rubbed his chin. "I'd like him to have a week living with my mother, then he can tell me all about being a man."

"So you're saying that if you had Lodestar back, your life would be back on track. You'd have your future mapped out."

His dark eyebrows lifted.

"Did you hear me?"

"I heard you." He cleared his throat. "If I could ever get Lodestar back, I think everything else will fall into place."

"Like . . . our future."

Jimmy ran his finger around his collar and smiled at her ruefully.

Lately, Jimmy Fisher had begun to feel something like . . . the word "panic" crept into his head, but he pushed it away. He didn't do panic. He just felt . . . unsettled, that was it.

As he had left Bethany last night, all the emotional jumble inside him came together in his stomach. He was crazy about Bethany Schrock. Her smile, when she turned it on him full force, was numbing. It made his bones turn to butter. She was the girl he saw himself growing old with. She was everything he'd ever wanted. Why was he scared to death to ask her to marry him? Was old Hank Lapp's prediction about him true? "Always shopping, never buying." He frowned, hearing Hank's loud voice echo in his head.

No. It wasn't that. There were just too many unsettled things in his life right now.

He adjusted the brooder lamps, checked the feeders, muttering away about how much he hated chickens, and walked over to the workbench to get a Band-Aid for his finger. He kept a big box of Band-Aids in the pullet barn, on the ready. There were a couple of hens who had it in for him. He was convinced they waited for him to enter the pullet barn, then sent a secret signal down the line of the nesting boxes so they would all come flying at him, beaks and claws sharpened. Today, one of them drew blood from his hand as he refilled the water trough.

He glanced through the open barn door and smiled at the sight of Honey, grazing in the pasture. She was a fine little mare, almost like a pet. He would take carrots from the garden and feed them to her by hand. He delighted in her so much that he always gave her a brushing before he harnessed her. He kept a little horse brush in his back pants pocket just for that purpose. This was the mare he had hoped to breed with Lodestar. The perfect complement to Lodestar. She was the one.

Galen King had given him Honey as a sorry filly and wouldn't take a dime for her. "Not fast enough to race," he told Jimmy, "too small for a full day's work, not strong enough to pull the team." But as smart as Galen usually was about horses, he wasn't thinking about Honey as a broodmare. And he certainly wasn't factoring in Lodestar's fine genes. A sorry filly, indeed.

If only Jimmy could find Lodestar's whereabouts. He was sure everything would work out once he had Lodestar back in his stall, locked up good and tight because that horse had a streak of Houdini in him, and his breeding business could begin. Bethany was right. Once Lodestar was back with Jimmy, everything else would fall into place. He swallowed past a knot the size of a goose egg in his throat. Even the part about Bethany Schrock.

The air smelled of lightning, and the breeze from the south carried a scent of heavy rain. All the signs were good that rain would arrive soon.

As soon as Naomi saw the barn door slide shut behind Galen, she pulled out her box of stationery from the kitchen desk and sat down to write a letter to Tobe. If she hurried, she could get it into the mailbox before the postman drove by.

Dear Tobe,

When I arrived home on Sunday afternoon, there, on the kitchen table, was the bus schedule. Just what I was afraid of! But you must have been praying: although Galen had beat me home, he hadn't gone in the house yet. The deacon and the bishop were waiting for him in the yard. They had a few suggestions for an apprentice for Galen's horse work, but he turned them all down. You know how finicky he can be about anyone around his horses. Anyway, I was able to dash into the house and hide the bus schedule before they all came in for coffee. My hands shook as I poured coffee in the bishop's mug. Shook like a leaf!

How much longer, Tobe? I can't keep this up. We need to tell him. Them. All of them.

Love,
Naomi

The storm that blew through Stoney Ridge this morning split two trees near the creek that ran alongside Eagle Hill. Water flowed over the road like a river. Behind the farmhouse, a trail that led up the ridgeline had turned into a small waterfall.

To Bethany Schrock, there were few displays on earth more thrilling than a thunderstorm. Her friend and neighbor, Naomi, felt quite the opposite. She was sure Naomi had passed the whole of the storm with a shawl pressed to her eyes.

By the time the rain was letting up, Bethany was on her way to the Sisters' House, where she worked a couple days a week for five elderly sisters. Once a week, she and Naomi made lunch for the down-and-outers of Stoney Ridge at the Second Chance Café held in the Grange Hall, but that was volunteer work. She'd been volunteered for it by the sisters. Her main job was the Sisters' House.

Her job entailed cleaning out and organizing the ancient sisters' home so they could take a long-overdue turn at hosting church, but it was an endless task. She loved them, though, each one. Ella, the eldest, insightful, kind. Ada, sensitive and cheerful. Lena, the middle sister, tender, a peacemaker. Fannie, efficient, determined, bossy. Sylvia, the youngest, capable, creative.

Today, Sylvia met her at the door and waved a letter in her face. "We have exciting news, Bethany! You have to stop your downstairs organizing and start right away on the guest bedroom."

"The second-floor guest bedroom," Fannie clarified.

"Yes. That's the one," Sylvia said. "I haven't been up there in years and years."

Bethany took off her bonnet and tried to find an empty

wall peg by the door, frowning because she had just emptied those wall pegs of umbrellas and old bonnets and a man's straw hat a few days ago, and they were completely filled up again. "Are you expecting company?"

"Yes!" Sylvia said. "A relation. He's come to Stoney Ridge to investigate the family tree. It's very exciting."

As they walked into the living room, Bethany nodded to Ella, Lena, and Ada, all seated in their favorite chairs.

"It's terribly exciting," Lena said, looking up from her knitting project.

"He told us he was hitting brick walls," Ada said, engrossed in a crossword puzzle in an old copy of the *Stoney Ridge Times*.

Ella, a woman with a soft fan of wrinkles beside each eye and curly gray hair that peeked from under her prayer cap, looked from sister to sister. "That sounds painful." At ninety-three, she was easily confused.

"I don't think he meant it literally, Ella," Fannie said. "It's genealogy lingo that means he is stumped."

"How do you happen to know about genealogy bingo, Fannie?" Lena said.

"Lingo," Fannie said in a brisk tone, "not bingo."

As Lena paused to ponder her response, Bethany knew she had to jump in and veer the sisters back to the original subject quickly or it would be lost forever. It often happened. Most of their conversation ended up on little bunny trails that led nowhere. "How close a relative is he?"

The sisters looked at each other blankly.

"Distant," Fannie said.

"Fourteenth cousin twice removed," Sylvia said. "He's coming soon, he said. By week's end. You can manage, can't you?"

Bethany sighed. If the second floor looked anything like the first floor, basement, and carriage house, her week had just taken a dismal downhill turn.

Five hours later, Bethany stopped by Naomi's house before she headed home to Eagle Hill. She was exhausted. Discouraged too. That upstairs bedroom was going to take her all week to clean out. And where would she put things? Managing that Sisters' House took every spare ounce of energy she had.

She was eager to show Naomi the quilt top she had finally finished last night and also to share a letter from her brother, Tobe. Under Naomi's tutelage, Bethany was finishing her first quilt for her eventual-but-not-official wedding to Jimmy Fisher. She'd started plenty of quilts over the years but abandoned them because she hated to sew. But Naomi was adamant that she needed to finish *something*. She gave her assignments to do and checked up on her tasks: cut, trim, sort, sew. Then: undo, rip out, redo. Bethany had hoped the quilt would be finished by now, but Naomi kept insisting it had to be perfect.

Good thing Jimmy Fisher didn't seem to be in a rush to get married, because this quilt wasn't making much progress. She frowned. *Shootfire!* What *was* taking Jimmy Fisher so long to propose? Just once she'd like him to behave the way she expected, but the fact that he never did was one more reason she couldn't seem to get enough of him.

As Naomi opened the door, Bethany inhaled a sweet scent of cinnamon and nutmeg floating in from the kitchen. "What did you make?"

"A new recipe for pumpkin cinnamon rolls," Naomi said. "I thought I'd practice the recipe before serving them at the next Sisters' Bee. Want to try one?"

Bethany nodded. Baking was her favorite thing in the world. Her younger sister, Mim, preferred to read or write. Naomi would rather quilt. But Bethany would rather be in the kitchen than anywhere else. As she grabbed a fork and sat down to eat, she slid Tobe's letter closer to Naomi and watched her reaction. Naomi stilled as she saw the thin gray envelope, addressed in Tobe's sloppy handwriting. Then she snapped to attention and went back to stirring sugar into her tea. "You brought the quilt top for me to see?"

"Yes, and I brought Tobe's letter for you to read, if you might be interested."

Naomi took a sip of tea. "Any news?"

"He hopes he'll be released soon. But no date yet. That lawyer is trying to pea bargain for him."

"I think you mean plea bargain," Naomi said.

Bethany pushed the letter closer to Naomi. "You can read it for yourself."

"No need," Naomi said breezily. "You've told me what's in it. Now, let's see about that quilt top."

Bethany was sure Naomi was sweet on Tobe, just *sure* of it, though she could never get her to admit it.

And wouldn't you know that Naomi insisted she rip out the last row of the quilt top just because a few corners didn't match up? "Why should it matter?"

Naomi sighed a deep sigh. "Bethany . . . imagine adding a tablespoon of salt into a recipe when you were only supposed to add a teaspoon. It would matter a great deal. Same with quilting." She held out the quilt top. "You need to redo the binding before the next Sisters' Bee. We had planned to help you quilt it."

Naomi was turning into a bossy hen, that's what she was.

Bethany took the quilt top back and examined it. She'd only been going to the Sisters' Bee for a few months and she was already tired of the quilting business. But she loved Naomi and she loved the old sisters and she was even feeling a twinge of affection now and then for Edith, Jimmy Fisher's mother. Nothing more than a twinge, but at least she wasn't frightened of her anymore. She might not be Edith's choice for a future daughter-in-law—everyone in Stoney Ridge knew her favorite girl was Naomi King—but at least she was accepting that Jimmy and Bethany had an Understanding.

At least, she thought they did, until last Sunday's unfortunate incident.

Bethany sighed. The wheelchair tipping might have set back her and Jimmy's Understanding.

After finishing the pumpkin cinnamon roll, she gathered up Tobe's letter—which Naomi never even bothered to read—and her quilt top with the unaligned border corners and went on her way.

Naomi snipped off the end of a piece of thread with her teeth. Last evening, Bethany had brought over her re-sewn quilt top and together they had spread it across the frame, over a layer of white batting and the backing to the quilt. She had promised Bethany she would help quilt it, but she was regretting that promise. It pained her to see the mismatched corners, the triangles with missing points, the crooked seams.

Naomi idly threaded a needle and bowed her head over a quilt square, making small, even stitches without the benefit of a ruler or a machine. She remembered what Tobe had said once about her stitches: "They're so tiny, they almost seem to disappear."

Her thoughts wandered to their brief time together last summer, when he had finally returned home after being a nomad for over a year. They spent every minute they could snatch together after that first time, when she had chanced upon him at Blue Lake Pond, sitting on an old log. He moved over to make room for her and she sat down, but he didn't say anything and neither did she. Somehow, she seemed to understand his need for silence. Instead, she had fixed her gaze out over the lake. It was so calm, not a ripple. A perfect summer day.

Naomi considered Blue Lake Pond to be one of the best things about living in a place like Stoney Ridge. A small town on the edge of a big natural pond. It wasn't much of a pond, considering other lakes in Pennsylvania, but it was a very nice one by any standards, full of little creeks and inlets, shaded by tall pine trees. It froze over in winter and transformed into an ideal skating rink. On that day, a hot August afternoon, stick bugs skittered over the surface of the water, while dragonflies buzzed in lazy circles.

A cottontail came and peered at them, looking curiously from one to the other before he hopped away. They laughed at the rabbit, which broke the tension between them, and soon they found they could talk to each other easily.

"Isn't it beautiful here?" she said. "Thinking out problems gets easier here at the lake."

He let out a snort. "I guess it depends on the problems. The problems I have—well, there's no one I can think them out with. Certainly not my family. And I really don't have any friends left."

She suddenly remembered a proverb her mother used to say: To be without friends is a serious form of poverty. "Hush." She spoke to him as a child. "I'm your friend. I'll listen."

He seemed to take a long time deciding and she wondered what he was thinking. She wanted to touch his hand, to squeeze it, to encourage him to confide, but she didn't. When he finally spoke, he refused to meet her eyes, but kept them fixed on the lake. "I just don't know how much to reveal about Jake Hertzler and Schrock Investments. Or whom to tell."

Once he started to talk, he was like a pent-up dam. He described his anguish over his father's death and the burden of guilt he felt, but what could he have done to prevent it? Tears rolled down his face as details of that unforgettable day spilled out. They sat for hours as the summer afternoon light came in patches between the hickory and beech trees that surrounded the pond.

Countless questions popped into Naomi's mind, but she held back and merely listened. She was surprised by what he confessed, and yet not at all surprised. She had always known there was more to the story of Dean Schrock's death. When he had run out of words, Tobe asked her what he should do.

"I think," she said, choosing her words carefully, "that you need to take responsibility for your part in it, and let God handle Jake Hertzler."

Tobe's eyes widened in shock. "*What?*" His lips clamped, his head came down with a snap, and he shot her a cautious side glance.

"Trust the Lord to carry out revenge, Tobe. He is a just God. He'll do what's right. Most likely, we won't."

The shadows grew longer as they sat on the log at the pond and talked. That was the day that began their dependence on each other—for him, it was the knowledge that she was the only person who understood the pressures, the pain, and the indecision he had been living with for the last few years. And for her, she had someone who viewed her not as fragile and timid but as strong and bold and wise.

They met each afternoon on the log, but their meetings had to be conspiratorial so no one, especially Galen, was wise to their rendezvous. There wasn't time to tell each other all the things still to tell, but by the end of the week, Tobe had agreed to speak to Allen Turner at the SEC and tell him about what had gone on, illegally and with intent, at Schrock Investments. "Almost everything," he said.

Naomi wondered what that meant, but from his demeanor she decided that it was best left alone for now.

Night after night, Naomi lay alone in her bed remembering that day Tobe had cried and she had held him in the woods. She could remember the way his body shook and how she could hear his heart beat against her. She could bring back the smell of him, of pine soap and coffee. She could remember the way his hair had tickled her neck and how his tears had wet her cheeks. And she remembered that final evening, when he had kissed her.

She had never imagined that a kiss could be so sweet, so natural, and so very easy. When they said goodbye to each other, they both had tears running down their faces, and he told her that he felt like a fool. "I should be strong and courageous for you, Naomi, not cry like a baby."

She smiled. "Rose says that men have tears, same as women. They just don't know that it's good to let them flow now and then."

After that week, Naomi King felt like a new person. She

was able to do more than ever before. She could scarcely remember the days when a headache pinned her down and time had seemed long and hung heavily around her, waiting for it to lift. Now there weren't enough hours in the week for all that had to be done.

But when the postman arrived and she bolted to meet him before her brother, hoping he wouldn't notice how terribly interested she was in the mail, or when Bethany spoke of Tobe and dropped hints that she thought Naomi was sweet on him—those were the times when her stomach tightened into knots of stress and she had to chew Tums like they were M&Ms.

She sighed and wondered how much longer this was going to last. She wasn't cut out for living a secret life. It was all wrong.

But it was so right too.

3

Now and then, Mim Schrock would stop by the Sisters' House on her way home from school to help her older sister Bethany with the endless task of organizing the elderly sisters' home. Bethany was quicker, but Mim was the one who hung about, who found excuses to have meaningless little conversations with the sisters, to try to find out more about the life they led in the white clapboard house with the lilac bushes and the tall hollyhocks that guarded the fence. It was a house filled with true stories from another time.

Her favorite sister was Ella, the eldest, who had good days in which she remembered all kinds of interesting details about her childhood and told her amusing stories about the people of Stoney Ridge, and bad days when she lived in a fog and got questions all mixed up. Last week, Mim had asked Ella if the gout in her big toe had eased up at all.

"Not bad," Ella replied. "Though it got away after I tried to wring its neck."

Mim tilted her head, puzzled. "Wring whose neck?"

Ella gave Mim a look as if she might be sun touched. "The chicken's!"

The sisters didn't have any chickens.

That was a bad day for Ella. Today, though, was a good day. Bethany had already finished organizing for the day and hurried home, but Mim stayed anyway to have a visit with Ella. She had all kinds of stories to report about the fourteenth cousin twice removed, who was soon to arrive and was, according to Ella, quite dashing and worldly and exciting. Mim often wondered if Ella had ever loved a man, if any of the five sisters had ever known the kind of love she felt for Danny Riehl.

The afternoon was cold as Mim set off for the Bent N' Dent to pick up a few things for her mother before she went home. The March sun shone weak in a pale sky, trying to break through the gray clouds to warm the air, then it would disappear again and Mim would feel a chill. "Come on, spring, hurry up," she whispered aloud. For a while she walked behind an Amish couple she recognized from church. The woman walked serenely at her husband's side, nodding to those he nodded to along the road, smiling at those he smiled at, head cocked to hear his every word. Even the sun seemed to cooperate and shone down on them, scattering and dispersing the clouds left over from the morning's storm.

That could be me with Danny Riehl, Mim thought with envy. And she watched until they crossed the street and disappeared down a long lane. Walking backward, still thinking about Danny Riehl, Mim tripped over something and fell hard onto her rump. The something proved itself to be the long legs of a red-haired boy of fourteen, fifteen tops, who sat with his back against a fence post, eyes closed, soaking in the sun.

The boy's eyes popped wide open, eyes that were as round

and brown as currant buns. Mim peered up at the boy: hair orange as a carrot peeping from beneath his black felt hat; a big smile that showed more spaces than teeth, and a face beslobbered with freckles, forehead to chin, ear to ear.

The irritation, the sting of her bottom, and the red-hot scrapes on her palms loosened Mim's tongue. "How dare you trip me!" she said as she picked herself up and brushed muck off her skirts. She gave the bow of her bonnet a straightening tug and smoothed out the now wrinkled skirt of her apron.

"I didn't," he said calmly, an ankle crossing a knee. "You were the one who was daydreaming and not watching where you were going."

Mim thrust her chin into the air. "Daydreaming? You were taking a nap without even worrying to see whose way you were in."

The boy shrugged. "I'm just passing the time, waiting for my sister," he said, gesturing toward the Bent N' Dent. "Enjoying the sun shining on my face." He radiated mischief, amusement, and mockery too.

"I've never seen you around Stoney Ridge."

He lunged to his feet. "My name is Jesse Stoltzfus." He introduced himself expansively, as if his name alone should bring her pleasure. "Nor have I seen you before. A girl with eyes as gray as a raging storm cloud, cheeks like Georgia peaches, and hair as dark as a black-crowned night heron."

Mim stared at him. She felt a blush creep up, no matter how hard she tried to stop it. She knew her face was turning the color of red raspberries. For some inexplicable reason, out of her mouth spouted something her grandmother would say: "The lowly woman and the meek woman are really above all other women, above all other things." She had just read that very thing in her grandmother's favorite book next to the Bible, *A Young Woman's Guide to Virtue*, published in 1948 and still as relevant as ever. According to Mammi Vera, anyway.

Jesse considered her words solemnly. "Then might I say, 'Never have I seen a girl with such beautiful meekness'? Or perhaps 'I am overwhelmed by your lowly spirited, meek-minded, lowly hearted, meek-looking humility, which meekly shines . . .'?"

Mim was staring at him with her mouth open. She knew it and she couldn't help it. It was the most ridiculous thing she had ever heard.

Jesse Stoltzfus doffed his hat and flourished it before him as if he were going to sweep the floor. He had wiry hair that grew upward from his head. It was sticky-up hair. When he straightened, he said, "No doubt we shall meet again. The glow from your jubilant meekness will lead me to wherever you are. Also your stormy gray eyes." He smiled as brightly as a full moon. "No doubt it was God's plan that we meet today."

Mim thought God might have better things to do than to concern himself with a chance meeting in the parking lot of a grocery store. Jesse Stoltzfus winked at her and strode off, whistling, toward a buggy his sister, another redhead, was loading with boxes of food. The girl looked over at Mim and waved in a friendly way.

Mim gave a halfhearted wave back to her and frowned at Jesse's back. *That* boy, she decided, thought he was *something*. She watched their buggy leave the Bent N' Dent and then she pulled a strand of hair out from under her black bonnet to look at it closely. Like a black-crowned night heron, he had said. It must be a bird, she thought, though she'd never seen one. Whatever it was, it had a crown as black as her hair, and she almost smiled as she skipped up the steps to the store. Almost.

Rose hadn't had a chance to talk to Galen since he'd asked to marry her. This morning, she caught sight of him striding across the yard and stopped what she was doing to watch him. She studied his familiar walk—the efficient steps, his long legs, the way one shoulder was a little lower than the other, the way he tapped his fingers against his thighs as he walked when he was puzzling over something.

He spotted her and walked toward her, meeting her by the privet. His hat brim hid his eyes, but there was a slight smile to his lips. "I was going to come over today. I've got a little spare time and want to get working on Silver Queen's training. It's time she learned how to be a buggy horse."

Rose smiled. She knew that Galen King didn't know the first thing about spare time. He worked. And worked and worked. Sunup to sundown, he never stopped. She knew he was just looking out for her. Her buggy horse Flash was long past retirement age and could only be used for short trips around town. He couldn't even stand and wait during church with the other horses because it made his joints too stiff.

"Now's as good a time as any," he said.

Side by side, they walked to the barn, the morning frost crackling beneath their shoes. Galen stopped by the oats bin and scooped up a handful, then slid open the door to Silver Queen's stall and offered her the oats. With his other hand, he stroked the horse's long neck and absently combed his fingers through her mane. That was one of Galen's ways, Rose realized. He taught a horse to trust him by giving her what she loved best: a handful of honeyed oats and a loving touch. In return, the mare gave him her best.

In the stall next door, Silver Queen's colt pricked up his ears, whinnied and stamped his foot, snorted, then tried to wedge his nose between the stall bars, eager for attention. Or oats. Or both. Rose stood by the colt's stall and let him nuzzle her hand.

Galen looked up. "Soon, it'll be time to get that one started."

"Oh, but he's young yet. Scarcely a year."

Galen slipped a bridle over Silver Queen's head. "Too young to pull weight, but not too young to condition to traffic."

Rose ran a hand over the colt's velvet nose.

Galen tossed the lead line over Silver Queen's neck and came back outside the stall. "Rose, I'd like to talk to the bishop. Make it formal, set a date for our wedding."

She looked at him in surprise. "I thought we could wait until Tobe is released from jail. It shouldn't be much longer."

"Why do we need to wait?"

"There's so much that needs to get figured out first."

"Like what?"

She could feel his gaze. She glanced at him and found him watching her with concern from beneath the brim of his black hat. "Where we'll live, for one. If we live in your house, what should I do about the inn? A guest is due in tonight. And I'm starting to take reservations for the summer. And who will care for Vera?" She took a few steps away. "But if we live at Eagle Hill, then what about your house? What about Naomi?"

"Naomi has a lot of options. Besides, the houses are only fifty yards apart. Hardly a difficult thing to navigate."

"Then there's Bethany. She's counting on Jimmy Fisher to propose soon."

"Really?" His brows lifted. "He hasn't said a word to me."

They looked at each other, sharing a mutual thought. Jimmy talked a blue streak about anything and everything. If he were going to propose soon, wouldn't he be crowing about it? "I thought, perhaps, Tobe might be interested in running the inn."

A moment passed, then Galen dropped his chin to his chest. "You're expecting too much of Tobe."

"Maybe you don't expect enough of him." Rose spoke the words and knew them to be true, and the thought behind them was true, and yet she was sorry she'd said them aloud. She found herself always defending Tobe, although she understood Galen's assessment. Understood . . . and even agreed with him. But unlike Galen, she wouldn't give up on Tobe. She held hope that he was becoming a new man. His letters, though infrequent, certainly seemed to be showing evidence of maturity. "Tobe is broken, Galen. You saw that when he was here last summer. He's lost. Sincerely lost. He needs us."

Galen made a small sighing sound, as if he'd heard this before. "I just don't think we should arrange our plans around Tobe."

Just then the wind kicked up hard, blowing through the open barn door, slapping her skirts and rattling the loose shingles on the eaves. The weather had turned cold again, with no hint of spring at all. She wrapped her arms around herself, feeling deflated. "I just need a little more time, Galen. To sort things out."

He walked up to her, put his arms around her, and gently pulled her against his chest. She could hear his heart beating, so steady, so sure. "Then take all the time you need," he said softly.

The temptation to pull the covers over her head and never get up was so strong that it frightened Brooke Snyder into dropping her legs over the side of the bed. Cold linoleum met the soles of her feet. She made her way across the bedroom to a utilitarian bathroom. Although small, it had been modernized. Perhaps this Amish inn wasn't quite as run-down as she'd imagined it to be when she arrived late last night. And it was thoughtful of the innkeeper to leave the guest flat open for her and a small kerosene light burning, though the hiss of the light took getting used to.

She stared at herself in the mirror, then her fingers constricted at the edge of the sink. Her face was haggard, gaunt, drawn. She looked like she had aged a decade in the last few weeks. She splashed water on her face, trying to detach herself from her bleak situation so she could make a new plan. She stared glumly down at the soap dish. Right. As if any of her big ideas had worked lately.

She showered, wrapped herself in a towel, and returned to her room, where she slipped into a pair of jeans and a comfortable sweater. She sat cross-legged in a chair and opened up a notebook, brainstorming ideas for a new life. She scribbled down a few, reviewed them, then tore out the page and balled it in her fist and threw it at the wastebasket. All the ideas she jotted down were awful. She was getting the uneasy feeling that she didn't know how she was going to get herself out of this mess. She closed the notebook, wondering when breakfast might be served. For now she simply wouldn't let herself think about her messy life. Maybe if she didn't dwell on her upsetting circumstances, they'd disappear.

And maybe not.

She walked over to the window and pushed back the curtains. A shower of lemony light drenched her. It streamed through the window as if it had been poured from a bucket, rays so intense she had to close her eyes for a moment. When she opened them, she saw the rolling hills of Lancaster County lying before her.

"Oh, my . . ." She rested her arms on the windowsill and took in the red barn, the pastures with horses and sheep milling around. And was that a billy goat? She wanted to see more, and she turned away from the window, then stopped as she saw how the light had changed the character of the room. Now the butter-colored walls were beautiful in their sparseness, and the simple furniture spoke more eloquently of the past than a volume of history books. She moved through each room, opening the curtains. The living room, which she'd barely glanced at the night before, felt cozy and homey.

The door opened and a woman in her sixties walked in. She had a dumpling figure, doughy cheeks, small dark eyes, salt and pepper hair that was primly twisted into a tight bun and capped with a white covering. Brooke had heard the Amish were known for their friendliness, but this woman didn't look at all friendly.

"You must be Rose Schrock," Brooke said.

"No." The woman set a breakfast tray on the kitchen table. "I'm Vera Schrock, Rose's mother-in-law."

"Denki." Brooke liked to demonstrate her exceptional mastery of the Penn Dutch language. She considered herself a whiz at foreign languages.

The woman didn't seem at all impressed. "Leave the tray outside the door when you're done."

"Do you happen to have a newspaper?"

"No. You'll have to go into town to get it yourself."

Vera opened the door, then stopped and looked back at Brooke. "If you don't eat everything, don't throw it out. We don't waste food around here."

Got it. Eating was serious business with these people.

Brooke looked past Vera at the door and saw a road curled against the hills in a pale, smoky trail. This beautiful place! To think that only yesterday she wasn't even sure she wanted to be here. The woman's dark mutter broke the peaceful mood, and she startled, realizing the woman was waiting for her to respond. "I'll do that. Thank you."

Even the dour expression of the woman couldn't detract from the enchantment of this quiet, peaceful location, and the knots inside Brooke began to loosen.

Finally, something had happened to ease her discouragement. She started the day with a much lighter heart. She walked to the window to gaze up at the sky. The high, fluffy clouds looked as though they should be printed on blue flannel pajamas.

It was a beautiful Sunday, and she wouldn't let even a surly Amish grandmother spoil it for her.

Mim and her brothers arrived at school just as Danny rang the bell. He had asked her to call him Teacher Danny like the other children, but she refused. Instead, she never addressed him at all. She hurried to put her lunch on the shelf in the back of the schoolroom and slipped into her seat. As she took out her books from her desk, she noticed a buzz of conversation in the classroom. She felt a gentle tap on her shoulder and turned to discover the horrible boy who had tripped her was seated next to her.

"Remember me, Miss Humility?"

Mim gave him the stink eye, a look usually reserved for her brothers.

"You never told me your actual name."

She turned forward in her chair, ignoring him.

"I'm Jesse Stoltzfus," he whispered loudly. "We moved in across the road from your farm. My father bought the Bent N' Dent."

Something red caught her eye and she realized there were more students in the schoolhouse. All redheads. Carrot tops. All with that same sticky-up hair. Her gaze traveled across the room as horror set in. There were so *many* Stoltzfus children! Were they all as awful as Jesse? "How many of you are there?"

"Six. I'm the only manchild. It's a sore trial." He motioned toward the teacher's desk. "She's the oldest. Katrina. Dad sent her to get us registered for school. She's seventeen, nearly eighteen. I'm fourteen. Nearly fifteen."

Standing next to the teacher's desk was that girl who had come out of the Bent N' Dent after Jesse tripped Mim. Danny was listening carefully to the girl, then laughed at something she said.

Jesse leaned across the aisle. "Boys go crazy over Katrina. They always have."

Katrina was beautiful, delicate yet curvy in all the right places. She had perfect teeth, and her neck was long, like a gazelle. She had a face like an angel. Mim, she hated her.

As soon as school let out that afternoon, Mim hurried

home, ran to her room, and locked the door. On the top shelf of her closet, too tall for snoopy Mammi Vera to find, she had hidden a hand mirror that she bought at a yard sale last summer. She took it out and examined her face in the mirror. It was a perfectly reasonable face. Why then was she lacking sparkle, like Katrina had? It wasn't a lively face. It looked flat somehow.

She turned to Luke's big dog, Micky, who was staring at her with a soulful look on his face. "What do you think, Micky?"

His tail thumped once, then twice. He seemed pleased. He stretched his big creamy limbs in front of her door.

"Move, Micky. I need to go downstairs."

She found her mother in the kitchen and grabbed an apple from a bowl on the table. "Mom, do you know anything about those Stoltzfuses?"

Her mother stopped chopping vegetables and looked out the window toward the Stoltzfus farm. "I know that their father is a minister, David Stoltzfus, and he comes trailing clouds of respect."

"I've heard he's a man to be reckoned with," Mammi Vera added.

Mim would not mind having David Stoltzfus for a neighbor. She was less sure about his son, Jesse, who both irritated and intrigued her. "His son Jesse is abominable."

"That's a very unchristian attitude," Mammi Vera said.

Mim shrugged. "Maybe so, but it's the truth." She cast a sideways glance in her grandmother's direction. "They've all got bright red hair. The whole lot of them."

Mammi Vera gasped. "Red hair means one is the devil's own. You know that, don't you, Mim?"

"Of course, Mammi Vera," Mim said, eyes widened in innocence. *I sincerely doubt it, Mammi Vera,* Mim thought.

It had taken two full days last week for Bethany to clean out the second-floor bedroom at the Sisters' House. The sisters' fourteenth cousin twice removed had arrived and settled in, though Bethany had yet to meet him. She brought fresh towels up to the second floor and knocked lightly on the door. "Hello?"

Silence.

The door was locked tight as a drum. She set the towels on a small hallway table and went back downstairs. As she picked up old *Stoney Ridge Times* newspapers from the dining room table, she asked the sisters, "So what is this fourteenth cousin twice removed like?"

Lena sat at the far end of the table, hemming an apron. "Very polite."

"Terribly polite," Ella echoed.

Fannie walked into the room with a pitcher of hot tea. "He has a good appetite."

"Oh, isn't *that* the truth," Ada said.

Bethany stacked the newspapers on a chair. It seemed as if paper multiplied in this house. "Isn't it creepy that he's been here a few days and I haven't laid eyes on him?"

"Why, no, it isn't creepy," Ada said. "He's busy."

"Terribly busy," Ella echoed.

"Where is he now?"

"He's off to the Lancaster Historical Society," Sylvia said, "to do some studying and research on family lineage."

Ada nodded. "He's not a bother at all. We hardly see him."

Fannie's sharp voice added, "Except for meals."

"Yes, that's true," Sylvia said. "He does love Fannie's cooking."

Fannie blushed, pleased to be singled out.

"He gives us the full report of our ancestry during supper," Lena said.

Fannie grabbed a newspaper from the stack to set under the tea on the dining room table. "Feels a little like having someone read you the book of Chronicles. So and so begat so and so, who begat so and so."

Ella wandered away to pick up a newspaper, then sat in a chair to read it.

Why, this was how it happened! Little by little, the sisters undid everything Bethany tried to do. And they were oblivious to the undoing.

Lena threaded a needle and knotted the end. "It turns out that we have an ancestor who came over on the *Charming Nancy*."

Bethany tilted her head. "What's that?"

"The Amish *Mayflower*," Lena said. "One of the first ships to bring the Amish over to America. 1738."

Sipping her tea, Fannie looked up. "1737."

"That's right," Lena said. "He did say that. Well done, Fannie."

"They came over on the *Charming Nancy*," Fannie said. "Enough Amish families to start the first congregation."

At that point the sisters' conversation quickly digressed into the unbearable living conditions of the eighteenth century. Bethany thought they should be more concerned they were living in an unbearable condition in the twenty-first century, but nobody in this room seemed the least bit concerned. She gave up on the living room with all those sisters planted in there talking about the *Charming Nancy* and set off to another room to work for the afternoon.

The next day, Bethany was back at the Sisters' House to work and slipped up to the second-floor guest room. She jiggled the door handle. Locked tight. She sighed, exasperated. That fourteenth cousin twice removed was turning into an irritating mystery.

4

Normally, Brooke Snyder thrived on self-discipline. On a typical morning, she would be out of bed at six for yoga and meditation. By eight, she would be in her lab coat in the dark basement of the museum, with the only light coming from infrared lamps so nothing would decay the paintings.

Instead, she spent her mornings strolling around an Amish farm.

Brooke Snyder was a professional art restorer, also called a conservator. She worked for a museum in Philadelphia—researching, cleaning, restoring works of priceless art.

She had been very bright at school; she had been good at everything. Her English teacher encouraged her to pursue a college degree in English Literature. Her P.E. teacher said that with her height—by the age of fourteen she was already nearly six feet tall—she could play volleyball or basketball, or both. But when it came to decision time, Brooke went for art.

She had learned to paint by studying the masters and copying their techniques—something that was part of every artist's training before they refined their own techniques. But Brooke never seemed to get that far. She had such a talent for reproduction that her art professor recommended her for a freelance job at a local gallery that needed help with a fire-damaged painting. One freelance job led to another, then another. She had a reputation for attention to detail, right down to the artist's signature. As soon as she graduated, she was offered a job at a museum.

If anyone asked Brooke about her work, she made art restoration sound like fascinating work, but the truth of it was that it was tedious, painstaking work in a windowless basement, where the average age of her boring colleagues was seventy, and the pay was horrible. Horrible! How could a person survive on such a low salary? She certainly couldn't. How could a young woman ever meet an eligible bachelor? She certainly hadn't.

And that was how she had been tempted to commit a grave error. She'd found herself facing some rather serious credit card debt and complained about it to a co-worker at the museum. It turned out he knew an art dealer who was looking for an artist to commission a painting. After meeting with the art dealer, she agreed to reproduce a Jean-Baptiste-Camille Corot painting for a handsome sum. She would have enough to pay off her credit card debt and some left over to put a down payment on a new car.

She worked extremely hard on that Corot plein air reproduction. She not only duplicated Corot's unique style, but she replicated his painting from every angle: back, front, and sides. She mounted and framed it in an identical way. She even copied the supplier tags. She did a stellar job.

So stellar that the art dealer passed it off as an original and sold it. The art dealer, who was now under investigation for selling several fakes to unsuspecting collectors, had gone missing. The museum curator was furious with her, though she claimed she knew nothing about the art dealer's unscrupulous actions. "Corot, of all artists!" the curator said. "One of the most faked artists of all time."

She knew that. A recent *Time* magazine article said that Corot painted eight hundred paintings in his lifetime, four thousand of which were in the United States.

"But it wasn't an *intentional* fake," she assured him. "My mistake was imitating the original too closely." It pleased her that she had fooled a collector—though, wisely, she kept that thought to herself.

"And adding the artist's signature instead of your own," the curator pointed out. "Intended or not, it is what it is. You created a forgery. A copy." He looked at her with disdain and told her she was fortunate to not be under investigation by the FBI—only because he had vouched for her innocence. And then he fired her.

Copied. There was *nothing* worse in the art world than that word. And yet . . . that's all she really had become, even her aunt Lois—Brooke's most favorite person in the world—had said so. She was a copier.

Brooke thought it might be wise to let things settle down and think out a new path for her future, which, according to the curator, apparently wasn't going to be in the art world. He told her she had committed a cardinal sin, crossed an unforgivable line, which she thought was a little extreme. However, getting out of town for a breather sounded like a good idea, so that's what she did. When her aunt Lois recommended a quiet little inn in Amish country as a place to recalibrate her life, she wiped away her tears, grabbed the idea, and ran with it.

And now Brooke was far, far removed from the art world. She watched the hens in the chicken yard, mesmerized, amused. When had she last stood still and just noticed something as silly and mundane as chickens? She wandered into the large vegetable garden, mostly dormant at this time of year, though she saw the tips of asparagus peeking through straw beds in tidy rows.

In her mind, she re-dressed it into a portrait of summer's full bloom: Glossy basil plants, snowy white impatiens, tomato vines, clay pots overflowing with red geraniums. Bright orange nasturtiums with the delicate blue flowers of a rosemary shrub, silvery sage leaves as a cool backdrop to a cluster of red pepper plants.

She smiled to herself. Maybe she should consider painting garden scenes. Claude Monet? No . . . too obvious. Philippe Fernandez? No . . . too odd. Perhaps Zaira Dzhaubaeva. Yes, she would be the one to study.

There I go again! Copying. She hung her head. She couldn't help it. Copying was what she knew to do. Aunt Lois had urged her to drop the copies, skip the restorations, and become an original at something of her own. Anything, she emphasized, choose anything! Become the real thing.

How insulting! Brooke *was* the real thing. She was gifted at what she did—everyone said so. If she studied others long enough, she could fix her mind to think like they thought, act like they would act, speak like they spoke, paint like they painted. Even write like they wrote. Why, she could do anything. "Except be an original!" she could just hear Aunt Lois say.

Two cats came up to Brooke and curled around her legs. She wasn't a cat person, so she untangled her legs and followed a path that led up a hill. Halfway up the hill, she stopped to absorb the view of the farmhouse from the back. The clapboard white of the house glowed in the sharp morning light. Ivy vines clung to the mortar of the brick chimney, climbing up a drain spout and curling near the green shutters at the windows. The main part of the structure was built in a simple, unadorned rectangle, the typical style of the Amish farmhouse that she'd read about in the tour books. A one-story room bumped haphazardly off the end, probably a later addition. The grandparents' quarters, perhaps?

Down below, she noticed a pretty young woman hanging brightly colored laundry on a clothesline. "Amish dryers" the tourist book had called those clotheslines. Brooke watched the Amish woman move efficiently down the line, with motions as graceful as a ballerina. She was petite, and her clear pale skin made an unusual contrast with her dark hair. She must be Rose Schrock, Brooke realized, the innkeeper. Or maybe she was Bethany, the older sister to Mim? Brooke might have all the women mixed up. Maybe everyone in Stoney Ridge looked the same.

If the woman was Rose the innkeeper, Brooke should head down and introduce herself. One thing she'd already noticed about these Amish—they were always moving on to the next thing. If she didn't catch Rose Schrock now, she'd miss her chance.

One of the cats had followed Brooke up the hill and rubbed against her legs. She scooped down to pick it up, trying not to think of the fleas it might carry, the ticks, the disease. She was doing her best to be fully present and enjoy this farm experience without overanalyzing everything. The sky felt bigger at Eagle Hill. It curved from one horizon line to the other. The fields that had been gray in the early morning had turned to a soft shade of amber brown in the midmorning sun. So beautiful.

It was perfect. Absolutely perfect. Aunt Lois was right. There could be no better place for what she needed right now: a reinvention of herself.

Brooke needed to be here. Every instinct told her this was the place she had to stay, the only place where she could find both the solitude and the inspiration to figure out how to resurrect her career. Her stubborn streak set in.

Right then Brooke made up her mind. She wasn't going to leave this humble Amish inn until she had her new life firmly in its grasp. A simple plan began to take shape in her heart and mind. *I won't leave until I find a fresh wind. A new life direction.*

But . . . what?

On a sunny afternoon, Galen led Silver Queen into the pasture, the foal following closely at her side. Rose closed the pasture gate behind her and walked up to Silver Queen, who bumped her with her nose. Rose scratched her between the ears as Galen put a nylon cord around the foal's neck. It was soft for him to wear for a while as he got used to the feel of something on his neck.

What a wonder a baby was. Rose never failed to appreciate the miracle of a new life, human or animal. So small and sweet, with overlong legs and a dainty little face.

Galen rubbed his legs and back, slow and gentle, until the foal quit fidgeting and stood still for it. "Every day someone needs to be stroking the colt's hooves so that he's used to getting his feet handled."

"He's still a baby."

"No, Rose. He's not a foal any longer. He's a yearling. And he's a promising horse—his conformation is good, his muscle development is right on target. In fact, most yearlings are gelded by now. This colt is far behind in his training from where he should be."

"The boys did a good job for the first few months, but after school started it slipped off to the back burner."

"It's not something that can be ignored and picked up again, on a whim. If you've ever had to shoe a horse that didn't like having his feet handled, you'd know how important this is."

She crossed her arms, annoyed. "I didn't say it wasn't important, Galen. It's just hard to keep up with everything."

Galen reached out and cupped her cheek with his palm, dissolving her annoyance in the time it took to draw a startled breath. "I know. I see."

"Deacon Abraham stopped by yesterday to remind me we're due to host church the first Sunday in May." As if she had forgotten. She thought of all the things that needed to be done to prepare for hosting church: the house would need to be scrubbed, top to bottom. The walls washed down, curtains washed and ironed. Every bureau and cupboard should be cleaned out and organized. The barn needed a serious sweeping out. The front porch was begging for touch-up paint. Windows had to be rubbed until they were squeaky clean. Everything had to be perfect—not for show, but to glorify the Lord God.

Her eyes noticed something new—a broken window on the second floor that looked like it was hit by a stray baseball. She blew out a puff of air. "So much to do."

Galen glanced up and saw the broken window too. "Make a list. I'll help."

"I can't ask that of you."

He took a step closer to her, his eyes smiling in that special way he had, just for her. He raised one hand to her temple and grazed her cheekbone with the tips of his fingers. "Yes, you can. You can ask anything of me." He leaned over to kiss her, gently, brushing his lips against hers.

Their lips had just touched again when they broke apart, startled by the sound of the kitchen door opening as Vera walked out on the porch and settled into the swing. Rose turned away, color rising in her cheeks. How ridiculous! Sometimes, she felt like a schoolgirl around Galen. "You've got your own farm and work to take care of. Spring is the busiest time for you. And you don't have Jimmy Fisher's help anymore."

"I'm surprised to discover how much I've missed his help. I have more work than I can manage." He leaned against the pen with his arms crossed over his chest. "Think there's any chance Edith Fisher would cut him a little slack and let him come back to horses?"

"I don't see how. She needs his help with the chicken and egg business, even more so after her bunion surgery." She bit her lip. "I don't suppose you'd consider taking on Tobe when he's released."

Galen's chin lifted. "Rose, we've been through this before. Tobe doesn't have the temperament for horses. What makes you think he'd even return to Eagle Hill?"

"This is his home. He can't keep running forever. I think he's starting to face up to things—after all, he's the one who pled guilty to withholding evidence. That's a step in the right direction, isn't it?"

"A step, perhaps."

A wave of irritation at Galen came over Rose suddenly. "Couldn't you even give him a chance? For your sister's sake?"

"Naomi?" He looked baffled. "Why would I want Tobe around Naomi?"

"Galen—you must realize there's something brewing between the two of them."

"Not while he's in jail, there's not."

"Definitely while he's in jail. Haven't you noticed the letters they write to each other? She runs to that mailbox every single day. I've seen her! And she walks back slowly, reading that familiar gray envelope."

Galen had a skeptical look in his eyes.

"Before you close your mind to their budding romance, have you even noticed that she hasn't had a single migraine since Tobe returned last fall? Not one."

It wasn't often that Galen King was confounded, but at that moment, he looked at Rose as if she was speaking another language. She turned her attention back to the colt and let Galen resume training Silver Queen. He didn't say another word about the subject of Tobe and Naomi. Neither did Rose. She thought she had said enough.

There was so much Naomi had to thank God for: she hadn't had a migraine since—well, not since Tobe had returned after he'd gone missing for a year. Naomi had suffered from headaches the doctors could neither diagnose nor cure.

It seemed trite, a cliché, but happiness had cured Naomi

of the headaches. Happiness and love. For she was in love with Tobe Schrock, and he loved her, and soon he would be released from prison and life could start fresh. Love, she had always thought, could do extraordinary things to people. Now she knew it to be true.

The Lord works in mysterious ways. She had always heard that phrase but never knew what it meant until she saw the miracle God was working in Tobe's life, even in jail. Especially in jail. For God was everywhere and all around and couldn't be kept out of any earthly place, not even a federal prison. A prison chaplain led Bible studies in the community area and delivered a Sunday service. Tobe was making strides in his journey of faith. "I feel a weight lift from my shoulders," he had written to her. And another time: "I'm beginning to realize a lot of things don't matter anymore. My chest is much less tight, the awful feeling of running down a long corridor gone." Only God could do this work in Tobe's life. He had been running for over a year and it took God to force him to stop, to take a breath, to catch up with himself. To be still and to know God was God.

And that's exactly what was happening, in a federal prison of all places. The questions Tobe had in his letters, the longings he expressed, the desire to know God, to be a man after God's own heart—why, Naomi fell in love with him all over again. She used to love what he could be, now she loved who he was becoming.

She was grateful for these blessings and many others, but she was also troubled, for when she prayed in her room at night, it was as much from worry as from gratitude. She picked up Tobe's letter that she had received today and re-read it:

Dearest Naomi,

You used to complain that I was too buttoned-up in my letter-writing. Now I wonder if you'll never write to me again after I pour my heart out to you. But here goes, here's the full whoosh of the waterfall.

Lately, I've thought of little else but your advice to leave Jake Hertzler in God's hands. The beliefs of the Amish church are easier to talk about in theory than to put into practice. They're counterintuitive to human nature.

Is it so wrong to want revenge on Jake Hertzler? So that he doesn't keep hurting others? Because he will, Naomi. Jake is made that way—to steal, to take, to harm, to not care a whit about the consequences. You've said we must forgive him and even to pray for him, but does that mean he doesn't have to face justice? Is that what nonresistance truly means?

I just can't do it, Naomi. I can't let him continue to hurt my family. I told the SEC lawyer most of the things Jake had done to Schrock Investments, but not all. A few important pieces—the most *important part—I kept to myself, because I want to get out of prison and face Jake myself. It's my responsibility to see it through.*

Problem is, I have no idea how to go about doing it. I spent a year trying to set a trap for him, but Jake was always a step ahead of me. In fact, he was the one who set the snare for me to step into. That's why I'm here, serving out a prison sentence, while he is off scot-free.

I love you, Naomi. And I do give serious consideration to what you have to say on the matter. Pray that I will do the right thing, sweetheart.

Pray for him? He didn't even need to ask! She prayed for him frequently throughout the days, and often at night. Naomi had been taught since she was small to be grateful in all things and for all things, so despite a feeling of foreboding for this unsettled issue, she gave thanks for it and for what lay ahead.

And then she ate a full roll of Tums.

5

Late last night, Mim was informed by her sister Bethany that Danny Riehl had driven Katrina Stoltzfus home from the youth gathering. Bethany felt she should know. "I went back and forth," Bethany had said, "on whether I should tell you or not, and finally decided I would want to know if Jimmy Fisher took another girl home."

Mim only shrugged and gave her a flat look. Why should it matter? Danny had become the permanent substitute teacher at her school. He had to stop inviting her to look through his telescope on starry nights because he felt it wasn't appropriate.

It shouldn't matter.

But it did.

Mim trudged down the driveway on the way to school with her brothers, who felt the need to crush the thin layer of ice that lined every puddle, then howl with approval and sock the air with their fists. She stayed clear of their splatters and wondered why boys always had the urge to break something, even at seven thirty in the morning.

"Yoo hoo!"

Mim spun around to find the new Eagle Hill guest waving to her from the door of the guest flat. She told Sammy and Luke to head off to school and she walked over to see what she wanted.

The guest, a very tall woman with spiky, short blonde hair, thrust her hand out to Mim. In it were dollar bills. "I'm Brooke Snyder." She motioned toward the guest flat. "I'll be staying for a little while. I'd like you to get me a newspaper each day. Preferably the *Times*."

Mim raised her eyebrows. "You want me to bring you the *Stoney Ridge Times*?"

Brooke Snyder blinked. "No. The *New York Times*."

Mim shook her head. "I've never seen that newspaper sold in Stoney Ridge."

She frowned. "Then bring me the closest thing to it. That's not asking too much, is it?"

"I suppose not," Mim said. "But I wouldn't be able to get it to you until late in the day. I have chores in the morning, then I have to go to school. And I have chores in the afternoon."

"That's fine. I'll just save it for the next day's breakfast. Old news is still news."

Mim considered pointing out that the very word *news* meant it was new, thus, old news was an oxymoron. But she didn't think her suggestion would be appreciated. Her family never appreciated her grammatical corrections, so why would a guest whom she'd just met?

"I'm not sure how long I'm going to stay here. Maybe for a while. I want a newspaper for the entire time I'm here, rain or shine. I'll pay you for your trouble." She pushed the dollars into Mim's hand.

"Sure." Mim pushed her glasses back up the bridge of her

nose. "Sure," she repeated, nodding vigorously. In fact, it was an ideal opportunity to read her Mrs. Miracle column. Usually, she only saw a copy of the paper if she was at the Sisters' House because her grandmother refused to subscribe. "Rubbish!" her grandmother called the newspaper. Mim spotted the black hats of her brothers as they disappeared over the hill and realized she'd better hurry or she'd be late for school. "Today. I'll bring you a paper later today."

As Mim ran up the hill, she tried to figure out why the guest would bother reading a newspaper like the *Stoney Ridge Times*. It was filled with stories about local people, stories like the one about the mayor who had just been reelected for the sixth time, which might sound impressive until you learned that no one ever ran against him. Then there was the police report, which mostly consisted of parking tickets. Once or twice a month, there were some scandals. Bennie Adams had been fired at the bank because he'd come to work drunk. Junior Jackson's wife had run off with the high school track coach. Those kinds of stories were why Mammi Vera called the *Stoney Ridge Times* the gossip buzz line. The sisters at the Sisters' House had a different point of view. They liked knowing what was going on in town. She wished for the hundredth time that Mammi Vera were more like the sisters—any sister, even Fannie, who was often prickly and her least favorite.

It wasn't that Mim didn't like Mammi Vera. After all, she was her grandmother. She had to like her, or maybe she just had to love her. Maybe it was the liking part she had a choice about. It wasn't Mammi Vera's fault that she wasn't like the old sisters.

That afternoon on her way home from school, Mim stopped

at the Bent N' Dent and bought the last copy of the *Stoney Ridge Times*. She spoke to the clerk Katrina, the sister of the incorrigible Jesse Stoltzfus, and asked her to save a copy each afternoon. The sister, she noted, was nice to her despite being irritatingly pretty. Katrina seemed to glide around the store, not walk like a normal person. Of course, *she* didn't wear glasses. *She* would never be called Four Eyes or Owl Eyes by the sixth grade boys.

The Mrs. Miracle column was running twice a week now, and the receptionist had confided in Bethany that there were even rumblings about expanding it to three times a week. Such an opportunity only filled Mim with panic: Someone, somewhere, was going to find out! Bethany was the only one who knew the true identity of Mrs. Miracle. No, that wasn't exactly accurate (and Mim prided herself on accuracy). Ella of the Sisters' House had guessed once, but she had memory woes and had already forgotten. No one else in all of Stoney Ridge suspected that Mrs. Miracle was actually a fourteen-year-old Amish girl.

Mim loved her role as Mrs. Miracle and took it very seriously. When she didn't know the answer to something, she would research it or carefully, cautiously, question the right people. She liked helping others and, not to brag, but she gave excellent advice. Excellent. Mostly, though, she was just reminding people to use common sense. It seemed to be in short supply.

But the Mrs. Miracle column was supposed to be a tiny little side job for her. It brought in only five dollars a week, and it gave her something interesting and challenging to do. No big deal. Just a once-a-week column.

She hadn't expected the readership to explode. She hadn't

expected the editor to expand it to twice a week. And now . . . three times a week? Each time she thought of it, she couldn't even swallow. What if she was found out? What if the bishop learned of her secret job? What would her mother say?

She walked as slowly as she could back toward Eagle Hill, reading the newspaper, admiring the Mrs. Miracle column. It was well written, and she tried not to feel proud, but she did. When she had nearly reached the driveway to Eagle Hill, she felt someone over her shoulder.

"My sisters love that column too. They fight over who gets to read it aloud."

Jesse Stoltzfus, of all people! Mim snapped the paper shut and tucked it under her arm. "Mrs. Miracle would say that it's only good manners for a person to let another person know that the person is there."

Jesse was staring at her with his mouth open, as if he didn't hear her properly. He thumped the side of his head with the palm of his hand, like he was shaking water from his ear. "But . . . I did." He tipped his felt hat back on his forehead. "Good thing you're not writing a newspaper column. That was the most confusing sentence a person ever said to another person." He grinned and took off his hat, bowing and sweeping his hat in a big arc. "This person needs to be on his way, if the other person will excuse this person."

Jackanapes! *That* boy always tried to best her. It irked her that Danny—who used to be her special friend before he got so high and mighty and puffed up—he only encouraged Jesse Stoltzfus's gargantuan ego. Just this afternoon, he had read Jesse's composition aloud. "I am sure," Danny told the class, "that all of you were as impressed as I was by Jesse's exciting essay."

Impressed? Mim was dumbfounded. Jesse wrote a heart-stopping composition about a time when he was lost in a snowstorm and had to make a snow cave to survive the night. Jesse described the sound of the wind and the bite of the cold so clearly she felt right there with him, in the middle of the blizzard, gasping for breath, trying to push down panic as he dug a snow cave deep down in a world of no light and little air.

How could she be all in a tremble just listening to Danny read about it? It actually hurt to listen—she was *that* jealous of Jesse's writing ability. Mim labored painfully over her writing, every single sentence; Jesse scribbled things down and turned them in before school or during recess. She had seen him! He had forgotten the essay that was due today and dashed it off during lunch.

On the other hand, Danny always caught Mim when her mind was on vacation, though he never suspected Jesse of not paying attention. Danny had one of those tricky voices. It would buzz along for several minutes quite comfortably, then *bang!* he was focused in and asking you a question.

Earlier in the week, Danny had cornered Mim with a question out of the blue, when she was a million miles away. Her mind went completely blank. Throughout the classroom she heard a shuffling of feet and paper, waiting for her to answer him. She could feel everyone's eyes boring into her. Mose Blank was staring at her so intently she thought his crossed eyes might switch sockets. "Parakeets can live nearly twenty years," she blurted out and the class roared with laughter. Turned out Danny had asked her the names of the different kinds of cloud formations in the sky.

Dumb, dumb, dumb.

Then he asked Jesse the names of clouds and of course

he knew the answers, including the Latin translations of the words: *cumulus,* heap; *stratus,* layer; *nimbus,* rain; *cirrus,* curl of hair. Wasn't that just like Jesse, to answer more than the teacher had asked for? Danny was delighted. Mim thought Jesse was showing off.

Jesse was one of those boys who sat quietly at his desk doing beautiful schoolwork, never daydreaming or shooting spit wads or chewing gum, and yet he was so full of shenanigans that if Teacher Danny could have once known what was running through that carrot-red-sticky-up-haired head, he would have thrown him out of the schoolhouse in horror.

She sneaked a glance over at Jesse. He was totally absorbed in his geography book, or so it would appear to anyone who didn't know. He must have sensed she was watching him, because he slowly turned his head in her direction. "I've always been fond of parakeets," he whispered, grinning widely.

Did Jesse Stoltzfus ever stop grinning? He grinned when he saw her come in the schoolhouse in the mornings. He'd grinned when she made a fool out of herself by spouting out the lifespan of parakeets (which, incidentally, was a well-known fact). He'd even grinned as he was bringing in wood to stoke the stove and a large spider crawled up his sleeve. *Who* could smile at a spider? She had never known anyone as maddening as Jesse Stoltzfus. Not even Luke, and he sorely tried everyone's patience.

They reached the turnoff to Jesse's driveway and he stopped at the mailbox, opened it, found it empty, then shut it tight. He started up the hill toward his farmhouse.

"Jesse!"

He stopped and turned to face her.

"Did that really happen? That snowstorm?"

He took a few steps toward her, grinning. "Now, why would I make something like that up?" Then he began scissoring up the driveway in great strides and Mim couldn't help but watch. He ran as though it was his nature. It reminded her of the flight of wild ducks in the autumn. Smooth and effortless. The word "glorious" came to mind, but she shook it away and hurried toward Eagle Hill.

The first time that David Stoltzfus delivered a Sunday sermon, a shaft of sunlight broke through the gray skies and came through a crack in the barn roof to touch his face, making him look more saintly than ever. In the short time that David had lived in Stoney Ridge, the people had quickly grown to love him, and in her heart Rose felt a little sorry for the other ministers, who were instantly overshadowed.

It wasn't the other ministers' fault; their sermons were full of good examples and strong admonishments. And yet Rose had to admit that David brought with him some new sense of excitement and inspiration that the other ministers, including the bishop, didn't have.

David fired the church members with an enthusiasm never before known in Stoney Ridge. He was so . . . clear, so vivid. He had a conviction that sermons should be kept to the comprehension level of children, to nourish the spiritual life of young people. He had confidence the adults would still be fed and, of course, he was right.

On this gray morning, he reminded them of how fortunate their congregation was to live in the safety of Lancaster County. He spoke of those, years ago in the Old Country, who had been martyred rather than renounce their faith. He described with vivid detail the horrific persecution their great-great-grandparents had endured. Even Jesse Stoltzfus, whom Mim called abominable, was on the edge of his seat, Rose noticed, listening to his father's sermon with rapt attention.

As they sat in the barn on that Sunday morning, the church of Stoney Ridge was transported miles away to another continent. They felt rich beyond the dreams of kings compared to their ancestors in Switzerland and Germany and France, who had cried out in their dying breath to hold tight to their faith. The barn might have been full of people sneezing and coughing, wet from the trek across miles of roads to get there on a rainy, blustery spring morning, but everyone felt warm and safe and grateful. Their life was a paradise compared to their great-great-grandparents'.

Rose gazed around the barn: at Mim and Bethany, seated behind Vera. At Sammy, at Luke, nodding off; at Galen, who nudged Luke awake with a jab from his elbow—and she gave thanks.

After youth group on Sunday night, Jimmy drove Bethany home. It was a cold night, but the stars were out and the moon was full and the brisk air gave them an excuse to cuddle. Jimmy took the long way home so he could pull up to the shores of Blue Lake Pond. Just to talk, he assured her, but she knew kissing was on his mind. Kissing was always on his mind and he'd been staring at her lips all night. Kissing Jimmy was one of Bethany's favorite things to do, so she didn't object when he stopped the horse and reached out to pull her close to him. But she also had something else to discuss.

"Jimmy," she said, pushing him back slightly. "Kissing is fun and all that, but it's time we started making plans."

Jimmy put an arm around her and wiggled his eyebrows. "I do have plans." He gave her one of his persuasive grins and cupped her jaw to kiss her with a tender consideration. As his lips joined hers, she swayed toward him, her fingertips grazing his chin. When at length he lifted his head, they were both breathing harder as they gazed into each other's eyes.

"Jimmy, don't you want more than that?"

His blue eyes widened in innocence. "Why, Bethany Schrock. I'm shocked!"

"Shootfire!" She snapped forward, cheeks flaming, and smoothed out her apron. "You know what I mean."

He took his arm back and sighed. "Bethany—we've been through this before. I'm trying to get all my ducks in a row." He wiggled his eyebrows again. "And you know how ducks can be."

"Jimmy, be serious, for once in your life. Are you or are you not planning on marrying me?"

"Well, sure. Of course. It's just that I'm not ready yet. I've got a few things I need to do first."

"That's what you told me months ago. It's that horse, isn't it? Lodestar." She crossed her arms against her chest. "You love that horse more than you love me."

"Now, sweetheart, that's not true."

She rolled her eyes. "You're going to keep pining over that horse and using it as an excuse not to get serious."

"I'm not pining for Lodestar. Not much." His smile faded. "I only think about him a few times a day now."

She huffed. "That's a few times more each day than you spend thinking of me."

"I think of you every other minute of every day. Especially how to get you up to the pond for some serious kissing." He leaned toward her to kiss her, but she lunged for the door handle. He reached out to grab her arm before she could slip out of the buggy. "Bethany, hold on a minute. Simmer down."

She closed the door and glared at him. "You just want to kiss so you don't have to talk."

He held his head to one side and smiled at her. "What kind of faith have you in me, that you give me such bad motives?" She ignored him. "Look, I don't want to be a chicken farmer for the rest of my life and I haven't figured a way out of it."

"Can't you get Hank Lapp to propose to your mother?"

"That wouldn't solve anything. Hank Lapp is not a chicken man." He relaxed his grip on her arm. "I wish my brother Paul would return to Stoney Ridge and take over for me."

"Ask Paul to come back."

"I can't. He's settled in at his in-laws, up in Canada. Besides, there were fireworks between my mother and Paul's new wife. I can't ask him to move home just because I prefer horses over poultry."

"But what you really want to do is work with horses."

"I know. But it would take a request from the bishop himself to convince my mother that horses are more important than her chickens." He picked up the reins and gave them a little shake to get the horse moving. "Give me a little time, Bethany." He turned toward her and wiggled his eyebrows in that way that made her smile. "What's the rush, anyway? We've got our whole lives ahead of us." He grasped her hand and wove his fingers through hers.

Later, as Bethany was getting ready for bed, she thought about Jimmy's dilemma and knew he was right, as much as she hated to admit it. He had done a good and noble thing to give up horse training with Galen to help his mother with the chicken and egg business.

But the facts remained: Jimmy loved horses and hated chickens. He had a dream to become a breeder for well-bred, well-trained buggy horses, filling an important need for their church and other districts. Galen had more demand for trained horses than he could fulfill. Last year, as Jimmy apprenticed for Galen, he had developed skills that proved his mettle. It wasn't easy to change Galen King's mind about anything or anybody, but he had grown impressed enough with Jimmy's way with horses that he called him a partner.

David Stoltzfus had just said in Sunday's sermon that God didn't give a desire without planning to fulfill it. Would the Lord give her the desire to marry and have a family if he didn't intend on fulfilling it? Would the Lord give Jimmy a desire to raise horses if he didn't plan to fulfill that?

There were many things about being Amish that frustrated Bethany to no end. What was good for the group was considered good for the individual . . . even if it wasn't. But then, to be fair, there were also many things about being Amish that made life worthwhile.

Have a little faith, Jimmy told her. Where was she putting her faith, anyhow? It had grown leaps and bounds in the last year since she had moved back to Eagle Hill. In many ways, she was a different person than she was a year or two ago.

But her main question wouldn't be silenced, and once again she was asking God: *Would you give us desires if you didn't plan to fulfill them?* She didn't receive an answer, but she didn't feel wrong about asking either. The silence that surrounded her was gentle, not accusing. Perhaps that was enough of an answer. To accept her desires, and Jimmy's, as a mystery.

For now, anyway.

The sun was cresting the hills that framed the back of the farmhouse as Brooke woke. The smoky scent of crisping bacon floated down from the kitchen and in through the open window of the guest flat. Brooke's stomach started to rumble. She threw on a bathrobe when a knock came on the door and there stood Mim, holding a tray that was covered with a red-checkered napkin.

Brooke was relieved whenever she opened the door and found it was someone else besides Vera Schrock, who always looked as if something had displeased her and she was about to issue a complaint. Vera had a tight, drawn look, a near permanent frown, solid and glum-looking. Brooke had expected a similar countenance from the innkeeper, Rose Schrock, and was pleasantly surprised to find Rose to be lovely, warm, and kind, dressed in soft, cheerful colors: turquoise or pink. Vera dressed in drab brown or olive green. No spark, no life. Brooke didn't know how the family abided Vera.

Mim's gaze was fixed on the sky. "The eagles are out." She lifted her chin toward an eagle, soaring above the creek. "They have an aerie in a tree on our property."

Brooke opened the door wide to let Mim cross the threshold. "What's an aerie?"

"It's an eagle's nest. It's huge. Made of sticks and lined with grass and moss. The eagles have been here two years now. Last year, they had one eglet but it died. We're hoping they'll have better luck this year." Mim set the tray on the table in the small living area. "That's why there's yellow tape around that far section of the farm. The Game Commissioner doesn't want bird-watchers bothering the eagles."

"Do they?"

"Yup. Bird-watchers are pretty intense around here. As soon as some eggs are spotted in the aerie, they'll be camped out across the street with their telescopes, day and night."

Brooke smiled. That was the longest speech she had heard come out of Mim Schrock. It pleased her. She was hoping someone, anyone, on this farm would slow down and talk to her a little. She was always noticing them darting around the farm, but rarely still. Especially not those two young boys with the black felt hats—they were in constant motion. Like a blur.

She lifted the large fabric napkin and found a bowl of baked oatmeal, toast with raspberry jam, four strips of thick-sliced bacon, scrambled eggs, orange juice, and a thermos of coffee. "Why, thank you. I thought I smelled bacon frying. It's perfect."

Mim gave a demure nod and darted out the door. Goodness, those Amish were always in a hurry. A cat rubbed against her as she settled at the end of the table. It must have slipped in behind Mim. Brooke thought about banishing it to the great outdoors but decided she didn't mind a little company. Not so much.

Brooke made a grab for the small spiral-bound notebook on the table. Tomorrow, she'd begin to follow the schedule she'd set up for herself:

Rise at 6:00 Meditation
Yoga or brisk walk or hike

She picked up her pen and added:

find eagles' aerie
Breakfast (but with such a large breakfast, perhaps she
    should eat, then exercise)
Construct new life plan
Lunch
Revise new life plan
Scheduled time for spontaneity. Sightsee, window-shop,
    explore, meet new people
Dinner
Inspirational reading, journal writing
Deep breathing exercises
Bedtime 10:00 pm

Her eyes slipped from the notebook to the *Stoney Ridge Times* newspaper that Mim had left under the breakfast tray. She skimmed the headlines and turned the page as her eyes caught on the Mrs. Miracle column. She nestled into the chair, happily distracted. She'd always loved advice columns.

She leaned closer to the newspaper. Interesting—this column was situated on the upper corner of page three, a perfect spot for the eye to land as the pages opened. She knew enough about newspaper layout from a journalism class in college to know this was no accident; the column must receive high traffic. She skimmed the column and found herself smiling at Mrs. Miracle's no-nonsense advice.

Dear Mrs. Miracle,
    My brother is always asking to borrow money from
me. He is divorced and never pays his child support.
He did, however, recently buy a 48" flat screen TV. He
says he needs it so his son will come to his apartment

and watch sports with him. What should I tell him the next time he asks me for money?

Yours truly,
Frustrated

Dear Frustrated,
It sounds as if your brother believes things, like a television, will solve his problems. Ironically, if he didn't have a television in the first place, perhaps he wouldn't be divorced and living away from his son. I wish more people lived without televisions, as I do. Maybe they would talk to each other instead of letting an electronic machine do all the talking for them. But to answer your question, the next time he asks you for money, tell him no.

Sincerely,
Mrs. Miracle

Brooke leaned back in her chair and wondered what Mrs. Miracle might say about her own current dilemma. She could just imagine how she would compose the letter:

Dear Mrs. Miracle,
I need . . . something. I need to reinvent myself. I need to change. A new mantra, a new tagline, a new reason to get up in the morning. Any advice?

Most sincerely,
Empty of Ideas

Or maybe . . .

Dear Mrs. Miracle,

My favorite aunt thinks I spend my life sailing on the wind of others' talent. She thinks I am avoiding something by not discovering my own self. I feel there's no point in reinventing the wheel. Why not borrow from the inspiration of others? Look at how the American public imitates celebrities. Is it so wrong to copy others? Any advice?

Most sincerely,
A Borrower

Brooke took a sip of coffee. Why not? Why not send a letter to Mrs. Miracle and see if she had an answer for her? She flipped the page of her notebook to a fresh sheet and started to write. When she finished, she found an envelope and a stamp in her purse—she traveled well prepared—addressed it, tucked the letter inside, and set it by the door to put in the mailbox on her brisk walk to find the eagles' aerie.

Why not? Why not see what wise old Mrs. Miracle has to say?

6

M im Schrock liked to collect wildflowers and press them
in a book, color intact. Virginia bluebells, coltsfoot,
Dutchman's breeches, sweet white violets. After they dried,
she would carefully glue them on cards and write their bo-
tanical names underneath in her most excellent handwriting.
Her mother said she was a real artist.

Bethany stopped by her room one afternoon as Mim was
gluing flowers on cards. "Those are pretty."

Bethany never said anything nice just to please you. If she
said they were good, then they must be.

"Maybe you could sell them at the Bent N' Dent. Maybe
it could turn into a card business for you. That would sure
make Mammi Vera happy."

Ever since Mim started eighth grade, Mammi Vera was
trying to spur Mim to think ahead about her future, what she
would like to do after she finished schooling. "Sie sehnt net
weider as die Naas lang is," Mammi Vera would say, with a
frown of concentration on her face. *She didn't see further than
her nose is long.* Her grandmother assumed Mim didn't have
enough on her mind, but the problem was her grandmother

had no idea of all that ran through Mim's mind. How could she? She never bothered to ask.

Bethany tossed a manila envelope on Mim's bed. Each week, Bethany dropped off this week's Mrs. Miracle responses and picked up the most recent letters for Mrs. Miracle that were sent to the *Stoney Ridge Times* office. "There's an envelope in there that's supposed to be important. Not sure what's in that, but the receptionist said to make sure Mrs. Miracle saw it pronto."

Bethany waited by the door, arms folded against her chest, as Mim opened and read the letter. It was from the features editor, a man Mim had never met and never wanted to. Bethany said he was quite unappealing, a real curmudgeon. "What's up, Mim? You look as worried as a duck in the desert."

Mim didn't even glance up. "You say that's how I always look."

Bethany lifted an eyebrow. "I've said it before and I'll say it again. I sure hope this Mrs. Miracle gig doesn't blow up in your face. First of all, you're supposed to be eighteen years old to have a column at the newspaper. Secondly, the bishop would not approve of you telling people how to live their life. Thirdly, Rose doesn't know anything about it, so you're being deceitful. Fourthly, Mammi Vera would blow an artery if she knew."

Mim kept her head down. Did Bethany think those concerns hadn't crossed her mind? They did! But Mrs. Miracle had a life of her own.

Bethany waited another long moment, then let out an exasperated snort. "Fine. I've got enough problems of my own." She spun around and walked down the hallway.

As Mim reread the letter, she could hardly breathe. The

editor said he had an offer to syndicate the Mrs. Miracle column. Was she interested? Because he was. Call me! he wrote, underlining it twice.

First, she had no idea what syndication meant. Secondly, whatever it was, she didn't want it.

She pulled the dictionary off her desk and looked up the word:

> **syndication** | ˌsin-də-ˈkā-shən | *noun* • publish or broadcast (material) simultaneously in a number of newspapers, television stations, etc.: *his reports were syndicated to 200 other papers.*

Oh, boy. Mim threw herself on her bed, headfirst.

Geena Spencer had once been a guest at Eagle Hill and liked Stoney Ridge so much she ended up moving here. She became the housemother to the Group Home for wayward girls, and Bethany couldn't get over the changes there—a person would hardly even recognize it anymore. If a house had a personality, the Group Home used to look sad, neglected, lonely. Now it was smiling, laughing, buzzing with activity.

The very first thing Geena had done as housemother was to get rid of the television. The previous housemother let the television stay on all day and all night. As soon as it had been given away, the wayward girls made noises about being bored and *boom!* That was the moment Geena implemented change number two: each girl would be required to work or volunteer ten hours a week in addition to attending school. But they had so much time, Geena pointed out as they howled and complained about the new rule, why not use it for good? So they did, and it did do good. Mostly . . . for the wayward girls.

On a rainy afternoon in early April, Geena stopped by Eagle Hill and Bethany invited her in for tea and fresh hot scones with a drizzled maple glaze. They had developed a comfortable friendship. By the time the two women came into the kitchen, Luke and Sammy were reaching for second and third helpings of the scones cooling on the countertop. Luke's and Sammy's appetites were a kind of natural calamity. Bethany had watched it with amazement for years and yet it still surprised her how much those boys could eat. Not only did they eat a lot, but they ate it fast. They were appalling.

It was always peaceful when Geena came for a visit; even restless Luke didn't need to be jumping up and moving about. He would hang around just to hear her stories about the wayward girls. They especially loved to hear about a tough cookie named Rusty who had blossomed like a summer rose at the Group Home. An aunt had emerged out of nowhere and asked Rusty to come live with her; things were going well, Geena said. A success story. Of course Luke and Sammy lapped up Geena's stories about her work with the Group Home. The boys hadn't been much of anywhere outside of Stoney Ridge, so it was all romance to them.

"Tell me something you learned at school today," Geena said to Luke as she took a third scone. Mid-bite, her eyes flickered to Bethany, who was staring at her. "Sorry," she said with her mouth full. She pushed the basket toward her. "I had a small breakfast."

Bethany had never seen a woman with an appetite like Geena's. It was impressive for someone who was barely five feet tall and hardly tipped the scales at one hundred pounds, soaking wet. She fit right in with Luke and Sammy.

Luke cut a grin at his brother. "We learned that Sammy thinks the moon was made of real cheese."

"It's a mistake anyone could make," Sammy said, scowling at Luke.

Luke got a devilish look on his face as he turned to Geena. "I just so happened to see you and that SEC lawyer driving through town last weekend."

"His name is Allen Turner," Bethany said, eyes on Geena to see her reaction.

Geena stirred sugar into her tea and held her peace. She never corrected anyone or told anyone he was being childish or immature, but often people seemed to realize it themselves. Not Luke, though. He asked her if she was sweet on Allen Turner, and Geena only sipped her tea, pretending he hadn't asked.

Soon, Bethany had enough of Luke. "You boys go outside so I can visit with Geena."

Sammy was no problem and quickly went his own way. He didn't want to hang around to hear their secrets. Luke needed to be asked twice, as usual.

As soon as the boys were out of hearing, Bethany fixed her gaze on Geena. "Is that true? Did you go on a date with Allen Turner?"

Geena waved that away. "We're old friends. You know that." She added another spoonful of sugar to her tea and stirred it, a little nervously, Bethany observed. "I came by to let you know we're going to set a date to turn the soil for the community garden beds."

Last summer, Bethany and Geena started the community

garden as a way to help the down-and-outers in Stoney Ridge. The Group Home worked a plot, and so did other families who were on government aid. The produce from the gardens helped supplement family groceries. It had been hugely successful; this summer there was a waiting list for the plots.

"Oh," Bethany said, but her mind was elsewhere, nowhere near the community gardens.

"You'll help, won't you?" Geena said, between bites of her fourth scone.

Bethany leaned forward. "Geena, I need your advice. What do you do when a person keeps avoiding something because he is overwhelmed by obstacles?"

"Deal with each obstacle, one by one."

One by one. Of course! Why hadn't she thought about that with Jimmy Fisher?

"So, I can count on your help?" Geena said, finishing off her sugary tea.

"Mmm-hmm," Bethany murmured, concocting a plan to knock down Jimmy's biggest obstacle to getting married.

The day suited Mim's mood—wet and cheerless. Earlier today, just after dawn, she was milking Molly only to have the dumb cow shift her big hip and knock Mim right off the milking stool, tipping over the full pail of fresh warm milk. Barn cats, who had been watching the milking from a safe distance, sprang on the spilled milk as if they had conspired with Molly for a free breakfast. When did milking Molly become Mim's job, anyhow?

She plodded along the road to the schoolhouse through the sodden countryside, alone, because her brothers had overslept and she refused to wait for them and risk being late. She made her way carefully around mud and puddles and drowned worms. Even the birds weren't singing this morning.

As Mim approached the schoolhouse, she felt a strange sense that something wasn't right. The schoolhouse was shrouded in mist, cloaked in an oppressive doom. And it was silent. None of the students were outside on the playground, which wasn't at all typical; even rain couldn't keep boys inside when they could be outside.

Something had happened.

Could she have mixed up days again? Was it Saturday? She had done that very thing once, at their old school in York County, and Luke still teased her about it.

But then she saw the backs of a few students huddled together at the open door. She walked up the steps of the schoolhouse and stopped abruptly as she crossed the threshold, expecting something horrific. A dead body, perhaps, or a sinkhole in the center of the schoolhouse that was swallowing it in one bite.

It was nothing like that.

The students' desks and the teacher's desk had been reversed. Everything was in the same spot but facing the opposite direction, a mirror image. Danny stood in the center of the room, a baffled look on his face.

No one had any idea how it had happened.

—⟨ ◊ ⟩—

Early one morning, while Brooke was still in her pajamas, she heard a knock and opened the door to find Mim Schrock with an empty laundry basket in her arms.

"Today's the day we wash sheets."

Mim always had a slightly anxious look, Brooke thought, as she stepped away to let her pass. She enjoyed Mim and tried to detain her with conversation each time she brought breakfast to her. Some might think Mim was dull because she was quiet and watchful, but Brooke could see there was more going on in her mind than she let others know. And it couldn't be a bed of roses living with the gloomy Vera Schrock, who probably hadn't cracked a smile in eons.

Mim headed straight to the bedroom. As she stripped the sheets off the bed, Brooke followed her in and asked, "What would you say, Mim, to a woman who is searching for a new identity? To find herself."

Mim straightened, blinked, pushed her glasses back on the bridge of her nose. "I've actually given this question a great deal of thought lately. What I've decided is that wherever she goes, there she'll be." She pulled the pillowcases off the pillows, one after the other, and bundled the sheets together. "We only have one set of sheets for your bed, so Mom will put them back on later today." She hurried out the door like there was a fire.

Brooke spent the rest of the morning pondering the comment made by fourteen-year-old Mim. "Wherever she goes, there she'll be." There was some truth in those words.

That afternoon, during her "planned spontaneity time," she drove to town to walk around Main Street. She passed the Stoney Ridge Wild Bird Rescue Center and saw a young man inside with a big bird on his gloved arm. Brooke stopped and watched him for a while through the large picture-glass window. If she wasn't mistaken, he was talking to the bird. She had never liked birds, so she moved along. In the air was the scent of bread baking and her tummy rumbled. She couldn't stop thinking about a certain pastry she'd had for breakfast at Eagle Hill yesterday morning. She noticed the Sweet Tooth Bakery and crossed the street.

Inside the bakery, everything looked so delicious in the glass case that Brooke couldn't decide what to pick out. "I'm staying at the Inn at Eagle Hill," she told the clerk, "and the innkeeper made blueberry lemon squares. They were—" Brooke's eyes went to the ceiling—"just amazing! Any chance you have any?"

"No." The clerk seemed greatly annoyed that Brooke would mention anyone else's baking while in her store. She glanced impatiently at the line that was forming behind Brooke.

What to get, what to get . . .

"Try the cinnamon roll," a man behind her in line whispered. "They're out of this world."

Brooke took his advice, bought a coffee to go along with the cinnamon roll, and sat down. She took a bite of the cinnamon roll and froze. It was . . . heavenly. Sweet, flaky, just the right amount of cinnamon.

"Was I right?" The customer who made the suggestion stood by her table.

Brooke swallowed down the bite, nodding, trying not to choke. "So right." He was possibly the most handsome man she'd ever seen. His dark blue eyes had the kind of lashes women envy, fair curly hair around his ears, his features had flawless symmetry and beauty. He was dazzling, startlingly attractive. Hard to tell how old he was—but she guessed he was in his late twenties.

He smiled at her, she smiled back, and she pointed to the empty chair. "Please, sit down."

His name was Jon Hoeffner, he said, a scholar, and he was

taking a sabbatical from the university to do some research in Lancaster on family ancestry.

"Interesting," Brooke said. "I'd love to hear more." Mostly, she'd love to hear more of anything from this gorgeous creature.

"And what about you?" Jon asked. "Did I happen to hear you tell the bakery clerk that you're staying at the Inn at Eagle Hill?"

Brooke nodded. "Do you know it?"

"I've heard good things about it." He took a sip of his coffee. "So, when you're not vacationing at a quaint Amish inn, what do you do?"

"I am a professional art restorer."

Mid-sip, Jon froze. Then he set the coffee cup down and leaned forward, fascinated. "Tell me more," he said, his smile wide and generous. "Tell me everything."

If it weren't for the fact that they were sitting in a bakery in a tiny Amish town, Brooke would have thought he was flirting, being suggestive. "Ask me whatever you want and I'll answer whatever I want," she said in exactly the same tone, and their eyes met.

7

Rose reminded the family of Tobe's mid-April birthday and even organized separate birthday cards from Sammy, Luke, and Mim so that they could each sign them.

This year, Luke was indignant. "Why should I? Tobe never bothers to remember my birthday."

Rose covered Luke's hand with hers, marveling at how big it had become this year. He was inching toward thirteen, an unsettled age. "That was last year. I think Tobe will remember this year. He wants to be part of the family again."

"I'm too old to be sending silly cards to him." Luke snatched back his hand. "It's not like he's my real brother, anyway. He's only my half brother."

Rose felt a flash of anger and gave him a sharp look. "Then why don't you just explain to me what is 'real'? Was it real that winter when Tobe fished you out of the pond you went skating on without checking first to be sure it was frozen over? Was it real when Tobe carried you home from school because you'd broken your arm after falling out of the tree? Tobe *is* your real brother and Bethany *is* your real sister and

I won't hear another word out of you on that subject. Is that clear?" She held a pen out to him.

He signed his name on the card and slunk away.

Luke's defiant nature wore her out. She feared there would always be a part of him that was drawn to risk, ignoring obvious dangers and warnings. He, more than the other children, was most like his father. So like Dean.

Today she had received a letter from Teacher Danny about Luke's bold behavior at school—just like the ones she used to receive from Teacher M.K. last year, on a regular basis. She thought he had turned a corner when Will Stoltz moved to town and took him under his wing at the Wild Bird Rescue Center. Luke's fiery temper was less likely to flare up at small things, his passion for birds motivated him to read and study. But Will had less time for Luke after he found his girlfriend, Jackie. Then Jesse Stoltzfus moved in across the street. Two years behind him in school, Luke admired Jesse's brash ways and tried to act and sound like him. He had no patience for Sammy anymore. Too much of a baby, he would tell him, when Sammy tried to follow the boys around.

Luke had slipped backward on his bumpy road to maturity.

Sammy picked up the pen after Luke had dropped it and studied the card before solemnly signing it, using his newly acquired third-grade cursive handwriting. He bit the tip of his tongue as he wrote.

Rose looked at Sammy affectionately. He was still a little boy, full of wonder. Everything fascinated him. A speckled bird's egg. A rainbow sparkling in the sun. He had made a pet out of a raccoon once, and Dean let him keep it for a spell before setting it free.

Sammy was such a funny little thing, quirky and serious

but never a moment's trouble to her. Unlike Luke, who was a source of constant mischief and friction. Luke would argue that a blackbird was white.

"I did it!" he exclaimed jubilantly, smiling up at her. He handed the pen to Mim, who had to stop and think carefully what she wanted to say before she signed the card.

Mim was so timid, so unsure of herself. She had inherited her grandmother's pessimism, Rose thought regretfully. She seemed to expect the worst from every situation. Well, perhaps it was better than having expected great things and having got so little, the way Dean had viewed the world.

Mim was losing the baby roundness to her face and turning into a young woman. It was funny how you could look at a person every day and not notice how she was changing until something startled you into seeing her with fresh eyes.

Such a gift God had given Rose when these children were born. The ups and downs, the joys and sorrows—motherhood made her life full and rich, to the point of overflowing.

Rose sealed the envelope and put a stamp on the corner. She hurried to put it in the mailbox before the postman came by. As she closed the lid to the mailbox, she watched a car slow and turn into the driveway. As the car sputtered to a stop, she walked toward it, assuming the driver was lost. Out of the car bounced a young woman, tiny and delicate, with hair the color of spice cake, and a belly bulging with pregnancy. She wore a tight T-shirt with an arrow pointing down toward her abdomen, the words *Under Construction* printed across her chest.

Rose slowed her steps. The young woman looked up at the farmhouse, blue eyes glittering, as cold as a February fog off Blue Lake Pond, before she settled on Rose.

"Do you need directions?" Rose asked.

"Not if this is the Inn at Eagle Hill."

"It is."

Luke's dog, Micky, came charging up to the young woman and she batted him away. "I don't like dogs!"

Rose called Micky back to her side.

"You must be Rose. Tobe's stepmother?"

Rose bristled. She disliked being referred to as a step-mother. She might not have been Tobe's biological mother, but she was a mother to him in every way that mattered. "I'm Rose Schrock."

The young woman smiled sweetly. "I'm Paisley. Tobe's girlfriend. And this," she patted her enormous belly, "is your stepson's soon-to-be-born child."

Rose's eyes swept down to the girl's round stomach. Her mouth opened but nothing came out for a full minute. Maybe longer. She was speechless. Paisley didn't even notice. She just beamed as if she was the happiest person on earth. Rose had no idea what to do or to say. She had never known Tobe to have a girlfriend, not ever, and with a name like Paisley, she was fairly certain she would have remembered.

Paisley waved in the direction of the kitchen. "Let's go inside so I can meet Mammi Vera. She's standing at the win-dow looking at us." Her face lit up even more so, if that was even possible. "Oh! There's the little boys! They're pressing their noses to the window. How charming! I can't wait to meet everyone!" She flounced toward the house, then stopped and spun around. "Rose, be a peach and bring my things." She pointed to the car. "Backseat. The trunk doesn't open."

Rose peered through the car windows. Crumpled bags and empty containers from fast-food restaurants littered the floor. She opened the back door and brought out a battered overnight suitcase and a bulky purse. A feeling of dread filled her, as if a tornado was heading her way but she wasn't sure which direction it came from.

In the kitchen, Rose cleared her throat and introduced Paisley to Vera as Tobe's friend and tried to smile but knew it came out forced and wrong.

Paisley smiled largely at Vera. "Oh, dear Mammi Vera! My sweet Tobe has told me so very much about you! He just adores you." Then she turned to the boys and spoke in a sugary voice to them. "Aren't you two munchkins just the cutest things!"

Mim walked in the kitchen and froze. For a long moment, everyone seemed completely dazed by Paisley's looks and by the way she talked. For a girl with such a small frame, she had the biggest, roundest stomach they had ever seen.

On and on Paisley went, oohing and aahing over what a quaint village Stoney Ridge was and how charming Eagle Hill was. Buttered up by the compliments, Vera's tight face softened. Rose thought Vera would recoil from such overfamiliarity but, to her amazement, she saw her almost preening.

The boys stared at Paisley, their mouths hung open, their eyes opened even wider. Rose put a firm hand on their shoulders and squeezed. "Close your mouths, boys, before a fly lands in them. Time to go feed the livestock."

"Aw, Mom," Luke said, eyes glued on Paisley.

"Go," Rose said, shooing the boys outside. Mim wasn't much better—she was still standing against the doorjamb with a baffled look on her face. "Mim, you help them." Sammy practically stumbled over Mim because he couldn't take his eyes off Paisley. Rose closed the kitchen door and turned to face Paisley. She tried to smile. "Tobe should have told us about you."

"I suppose he's shy like that," Paisley said. "But he'll have to get used to having a wife."

Rose froze. "A wife?"

Paisley laughed at the shocked look on her face. "We haven't tied the knot yet. Soon, though. As soon as he gets out of jail. He needs to make an honest woman out of me."

Vera's eyes went wide and she clutched her chest. Rose wasn't too worried. Vera clutched her chest a lot.

"When did you last see Tobe?" Rose asked.

"Before he went into the slammer." Paisley laughed and patted the bump of her stomach. "Obviously." Her blue eyes darted around the room, taking everything in. "Do you happen to know when he'll be released?"

"Any day now," Vera said firmly, though Rose knew she had no idea.

"Soon, you'll be admiring all this," she said to the unborn baby.

"And how did you say you met Tobe?" Rose said.

"Actually, I didn't say." Paisley peered out the kitchen window. "He was a customer at the restaurant where I worked. It was love at first sight."

"Paisley," Rose said carefully, "do you have any proof?"

"Proof?"

"About Tobe. Try to understand—you seem to know a great deal about us and yet we've never heard a word about you."

Paisley looked at Rose for a long moment, then went to her luggage that Rose had set in the corner of the kitchen. She rummaged around, and then held up a blue shirt.

Rose took the shirt from her. She had made Tobe that shirt three Christmases ago. She remembered every stitch, every seam. Big and square, narrow at the waist. Paisley pulled something else out of her battered suitcase and thrust it at Rose. It was a picture of Tobe with his arm around the shoulders of a then-thin Paisley. "That was taken a year or so ago."

Vera took the photo from Rose and sat down to examine it.

"I can hardly wait to meet the girls and see more of your wonderful house and farm." Paisley peeked into the living room. "It must be wonderful to be so rich!" Her face was flushed and eyes bright, much too bright.

Rich? *Rich!* Rose nearly laughed out loud but didn't dare, with Vera only a few feet away.

Just this morning a neighbor brought over a bushel of cabbage claiming they'd had a bumper crop last fall and needed to start cleaning out the root cellar to get ready for spring. Lately, it seemed, everyone thought of the Schrocks when they needed to share their over-wintered fall vegetables. Eagle Hill had more onions, carrots, turnips, and cabbages than Rose knew what to do with, yet she was grateful for the kindness of their neighbors.

Sammy and Luke felt differently. They would bitterly complain when they faced yet another bowl of stewed cabbage or boiled turnips. She could just predict the scene: one or the other boy would make a face and ask why neighbors never seemed to have an abundance of ice cream or cake. Their ungratefulness would prompt Vera to launch into a long lecture about children in other countries who didn't have enough to eat, then she would wind down by tossing proverbs at them.

Paisley turned to Rose. "Just tell me where to go unpack and I'll take care of myself. I'm very low maintenance."

There was an awkward silence as Rose realized Paisley aimed to stay at Eagle Hill.

Finally Vera broke in. "You can settle into Bethany's room. It has the best view in the house. Second story. It's the room to the right of the stairs. Make yourself at home. Just let Rose know if you need anything."

"Second story? My, how grand!" Paisley flounced up the stairs with her little suitcase.

Rose turned to look at Vera. "You *want* her to stay?"

"Of course I do. If she's carrying Tobe's child, I want her to settle in and make herself at home. Don't you see? She's going to tie him down to the farm. He'll stay here, if he has a wife and child to care for. He'll settle down for good. I always knew it would happen." Vera was fairly glowing with happiness. "Kommt zeit kommt ratt." *When the time comes, there will be a way.*

"Has Tobe ever mentioned her name to you? Because he certainly never said a word to me about a girl named Paisley."

Vera's smile faded. "Love at first sight, she said."

"I find it hard to believe you're not horrified that Tobe might be a father without benefit of matrimony."

Vera patted the hairs at the back of her neck. "Well, sometimes the young get a little ahead of the wedding."

"And what if the child Paisley is carrying isn't Tobe's but some other man's child?"

Vera clutched her chest. "Oh my soul. Why would anyone lie about such a thing?"

"I don't know. But doesn't it seem fishy to you?"

"Maybe you're just being suspicious."

"Vera, I'm just trying to be cautious."

"And I'm trying to be positive. Don't you see? This could be the very thing Tobe needs to join the church."

Rose raised her eyebrows. "And you think a girl like . . . Paisley . . . would want to join the Amish church?"

"Love at first sight, she said." Vera's chin jutted out. "She loves Tobe and a woman will do anything for the man she loves." She sat heavily in a chair, as if exhausted. "Why else would she be here?"

Maybe . . . maybe Vera was right. If Paisley were carrying Tobe's child, maybe he would finally settle down and become the man he was meant to be. Just when Rose thought Vera might be suffering from a little softening of the brain, she up and surprised her with some insightful thing she said. From time to time, Rose felt a surge of affection for Vera, but mainly she felt she brought a lot of unhappiness on herself. Goodness, she went out halfway to invite it.

Rose gazed at Vera, a stout, sad woman in her sixties, a widow, her only son gone. Let her have this hope.

Then another thought crowded in: What about Naomi? What would that hope mean for her?

Naomi felt unsettled, the way air shifted right before a rainstorm was due in. But the sky was delphinium blue and empty of clouds. Restless and at loose ends, she picked up her scissors, grabbed a swatch of pink fabric from her scrap basket, and cut triangles for a new quilt. She needed a new project, something to calm her mind. Her fingers flew without needing a pattern, a skill that irked Bethany. Each triangle was identical to the one before it. When she had finished with the pink fabric, she glanced up and noticed Bethany come up the driveway. She had been working at the Sisters' House today and was on her way home. Naomi thought she might stop by the house, but she beelined into the barn. She set the scissors down and stared out the window, still bothered by something she saw earlier today. Or thought she saw.

Earlier this afternoon, Naomi had dropped off a package at the post office and she spotted a man walking down Main Street. She didn't immediately recognize him until he crossed the street. There was something familiar about the way he walked, arms bent and aggressive. If she didn't know better, she thought the man looked like Jake Hertzler . . . but that was impossible. He was long gone and good riddance to him. She never—not ever ever ever—wanted to set eyes on that horrible man again.

Naomi had only seen Jake Hertzler one time, late at night, though she would never forget it. It would be easy to give in to feelings of hatred for that awful man. But she refused. Instead, she prayed for his soul whenever she thought of him because she knew it was in jeopardy. It was impossible, she knew, to allow hatred to grow in your heart if you prayed for that person. Hatred may visit your heart, but you needn't invite it to stay.

She picked out another scrap of fabric from her basket—another soft shade of pink—and set to work cutting out pieces. She felt a little better, but not much, and she reached into her pocket for a Tums. Something just didn't feel right today.

───◦ ◊ ◦───

Bethany went hunting for Galen in his barn and found him, head bowed low, in the tack room, where he was rubbing down an enormous oval collar with a rag of liniment. She watched him work for a moment, breathing in the smell of saddle soap and oil and horses. Galen looked at home in the tack room, but he looked lonely too. "Do you use that for training buggy horses?"

He spun to face her, startling at the sound of her voice. "This collar? No. But Amos Lapp bought a new Belgian for fieldwork and he shies at the collar. He asked me for help, so I thought I'd start with a larger collar so it's not rubbing the horse's neck. I wanted to clean it first."

Clean it? Why, every piece of equipment in this tack room looked like it had been spit and polished that very morning. Meticulous. Fastidious. Galen didn't even use metal nails to drape the leather bridles—only wooden pegs, so nothing would crimp or crack. Curry combs, leather hole punchers, hoof trimmers, shears were hung in designated spots. Rolled leg wraps, bandages, tins of liniment and oil and saddle soap were arranged in a single row above the workbench. Lead ropes were coiled as neatly as lariats. Stacked on a tack trunk was a pile of clean horse blankets.

"Is it always like this?"

He looked around the small room. "Like what?"

"So . . . scrupulously tidy?"

"Yes, except after one of your brothers have been in it." Galen glanced up at the wall wreathed with neatly hung harnesses. "The tack room is one of the most important places in the barn. Everything in its place, and a place for everything."

Why, Bethany should bring the old sisters over to this tack room on a field trip, that's what she should do. They could take a lesson from Galen.

He took the soiled liniment rag, folded it in half, and

draped it over a wooden peg as precisely as Rose draped a dish towel over the kitchen sink faucet. "If you're looking for Naomi, she's in the house."

Oh! She had become so fascinated with the orderliness of the tack room that she forgot why she had come. "Galen, would you help me find Lodestar?"

He looked up at Bethany in surprise. "You think that horse is around here? I figured he'd be long gone by now."

"Maybe. But maybe not. Jake Hertzler stole Lodestar from Jimmy to make sure everyone knew he had the upper hand, but I don't think he ever cared about the horse other than turning a profit. So wouldn't it make sense that he would try to sell Lodestar again? He's a pretty valuable horse. There are warrants out for Jake's arrest—I doubt he wants to drag a horse around with him while he's on the run."

"I doubt even Jake Hertzler would be bold enough to sell such a distinctive horse at an auction in this county."

"You never met Jake, did you?"

Galen shook his head. "I saw him once in his truck, but it was getting dark. I'm not sure I would know him if I saw him."

"I just have the strangest feeling that he's nearby. I can't explain it."

Galen's dark eyebrows shot up. "Have you seen him?"

"No. Maybe I'm just hanging around Naomi too much. She's always sensing things that aren't visible."

Galen stiffened. He didn't like to hear any implied criticism about his sister. "Naomi has good intuition."

Bethany nodded. "I know, I know. I think that's what I'm starting to pay attention to."

"Maybe you should call that SEC lawyer Allen Turner and tell him what you told me."

"I thought of it, but I haven't actually seen hide nor hair of Jake. It's just a hunch. A feeling. I have no proof."

"The spring auctions are just starting up again. I could ask around about Lodestar."

Satisfied, Bethany turned to go.

"The chance of finding Lodestar again is low, Bethany. But even if I did find him, would you really want him back? I thought Jimmy had made up his mind to give up horse breeding."

Bethany kicked a piece of straw with her shoe. "Haven't you noticed a change in Jimmy? Something's wrong. He's missing his spark. I think he needs that horse back. Maybe once Lodestar is back, everything else will fall into place for him."

"Like . . . proposing?"

Shootfire! How did everybody seem to know she had matrimony on her mind? She put her hands on her hips. "I don't know what you're talking about, Galen King."

He grinned. "I'll do what I can. If Lodestar is anywhere in Lancaster County, I'll find him."

⁓ ◊ ⁓

Rose made a phone call to the minimum security federal prison where Tobe was being held, saying she had an emergency and needed to get a message to him.

"Just one moment," and there was a shuffling of papers before the voice came back. "Is this a documented emergency?"

"In what way?"

"Is it a matter of life or death for an immediate family member?"

Rose had to admit that no, it wasn't. The operator then

suggested she had three choices—she could send a letter to the inmate or have his lawyer call and speak to him or wait for the inmate to use his prepurchased minutes during his free time. Then she hung up without a goodbye.

Rose pressed her forehead against the phone's receiver. Frustrating! Today's mail had come and gone, though maybe Mim could take the scooter into town and deliver it to the post office. Even so, a letter wouldn't reach Tobe for a day or so. Then an answer back might take another few days. It might be four or five days before she heard back from him. Should she try to go visit him? She had offered to visit him but he had discouraged her, telling her he'd prefer letters. To be frank, visiting a prison filled her with panic.

Should she call Allen Turner? He was a go-between for Tobe and his court-appointed attorney. But then she dismissed that thought. She couldn't involve him in a family issue like this.

Back in the house, Rose dashed off a letter to Tobe to find out if he knew a woman named Paisley. She had just arrived at Eagle Hill, with plans to stay. Also, with plans to deliver a baby. His baby.

And did he have *any* idea yet when he might be released from prison?

She had just sent Mim off to town with the letter when she heard Paisley call out to her. "Oh Rose. I've had a little accident. Can you come here? Quickly?"

Rose hurried upstairs to Bethany's room. There in the middle of the quilt Bethany had just finished—the first quilt she had ever made—was a tipped-over bottle of bubble-gum-pink nail polish. The polish had started with a puddle and was now spreading out. Paisley stood in the center of the room, a blank look on her face. "I was polishing my toes and must have knocked the bottle over."

Rose quickly picked up the bottle and lifted the quilt as carefully as she could, so the rivers of polish would remain on that one quilt block and not spread onto others.

"Oh dear, oh dear," Paisley said, fanning her eyes with her hand as if she was trying not to cry. "It's my condition, you see. I have become so clumsy."

Rose's first inclination was to ask her why she would paint her toenails on someone's handmade quilt, but instead she said, "It'll be all right. Bethany can replace that quilt block and it will be good as new." She was trying to be polite to the girl. It would be a painstaking task to fix this quilt.

"Well," Paisley snuffled like a little child. "If you're sure."

As Rose carried the quilt downstairs to the basement to try to get the stain out, she cringed, thinking of Bethany's reaction. She was going to hit the roof when she saw her spoiled quilt. She had just finished it! Her first quilt.

After Paisley had recovered from her episode of near tears, she found Rose hanging the quilt on the clothesline and said she wanted a tour of the whole farm. Rose showed her the garden, the henhouse, the pastures, Silver Queen and her colt, and the barn. As they walked, Paisley was full of questions like how fast do chickens lay eggs—daily—and how long did it take for a horse to have a colt—about eleven months—and were sheep a good investment—no—and how much money did Rose think the whole place was worth? She asked Paisley what made her so curious about Eagle Hill and she said, "Oh, well. Tobe can't stop raving about the place." She peered into Flash's stall and the old horse peered back at her. "I suppose it's become like home to me."

Rose was just about to ask Paisley where *her* home was, when Sammy came out of the feed room, pushing a wheelbarrow filled with hay. Paisley made a big fuss over him. "You're such a little boy to be pushing that big wheelbarrow!"

Rose cringed. She knew how sensitive Sammy was about his small stature. His cheeks turned red and he got flustered and called her Parsley. She laughed the first time, then she got irritated when he called her Parsley a second time.

"Sammy," Rose said, "I hear Silver Queen neighing for her dinner. Why don't you head out to her."

Sammy grabbed the handles of the wheelbarrow and hurried out the barn door.

As soon as he was gone, Rose turned to Paisley. "Please don't embarrass him. He'll learn your name. It's just a little . . . unusual."

Paisley lifted her eyebrows at Rose and then nodded as if she understood a great secret. "Oh! Tobe didn't tell me that Sammy was developmentally delayed."

"What?" Rose said. "No! Not in the least."

Luke came out of the feed room holding two buckets of oats. He walked through the aisle and out the barn door without a word, his face tight. A moment later, Rose heard a bloodcurdling scream come from the front yard.

"Luke Schrock! What have you done?!"

Oh dear. Bethany must have returned from the Sisters' House and seen the quilt hanging on the clothesline. Rose had tried everything she could think of to remove the nail polish from the quilt, but the stain was permanent. She flew outside and dashed to the clothesline. Tending to the horses in the pastures, the boys dropped the feed and came running toward the clothesline with all their might. Bethany stood by the quilt, examining the stain.

"It wasn't Luke, Bethany," Rose said, trying to stave off an explosion of words aimed at Luke. "It was Tobe's friend, Paisley."

Bethany looked like she was trying not to cry. "What? Who?"

"Her!" Luke pointed to Paisley, walking toward them from the barn, as if she didn't have a care in the world. "And she's staying in your room." He was scowling at Paisley as she approached them.

"That would be me," Paisley said, with an apologetic smile on her face. "I spilled my nail polish while I was doing my toes." She stuck a hand out to Bethany, who was staring at her with a baffled look on her face. "Let's see. You must be Bethany. I'm Paisley. Tobe's Paisley. He's told me all about you."

Off in the distance, Rose noticed something awry. "The goat!" It had gotten into Silver Queen's pasture and pulled hay off the wheelbarrow. The buckets, now empty of oats, lay on their sides, abandoned by Sammy. Silver Queen and her colt were helping themselves to the hay. Rose shooed Luke and Sammy off to finish feeding the rest of the stock.

Rose rubbed her temples. Could this day get any worse?

8

Brooke liked Jon Hoeffner. She liked him quite a bit. He was possibly the most charming and easy-to-talk-to man she had ever met. He must be spoken for; a man like him wouldn't be unattached. Could he?

She was taken aback when Jon waved to her at the Sweet Tooth Bakery the very next day when she dropped by.

"Good. I was hoping you'd be here," he said, and her heart skipped a beat.

He seemed to be especially fascinated with her work and asked numerous questions, which was so different from other men who only talked about themselves. "But how," he asked, leaning toward her, resting his forearms on the table, "does restoration differentiate itself from forgery?"

"It's entirely different," Brooke said, trying not to sound a little touchy on the subject. She was still sensitive about the museum curator's accusation that she had been treading in dangerous waters. "Paintings are like fingerprints—they're very unique, and for most forgers, there's simply too much for them to duplicate. People get fooled when they're only familiar with an artist's name and not much else. You need to know what an artist's brushstrokes look like, what his or her favorite subject matters and compositions are, what kinds of mediums, materials, sizes, and formats they usually work in."

Jon didn't seem at all bored, quite the opposite. How refreshing! "I think it's also important to know what the art looks like from the back, how it's usually framed, mounted, or displayed, how and where it's titled or numbered, what gallery it's been in, what labels it's likely to have."

She paused again, aware she was doing all the talking, giving him an option to change the subject if he wanted. But his eyes were glued on hers and he nodded to encourage her to continue. "Then, of course, there's signatures. A lot of forgers make the mistake of not studying an artist's signature. You'd be amazed how many forgers miss something as small as setting the signature where an artist typically locates it."

"Signatures?" Jon said, eyebrows lifting in surprise. "You can duplicate an artist's signature?"

She smiled. "That's one of the easiest things in the world for me to do."

"And you've never gotten caught?"

She bristled. She could practically feel the hair rise on the back of her neck. "I'm a legitimate art restorer. Besides," she tore off a bite of her cinnamon roll, "it's hard to fool someone who knows how to analyze art."

"Show me. Can you copy my signature?" He wrote it out on a piece of paper and slid it toward her.

She picked up the paper and studied his signature, noticing the way he curled his *H*, closed the circles on his *O*. He handed his pen to her and she wrote out his signature, then handed it to him.

"Amazing! It's . . . nearly identical."

She grinned at his response. "It's easy when you know what you're looking for."

"Yes." He smiled back at her. "I can see how that would be true."

⌐ ১ ◊ ৹ ⌐

Vera marched into the kitchen where Rose was preparing dinner. "Those boys need to keep quiet. For Paisley's sake. She's trying to rest in the living room before supper."

"I just sent them outside to play. They're tossing a ball back and forth."

"They're too loud. They're always loud. They can't do anything quietly."

Rose was cutting an onion to make chicken soup. With a match, she lit the blue ring of fire on the stove top and placed a big soup pot on the burner. She started to sweat the onion with a little olive oil, then added chopped carrots and celery. "Well, they are boys, Vera. They aren't doing anything wrong."

"It's not good for her to be stressed. She says her nerves get easily frazzled."

"Then why did she arrive at a stranger's home toward the end of her pregnancy?" Rose added chicken broth to the pot, shredded chicken, noodles, minced parsley. "What could be more stressful than that? She should be with her own family."

"She doesn't have any family. She told me so." Vera's lips fit into a tight line. She crossed her arms against her chest. "You will try to treat her nice, won't you?"

The soup began to simmer and Rose stirred it with a wooden spoon. "Oh, certainly," she said, feeling more than a little bit aggravated at all the fuss. As Vera went outside to tell the boys to stop playing so loudly, Rose turned her attention back to making dinner, with enough banging and clanging to shake the teeth loose in Paisley's head and frazzle her nerves good.

Finally, Paisley came in from the living room. "Is there any way I can help get dinner ready?"

Rose looked up from stirring dough for biscuits, surprised and pleased. "Would you wash and dry these dishes?" She tilted her chin to motion toward a small mountain of dirty dishes in the sink.

Paisley craned her neck to look behind Rose, frowning. "There's no dishwasher."

"No. We hand wash all the dishes." She set the bowl of biscuit dough to the side and reached for the hot water faucet. Water started to fill the sink as Rose squirted some dish soap into it. She swirled her hand in the water to suds up the soap. "All ready for you."

Paisley took a few steps back. "Oh, bummer. I wish I could help, but I have very sensitive skin."

"Sensitive skin?"

"Yes. Haven't you ever noticed all the skin lotion commercials on TV? The actors are always redheads. Like me." She pulled a ringlet out of her ponytail and twirled it around her finger. "Of course you wouldn't! You don't have a TV!" She held out her hands. "Anyway . . . my hands need special care or I break out in a terrible rash. I wish I could help. I really, truly do." She smiled a weak attempt at an apology and went outside to sit on the porch swing in the sun.

By the time Bethany had moved a few things out of her room to make space for Paisley, she was calming down from the quilt disaster. A tiny little bit. *Shootfire!* Who was this pregnant Paisley, anyhow? Bethany didn't like her and didn't know why the family was welcoming her with open arms. *Double shootfire!*

She came downstairs to help Rose get supper ready, but the kitchen was empty. There was something good-smelling on the stove top and Bethany peeked inside, hoping Rose had made a broth-based soup and not that awful cream of mushroom that Mammi Vera was so fond of. Whatever it was, it would need to be stretched tonight. She had learned quite a bit about stretching soups from her weekly meal preparation for the down-and-outers at the Second Chance Café. Stretching a cream soup meant dumping in more cream. You ended up with a bowl of hot salty milk. Disgusting.

Bethany had seen Jimmy Fisher earlier in the day, and when she heard he would be dropping by Galen's to talk horses, she invited him for dinner. She peeked out the window, hoping to catch sight of Jimmy, and noticed Paisley walking around on the wooden porch. Then she saw Jimmy come through the hole in the privet.

Before Jimmy reached the porch steps, Bethany saw him stop abruptly, startled, as he realized there was a stranger on the porch. "Hello," he said to Paisley, and Bethany leaned closer to the window, opening it up a crack.

Paisley perked right up and said, in a giggly voice, "Well, hello to you. My, my, my. No one ever told me that I'd be encountering such a handsome man on a dusty old Amish farm."

Jimmy grinned that devilish grin of his, which made Paisley practically swoon. She giggled and held out her hand to him. Paisley's voice dropped to a whisper, but Bethany could tell she was talking up a storm. Jimmy laughed, which made Bethany all the more suspicious of Paisley. If she was so in love with her brother Tobe, then why was she flirting with the first fellow who came along?

Bethany saw Paisley grab the crook of Jimmy's arms and cling tightly. She jumped away from the window and plastered a sweet smile on her face as they entered the kitchen.

"How nice," Bethany said, trying to keep her voice in check. "I see you've met Paisley." She smiled as sweetly as she could. She took a handful of spoons and grabbed some napkins and put them on the table. "Paisley, perhaps you could help set the table for dinner."

Paisley let go of Jimmy as if it took all her strength to pull her hands off him and said she didn't know the first thing about setting tables, but perhaps Jimmy could help? She flashed her dimples at Jimmy and he quickly jumped to her rescue. In fact, Jimmy ended up setting the table as Paisley giggled and told him how clever he was, and Bethany smoldered as she set out butter and jam for the biscuits.

As if stomachs had an alarm clock, the boys and Mim appeared in the kitchen. Rose helped Mammi Vera in from the living room.

"Supper's ready," Bethany said. "Paisley, why don't you sit between Sammy and Luke." She pointed to a chair to sit in, but Paisley had already darted over to be next to Jimmy.

"You can sit there, sister Bethany, and mind those two little rapscallions. I'll keep an eye on this special guy." Paisley offered Bethany her sweetest smile.

Jimmy wiggled his eyebrows at Bethany, which only made her all the more annoyed.

Rose had a belief that many a skirmish could be avoided by the timely appearance of food, but Bethany figured she hadn't shared a meal with someone like Paisley before. All during dinner, sparks flew between Bethany and Paisley like a house cat in a thunderstorm. Jimmy, Bethany noticed with annoyance, had a foolish grin on his face the entire meal, like he was having a wonderful time.

Later that evening, after Rose had cleaned up the kitchen from supper, she heard a knock at the kitchen door and opened it to find Galen smiling down at her, handsome in a black coat and trousers, with Paisley hanging on to his arm. "I just met your newest guest." His voice was happy sounding, but his face was curious and stunned.

As they walked through the door, Galen unhooked Paisley's hand from his and stood near Rose.

Paisley flashed him a saucy smile. "I just can't get over Amish men! Every time I turn around, another dashing fellow appears out of nowhere."

Rose saw the look on Galen's face go from puzzled and amused to wary and cautious. He ignored Paisley's overly effusive comment and turned to Rose. "Would you like to go for a walk?"

"Absolutely." She grabbed a shawl off the wall peg and noticed Paisley's mouth open as if she was going to invite herself along and quickly closed the door behind her. Paisley would have to fend for herself. Something, Rose suspected, she was probably quite good at.

With the barest turn of the head, Galen said, "I've been told you had an eventful day."

"Indeed it was. I'll tell you about it on the way. Who told you?"

"Jimmy filled me in before he headed home tonight."

There was still some fading light left in the sky as they walked behind the house toward the ridge. From somewhere far off came the bellowing of a cow. The chickens had gone to roost in the henhouse, and the chill of evening had begun settling in. Once they had reached the trail that led up the hill, Galen reached out and took Rose's hand.

"I thought you already had a guest using the flat."

"She's not a guest of the inn. She's a guest . . . of the family."

"She's staying in the house?"

"At least for tonight. She says she's a friend of Tobe's."

Galen's eyebrows lifted sharply.

"I sent a letter to Tobe to find out if he does, indeed, know her."

Galen tilted his chin. "Why is she here? She looks like she's about to . . . fresh." Color rose in his cheeks.

"Good grief, Galen. She's not a cow. She's a woman. I'm . . . not exactly sure why she's here. Why now."

Understanding filled Galen's eyes. "So she's carrying Tobe's child?"

Rose yanked her hand out of his and wrapped the shawl tightly around her. "There's no proof that her baby is Tobe's. Only Paisley's word. We've never seen her before in our lives. I tried calling the prison to see if I could get word to him, but it wasn't possible. My letter to him won't even arrive until midweek. Until then, it seems best to be hospitable to the girl."

"Why would she make such a thing up?"

"I have no idea."

"Do you believe her?"

"I . . . can't quite read her. I don't trust her." She walked up the ridge trail ahead of him. "Galen, are you going to tell Naomi what I've told you?"

"Is it a secret?"

"Yes. No. I just . . . would rather wait until I hear something from Tobe."

"But why should it matter to Naomi whose baby it is?"

She stopped and spun around. "You must be joking."

Galen looked at her blankly.

"You must realize Tobe and Naomi have some kind of understanding."

He shook his head, a little too forcefully. "No, they don't. You're mistaken."

"Galen, you think of Naomi as a child. She's a grown woman. She's old enough to make her own choices."

"Tobe might be interested in her, but she has too much sense to—"

"To fall for a Schrock?" That wasn't fair. She regretted saying it as soon as the words spilled out of her mouth.

He looked hurt. "That's not what I was going to say."

"I know you have doubts about Tobe. Naomi knows that too. But you can't predict who you'll fall in love with, can you? No wonder she can't talk to you about their relationship."

"Relationship? He's in jail! They don't have a relationship."

"Once you see Naomi and Tobe together, I believe your doubts will vanish."

"No, I don't think so, Rose." Galen offered a shaky smile. "Why are we talking about such a thing on a beautiful night like tonight?"

They walked up to the ridge in silence, each alone with

their own thoughts, a wedge between them. As Rose tried to cope with all the day had brought, she was glad she had come to the top of the ridge to stargaze on this dark night. The clouds kept racing across the moon like smoke from a fire. Drinking in the beauty of a night sky always reminded her of the infinite majesty of God and the finite trivialness of her problems. God was bigger than any problem life could throw at her.

She leaned against him and he put his arm around her.

"Can I do anything? I'd do anything to help."

"I know you would." And Rose did know.

The next afternoon, Naomi walked over to Eagle Hill to see if Bethany wanted to ride with her to the Sisters' Bee over at Edith Fisher's house.

Bethany came out of the door before she reached the porch, an anxious look on her face. "Did Galen tell you?"

"Tell me what?"

Bethany glanced at the house. "Jimmy didn't say anything?"

The pinched look on Bethany's face worried Naomi. "What's wrong?"

"Nothing, really. Well, something is wrong, actually. Someone is terribly wrong, I suppose you could say. And I'd rather you hear it from me first." She sat down on the porch steps and patted a spot next to her for Naomi. "A girl showed up out of the blue yesterday." She pointed to a rusty car that was blocking the driveway.

Micky ran up to Naomi and curled up beside her. "A new guest?" she said, stroking his big head. She loved this silly dog.

"No, not a guest at the inn. She says she's a friend of Tobe's."

Naomi's hand stopped in mid-pat, but Micky looked up at her and she finished the stroke. "Oh."

"A close friend. She says she was his . . . girlfriend. Her name is Paisley. Does that name ring a bell to you? Did Tobe ever mention a Paisley?"

Naomi looked away. "No." She felt a sudden chill.

"I didn't think so." Bethany took in a deep breath. "I have to tell you this before someone else does. This Paisley is pregnant. Very pregnant. Soon to deliver. She says . . ."

Naomi could feel the back of her neck get cold and clammy.

"She says . . . that Tobe is the baby's father." Bethany's fists clenched. "But I don't believe a word she says, Naomi. You shouldn't, either."

In instant response, Naomi's throat tightened with fear and her pulse thrummed fast in her ears. She knew, in a disembodied way, that she would remember this moment forever. She knew the time and the date, and the way she sat on the porch steps with her hand stroking the head of the dog. She knew, with a certainty that she had never felt before about anything, that Paisley was going to bring trouble into her life. Real trouble, threatening everything she had hoped for.

Out the kitchen window, Rose noticed Bethany and Naomi with their heads bent together outside on the porch steps, then she saw Naomi walk back toward her home, shrinking away like an animal that had received a blow. Shoulders slumped, chin down, hands clenched in tight fists. It was a look of Naomi's with which Rose was familiar; it usually was a sign that she was suffering from a headache.

But just ten minutes ago, she had slipped through the privet looking entirely different. Happy, lighthearted, practically glowing.

Rose's heart skipped a beat. *Oh no. Oh no no no.* Bethany must have told her about Paisley.

9

Brooke Snyder set out on her twenty-minute walk eager and happy, her step animated as she strode along the crunching gravel. She walked down the road beside green shoots of new grass that were sleek with dew, glistening in the morning sun, quivering now and then from a breeze. The world was resplendent, quiet and fresh, with sights and sounds of a new day. The creak of a windmill's turning arms, the whinny of a horse in a pasture, the cawing of crows on a sagging telephone line.

Why, the weather alone made her spirits dance. The mid-morning sun felt like a golden caress on her back. A few meringue puffs of clouds floated high in the blue sky, a blue so rich it startled the senses.

She passed by an Amish farmer and his son tilling fields, their plows harnessed to six brown, long-eared mules. When the breeze changed direction, she could even smell the good earthiness of the freshly turned dirt. A number of black-and-white cows stood along a wooden fence, rhythmically chewing their cud, regarding her with mild interest as she walked past them. A patchwork cat sat on a fence post, washing its face with an orange paw. A clumsy bumblebee buzzed around her, then dipped into a patch of yellow dandelions. An Amish woman walked briskly past her on the other side of the road, turning her bonneted head at the last moment to give her a shy smile.

The Amish were such ordinary people, but in that very ordinariness Brooke saw goodness and decency. The men were built broad and strong, their thick hands calloused and hard. The women were truly plain by modern standards, with no makeup or hair coloring to camouflage the effects of aging. Clearly, they dressed for comfort rather than style, though she was surprised to see orange crocs on the feet of the woman who just passed by her. They surprised her, these people.

Suddenly inspired, she wished she had brought her sketchpad with her to capture these bucolic scenes. With a start, she realized it was the very first time she'd had such a thought, in which a germ of an idea welled up inside her and she wanted to see it bear fruit, to become something. Her gait slowed as she tried to memorize all she saw on her walk. As soon as she returned to the guest flat, she would get those images down on paper before she forgot them.

But to her surprise, she didn't return back to the guest flat at Eagle Hill for two hours and then she had to hurry. She wanted to find a new outfit in town to wear, one that would bring out the gold flecks in her eyes, hoping she might accidentally-on-purpose bump into Jon Hoeffner later today. The sketches were forgotten.

Later that morning, as soon as Rose saw Brooke Snyder's car drive off, she hurried down to the guest flat to do a quick dusting and change the bed sheets. Brooke Snyder could be a talker, as she had discovered one morning when she brought a breakfast tray to her. She didn't mind chatting a little with the guests, but today she was already behind in her morning work and it was nearly noon.

She was pulling the top sheet off the bed as Paisley walked in and announced, "I'd like some breakfast. Would you mind bringing it to me? I'll be in my room."

Rose's teeth clenched. "Breakfast was hours ago, Paisley. But lunch will be on the table before too long." She yanked the bottom sheet off the bed, a little more firmly than she needed to. "In the kitchen. That's where we eat."

Paisley tilted her head at Rose, then walked around the rooms in the guest flat. "You know, this should do nicely for us. For a while, anyway."

Rose gathered wet towels from the bathroom. "I beg your pardon?"

"I think Tobe and I and the baby will move in down here. Until you can find someplace else to live."

Rose stiffened. "Excuse me? Why would I need to find someplace else to live?"

"Eagle Hill is our home. Tobe's, mine, and the baby." She caressed her high stomach, as if to remind Rose that she was about to deliver a child. There was something about her blue eyes, though, that looked like she was shooting poison darts. She'd never seen blue eyes that were so cold, like arctic ice.

"Paisley, I don't know what Tobe might have led you to believe, but this farm belongs to his grandmother."

"When she dies—and that day doesn't seem too far off, judging from the looks of her—he'll get it all."

Rose bundled the sheets into a ball and tossed them in a wicker laundry basket. "Such news might surprise Vera."

Paisley hesitated. "I'll move down here until it all gets sorted out."

"This guest flat is a business for us. I have reservations for it throughout the summer. Hopefully, even more in the fall. We need the income. I count on it to support my children."

Paisley narrowed her eyes. "I was told that Tobe came from a well-to-do family."

"Tobe might have exaggerated."

"I don't believe you!"

"I'm telling you the truth, Paisley," Rose explained patiently. "There is no money."

Paisley was having none of it. She spun on Rose, lines of stubborn determination forming around her mouth. "Or maybe you're just angling to keep it all for yourself." Her voice grew bitter. "I've read all about your husband in the papers. I know there's money. Somewhere. There's money someplace in this old rat trap of a farm."

Rose struggled to hold on to her temper. "I don't know what you've read or what Tobe has told you, but there is no money."

Darting Rose a last hostile glance, Paisley shot out of the room.

Rose watched her go. She wished she could talk to Tobe. She needed to find out the truth, but at the same time, she didn't want the truth.

As soon as Galen had left for the auction in Mount Joy the next day, Naomi made up a bagged lunch, brushed her teeth, and waited outside for the driver to pick her up. Since she had learned about Paisley yesterday, her anxiety escalated with each passing hour. Today, she was determined to go to the federal prison to talk to Tobe about this Paisley woman. Hiring a driver would cut time off the trip, both ways, faster than the bus. Galen would be gone until late afternoon, and Jimmy Fisher had already agreed to feed the livestock. If things went well, she would be back by suppertime and no one would be the wiser. Except she hoped she would be made wise to the Paisley situation.

As she waited, she felt all those unruly vines of emotion within her start to settle. Of course, of course Tobe would tell her that he had never known a woman named Paisley. Everything would be sorted out as soon as she talked to Tobe. Of course it would.

She reached into her pockets and realized she'd forgotten her Tums, so she hurried back inside to get a new pack, maybe two packs, just as she heard a car turn into the driveway.

She chose this particular driver, Mr. Kurtz, to take her to FCI Schuykill for three reasons: one, he drove fast, and two, he didn't like to talk, and three, he didn't gossip about where he drove his passengers. He never spoke about other people so everyone knew their secrets were safe.

She stared out the window through most of the trip, growing more anxious by the minute. Thoughts of Paisley dogged her, twining together the worry about her and Tobe's future. Would there be a future for them at all? She thought of Bethany's remark that her grandmother was delighted with Paisley's arrival—convinced this young woman was the way to keep Tobe in the fold. Was that what it would take? Could this be God's plan for Tobe? If so, she had completely missed the signals from God and that created another tangling vine of worry. Her stomach tightened into a burning ball, making her regret what she'd eaten for breakfast. *Breathe, Naomi.*

Deep, deep breaths. Six in, seven out. Or was it seven in, six out?

She might be worried for nothing. Tobe might tell her that he didn't know a girl named Paisley. That was her best hope. That was what she had come to hear.

Minutes slid by, one into the next. She had chewed through one roll of Tums by the time Mr. Kurtz pulled over in front of the prison. "Want me to come back in a few hours?"

"Do you mind waiting? I don't think I'll be too long. I don't think there will be a wait to get in like there is on weekends."

"I don't mind at all." He gave her a sympathetic nod. "Is it as bad as they say?"

"He says it's not too bad. He's in that adjacent building there, the minimum security prison." She pointed out the window to a nondescript building. "He's not in a jail cell. He says he sleeps in a room with bunks."

"Do you get up here to visit a lot?"

"No. He only gets eight points a month and each weekend visit requires two points. Weekday visits are only one point." That was one of the reasons Tobe didn't encourage his family to visit him—he wanted to save his points for Naomi's visits.

"I've seen on the television that you have to talk to prisoners through a glass partition."

"Not here," Naomi said. "It's a big room with chairs, all in a row."

Mr. Kurtz lit up. "So at least you can hold hands with your fellow."

Naomi felt a blush creeping up her cheeks. "The guards walk around the room, watching everybody."

He opened his palm to reveal a few dollars. "Give them to your young man. I hear money talks in the pokey."

He was such a nice man. She tried to smile, though she knew it came out all wrong. "Thank you, Mr. Kurtz, but money has to go straight to the prison commissary accounts. Tobe says inmates aren't allowed to handle any money." How strange it was that she knew that fact and so many others about prison life.

Naomi was briefly detained while her clearance on the pre-approved list was verified at the security gate. Then she was asked to put her house key and the money she'd brought to pay Mr. Kurtz into clear plastic bags before she was led into the visitation room. She sat down on a hard plastic chair to wait for Tobe. Her breathing grew shallow, and she started to feel like she couldn't get enough air. Pins and needles pricked the ends of her fingers, and her whole body began to quake as if she had chills. Over and over she said, "Oh-God-help-me-help-me-help-me please." She kept saying it until she found her muscles start to soften, and then, her symptoms began to relax their grip on her.

Ten minutes later, Tobe was brought in, wearing the prison garb: a khaki button-up shirt and khaki pants, his dark hair shaved close to his skull. Such short hair would have made any other Amish man look like a plucked chicken. But not Tobe. He was so handsome he took her breath away. He saw her and rushed to her. They hugged like long-lost lovers parted unwillingly, which is exactly what they were. Then he kissed her until she felt dizzy and breathless and thoroughly confused.

Some caution seemed to seep back into her and she pulled back, embarrassed by such a public display of affection. He tucked her arm into his and they sat in chairs, facing each other, holding hands.

"I couldn't believe it when I was told I had a visitor today. You were just here, Naomi. Why now?"

"Something has happened."

His smile faded. "Mammi Vera has passed."

"Oh no. No." She shook her head. "Nothing like that."

His smiled returned. "What is it? What brought you all the way to Minersville?"

She looked down at their intertwined hands. "Do you remember a woman named Paisley?"

Tobe stilled. "Yeah. Sure. Why?"

"When did you meet her?"

"Awhile back, while I was scrounging around for that year, living from place to place. She was a waitress. I guess she sort of took a shine to me."

"How well did you know her?"

"She let me crash at her place when I had run out of options. Just for a few nights—then I found a construction job over in Mount Joy and I didn't see her anymore." He tipped his head. "What's all this about?"

She peered at him. "But what I'm asking is, how well did you know her?"

"I told you. Not well."

"Did you know her . . . in the biblical sense?" Naomi's tone was light, her question deadly serious.

Tobe's face went slack. "Why would you ask me a question like that?" He pulled his hands away and leaned back in the chair. "Why in the world would you ask me such a question?"

"Paisley has come to Eagle Hill. To stay. To deliver a baby she says is yours."

Tobe looked at her in disbelief. "Impossible!"

"Is it, Tobe? Is it truly impossible?" She kept her eyes steady on his. She didn't want him to back away from the question. She needed an answer.

In a flash, his face went from fury to guilt to resignation. "No," he said quietly, as the color drained from his face. He looked up, drew a deep sigh, and spoke very gently. "No, it's not *entirely* impossible."

Naomi would remember forever how it felt when Tobe told her that indeed, he had known Paisley, in a biblical way. She felt the shock rush through her, prickling her skin and making her head tingle.

"She's lying. It's all a terrible mistake, Naomi. I would *know* if I had fathered a child with that girl. I would *know* it. I can't imagine why she would do this, out of the blue. But I don't know the kind of person she is."

Naomi squeezed her eyes shut at that last sentence. And yet he knew her well enough to *know* her.

She was very still as she sat and listened to him. Her face changed from time to time, concerned and distressed and compassionate as Tobe explained his tale of loneliness and misery, hastening to put her anxieties at rest: he was just with Paisley a few times and it never meant anything to either of them and he was having such a terrible time when he was in self-exile. She had to force herself to keep from looking stricken, horrified, when he said Paisley must be crazy because he was the last person in the world anyone should choose as a father for their child.

"Could she be lying about the timing? Would you have . . . known her . . . last August? Before you returned to Stoney Ridge?"

Tobe dropped his eyes. "Yes. I was with her one last time, before I returned home. I was a mess, wrestling with coming back home, and I got really drunk. I don't remember much of anything except waking up in the morning at her place again, with people there I didn't even know. I decided right then that I'd go home." He looked up, misery flooding his eyes. "I'm sorry. I'm really sorry."

For a moment, Naomi couldn't breathe. When she took in a full breath, her eyes started to sting. *Oh Lord, don't let me cry. Not here. Not now.*

"Say something, Naomi. Anything." His voice was only a whisper.

She tried to respond but the torrent of words welling up inside her wouldn't budge.

"You're as white as a sheet."

"I'm fine." She wasn't fine. Her muscles and emotions had all turned to jelly.

"Please believe me. I'm begging you. Begging you, Naomi. You're my only sure center. The only thing I need."

"But I'm not, Tobe," she said, strangely calm, though her temples were starting to pound and spots had started to dance before her eyes. "No one can ever be another person's center. That position belongs only to God." She glanced at the clock and said she thought she should leave.

His dismay was enormous. "You can't go now, you've only been here a short time."

"But you've told me everything."

"No, I haven't told you anything really. I've only skimmed the surface."

But she had heard what she came to hear. "I have to go back, Tobe. I would have, anyway, no matter what you told me. I need to get home before my brother returns from the horse auction."

They rose to say goodbye.

"I never, ever intended to hurt you," Tobe said.

Her stomach knotted with worry and she put a hand to her head as if she were coming down with a dreadful headache . . . which she was. "It doesn't matter what you intended. What matters is . . . what is."

What matters is what is.

"Did I do the wrong thing, telling you the truth?" He was a child again, confused and uncertain.

When she first arrived, she had hoped that Tobe would smile his lovely, familiar, heart-turning smile and say, "I've never heard of anyone named Paisley," and they would fall happily into each other's arms. But Tobe didn't say such a thing. It felt like the time when they all thought that Luke had drowned in Blue Lake Pond and it turned out later he'd just gone on home the other way. Well, that's the kind of fear she had now. She knew this kind of fear—it went bone deep.

He reached out to hold her hand. Her throat swelled and tears rushed to her eyes. "I need to go home," she said, backing away from him.

It had begun to rain as Mr. Kurtz drove her home, passing by the fields of green, each surrounded by a hedge of darker green; and Naomi stared hard out of the window willing the tears back into her head. But they came, one after the other, cascading down her cheeks. Her emotions felt like tangled vines, difficult to pull apart, no idea of where they began or ended.

What Naomi had felt as she sat on that porch swing yesterday with Bethany had not been a suspicion, it had been a foresight. She didn't just fear what Paisley's arrival might mean, she knew it.

What matters is what is.

10

Mim set her diary down, filled with notes and ideas about how to answer letters to Mrs. Miracle. She was stumped by a recent letter:

Dear Mrs. Miracle,
My father insists that I follow him in the family business. He's worked very hard at establishing a successful business and I admire what he's done. But here's my problem: he's a butcher and I'm a vegetarian.
What should I do?

Signed,
Animal Lover

"Honor thy father." The words slipped through her mind as she glanced over at her Bible on the corner of her desk. Could you honor your father and still choose a different career path?

She closed her diary, hid it under her mattress, and went next door in search of Naomi, who knew the answer to these kinds of questions.

"Looking for Galen or Naomi?" Jimmy Fisher said as Mim came into the barn over at the Kings', blinking her eyes rapidly as they adjusted to the dim lighting. Three horses stuck their heads over their stall doors, regarding her with interest. Barn swallows swooped from their nests and flew past her toward the open door. Jimmy was brushing a horse held in crossties in the middle of the barn aisle.

"I wanted to talk to Naomi."

"She's away, and so is Galen. I'm helping him out today."

Mim glanced at him with surprise. "Who's minding the chickens?"

He frowned. "I got up extra early and I'll stay up extra late tonight."

Jimmy walked the mare outside to the round training pen and Mim followed behind to watch the training session. He stood in the center, holding on to the long lead line, and made a clucking sound with his tongue to get the horse circling around the pen. He watched the mare's gait with a practiced eye. Now and then, he flicked a whip at her rear hooves to keep her in a gentle canter.

Mim leaned her elbows on the pen's railing. That pinched look Jimmy got on his face when she had asked about his chickens was gone. Come to think of it, that pinched look was on his face rather a lot lately, like his stomach hurt or he'd gotten a popcorn kernel stuck between his teeth. She felt a stab of pity for Jimmy. Here, as he concentrated on the movement of the horse, chirping to her when she slowed from a lope to a jog, praising her when she kept a steady pace, he seemed more like the old Jimmy. Happy, lighthearted, quick to smile.

Bethany was right. Jimmy was in danger of losing his sparkle. Or did she say spark? Either way, it had gone missing.

After the horse had been warmed up, Jimmy unhooked the shank from the mare's halter. He walked over to Mim to set down the whip and pick up a few training tools. "Jimmy, can a son honor his parents but not agree to work in the family business?"

Jimmy's face went blank. "What did Bethany tell you?"

"Tell me about what?"

He looked confused. "About how much I hate chickens."

"She didn't say a word." She didn't have to. Everybody knew that. Everybody!

"Then, why did you ask me such a question?"

"I just . . . was wondering. So what do you think? Can you honor your mother and quit the chicken business?"

Jimmy leaned against the pen railing. "I've been giving this a lot of thought lately."

"Honor thy father. It's in the Bible."

"I know it is." Jimmy looked out at an eagle, drifting high on an updraft, its wings as still as the grasses below, circling and searching for its dinner.

Those words were there. She couldn't deny that. But other bits of verses came to mind. "It also says to walk in truth. And the truth shall make you free."

Jimmy's head snapped around to look at her. "What did you say?"

"Those are someplace in the Bible but I don't know where, exactly. My mom has them written out on index cards and taped to the refrigerator."

Jimmy rubbed his face with his hands.

Mim wasn't sure what she had said that made Jimmy seem bothered.

He picked up a bucket of tools used to condition the horse

to unexpected noise. "I'd better get back to work." He walked toward the horse, then spun around. "Thank you, Mim. You've been a big help. You know . . . you give pretty miraculous advice." He winked at her.

What had she said?

After a few casual meetings, Brooke decided to go each day at the same time to the Sweet Tooth Bakery. Jon Hoeffner was always there, in the same seat and table that faced the door—as if he might just be waiting for her. His smile was warm, but it made her nervous. It had been a long time since a man had given her this kind of attention.

And this was the kind of man you could dream about night and day, someone who would occupy all your thoughts. There was a definite undercurrent of romance between them. Jon was strikingly handsome, charming, easy to talk to, and most importantly, he didn't wear a wedding ring. He mentioned very little about his private life, but he spoke well of everyone and badly of no one.

Was Jon toying with her? She couldn't tell. Her intuition read kindness and genuine goodness in him, but she'd been wrong about people in the past.

Brooke was hoping Jon might suggest going out on a date. She thought about asking him—after all, this was the twenty-first century, but some warning voice made her think that she could only keep his attention if she didn't seem to care. It was so silly, all this game playing, yet it appeared to work. "Will you stay in Stoney Ridge long?" she said nonchalantly. It was an act.

He shook his head. "As soon as I wrap a few things up, I'm on my way."

She felt a twinge of disappointment. "Don't you like it here? I do."

"It's a one-horse town and a pretty poor horse at that."

"I don't know about that," she said, stirring her coffee. "There's certainly a lot of drama at the Inn at Eagle Hill."

"Oh?" he said. "What kind of drama could be going on at a quiet Amish farm?"

She told him about the pregnant girl named Paisley who had arrived, out of the blue, claiming to be carrying the oldest son's baby, and how the family was reeling from the news. Come to think of it, she had learned quite a bit about this family just by paying attention. If only more people would learn to listen, they could pick up all kinds of amazing information.

Jon, for example, was a wonderful listener. He leaned close to her as she talked, nodding in all the right places, eyes lighting up as he heard the Schrock family gossip. How many men would find it interesting to hear about an Amish family?

She smiled at Jon. Stoney Ridge was turning into a surprisingly delightful place for her life to find new direction.

She took a sip of coffee and gave a sigh of pure pleasure.

"It's good, that coffee, isn't it?" he said.

As far as Brooke was concerned, it could as well have been turpentine.

Naomi arrived home to find the house was still empty. Relieved, she made up a sandwich for her brother Galen, left it in the refrigerator, and got ready for bed. She could tell that a migraine had begun and was moving from the first phase, which she had felt at the prison—where every sense felt on high alert and almost unmanageable, to the next phase, where a flickering blind spot occurred in the center of her vision, like a spinning black penny. Soon, she knew, the pain would start to throb on one side of her head or the other.

The weather had taken a turn for the worse as the evening wore on. Lightning lit up the room; raindrops splattered the windows. She tried to sleep, then gave up and went down to the basement to the little cot. It was dark in the basement, no sound of crashing thunder, no bright streaks of lightning, no pounding rain.

When Naomi was a child, she used to play the game of "if."

If she got up the stairs before the grandfather clock in the hall stopped striking, then the teacher wouldn't be in a bad mood tomorrow. If the daffodils planted by the front of the house bloomed by April first, she'd get a circle letter from her sisters.

Now she sat in the dark basement with her arms around her knees. If the rain stopped soon, everything would be all right. It wouldn't have happened at all.

But it did. There was no point in pretending it hadn't. The anxiety of what she had learned from Tobe kept coming back—things changing, not being safe anymore.

She dozed off and on, but in the middle of the night, she woke with a start. The panic over Paisley seemed unbearable. She tried to beat back the wild fears that kept shooting through her mind, like violent streaks of colors.

All sorts of horrible possibilities presented themselves in her mind, troubling thoughts that she might be able to dismiss in the daytime but that took hold of her in the dark of night and seemed completely real. As she lay there, she became convinced that Tobe would want to be—and *should* be—with Paisley and her baby, and her breathing quickened and her heart began to beat so hard that it was all she could do not to cry out. She felt so sad, so alone, so lonely. She was ashamed of her own lack of faith, but she conjured just enough to whisper, "I am afraid." She hardly slept the rest of the night.

By noon of the next day, Sadie Smucker came down the basement stairs to check on Naomi. "Galen asked me to come and see if I could help you. He's worried about you." Sadie's voice was sweet and reassuring and Naomi felt thankful she was there.

Sadie placed a cool compress on Naomi's forehead and encouraged her to drink an herbal tea remedy made of Ligusticum. Naomi's body ached, her chest was tight, her head throbbed. She had never felt so sick. "I don't know what's wrong. I've never felt like this before. It must be the flu."

"Can you think of what triggered this migraine? Any food you ate?"

Naomi shook her head. Sadie had helped her create a diet high in magnesium and omega-3 fats to prevent migraines and taught her to avoid other foods that might act as triggers. "Nothing." She put her elbow over her eyes. "I've been so careful, and I haven't had a migraine in months. I thought I was finally getting past them."

Kindly, Sadie said, "I don't think it's the flu. Those migraines have always been your Achilles' heel. Did something happen to upset you?"

Naomi lifted her arm to look at Sadie. She and Sadie had always had a special understanding. Sadie said she used to be very much like Naomi: shy and timid and scared of her own shadow. Naomi couldn't imagine Sadie like that. She might be a quiet person, but she oozed a strong, reassuring presence.

"Naomi, you are sick from despair. This is how the heart

speaks to us, through our illnesses." Sadie tipped the cup of tea for Naomi to take another sip. "But you're not alone in this, whatever it is that's troubling you. You're never alone. God hasn't left you. He'll see you through."

Naomi knew that. She knew that God was holding out his hands to her through this situation, asking her to trust him completely. She was trying! She truly believed that God hadn't given her a spirit of fear. This wasn't how he intended her to be. She'd been doing so much better, feeling so much stronger and more sure of herself. Then this situation popped up with Tobe . . . with Paisley . . . and now she was a frightened rabbit again. Afraid of her own shadow.

After finishing the tea, Sadie rested her hand on Naomi's back and began to trace circles with her fingers—across her shoulders and down her spine, back and forth, up and down, again and again. As she did, Naomi's heartbeat slowed and her chest relaxed, and she began to feel calmer.

"Nothing controls and calms the mind like full, deep breathing," Sadie said. "Do you remember what I told you about breathing?" She had taught Naomi how to breathe deeply when the pain was at its worst. When you breathed deeply into the lower lobes of the lungs, she explained, you activated the parasympathetic nervous system, which produced endorphins, which in turn made you feel relaxed and calm and helped you let go of distractions.

Sadie told Naomi to match her breathing to hers, and as she did, in and out, in and out, her fears subsided and she fell asleep.

When she woke again, Sadie was still there, with a small plate of apple slices and cheese. "It would be good if you could eat a little bit."

Naomi sat up slowly. The worst was over, the pain had ebbed. She ate a few bites of apple and was relieved when her stomach didn't reject them. "Sadie, have you ever had second thoughts about Gid?"

Sadie's head lifted in surprise. "What? Where in the world did *that* come from?"

"I just wondered . . . did you ever think you might have made a mistake?"

"I made a promise, Naomi, up in front of the church. You were there. You heard me."

"Yes, you said some words . . ."

"Not just words, Naomi, a promise. A solemn oath. For better or worse, sickness or health. I meant those words." She smiled. "Now, I will admit that I probably expected married life to be all sweetness and light and it's not. Not every day, anyway. Life wasn't meant to be easy. But those are the days I remind myself of that promise I made."

"Yes, but does your marriage make you feel safe?"

Sadie tipped her head to one side and peered at Naomi. "There are more important things in life than being safe."

Naomi stared at Sadie and felt as if she'd just pushed open a window and light flooded into the basement to surround her and lift her, helping her mind shrug off the darkness and take wing. Her heart felt free to beat again and her stubborn streak set in. She was tired of worry and what-ifs. Was she going to let herself be chased away from something precious? No, she certainly wasn't, she decided with sudden conviction.

Right then she made up her mind. She wasn't going to be afraid of this woman named Paisley anymore.

◇

As great with child as she was, Paisley walked with a swish and a certainty. There was nothing demure about her. She was flashy—even Mammi Vera agreed on this. Bethany heard her grandmother tut-tutting about Paisley when she thought no one was listening. Her back hurt terribly, though, she said, and that's why she couldn't help with chores around the farm.

Whenever Bethany would ask when her baby was due and where did she expect to deliver this baby, Paisley would turn the full force of her smile upon her. "There's plenty of time for all that," she would say with a wave of her hand. Bethany would smile back and think to herself, *Paisley is delusional on top of being flashy*. That girl looked full of child, like she was ready to give birth any minute.

But soon, Bethany stopped smiling back. Anytime Paisley was in close proximity to Jimmy Fisher, she found a way to bump against him or touch him.

By week's end, Jimmy wasn't coming around anymore.

One sunny afternoon, Danny asked Mim to stay after school. He waited until the students had all left, then locked up the schoolhouse and walked beside Mim toward Eagle Hill. On the way, he explained that Nancy Blank, mother of Mose, an easygoing ten-year-old boy who was often teased by the others, had come to the schoolhouse earlier in the week. "She's worried about Mose—he's getting pushed around by the big boys on the way home from school each day. She said if she mentions her concern to his father that he tells her to stay out of it. Leroy Blank is the type who thinks being bullied will make a man out of his son."

From the disdainful look on Danny's face, Mim could

tell what he thought of that kind of parenting. In an odd flash of maturity, she realized that Danny was probably much like Mose as a young boy—gentle, kind, and a target for bullies.

"I've been watching how the older boys act toward Mose," Danny said. "I haven't actually seen anything to worry about during recesses, but I don't doubt Nancy about the walk home. I wondered if you had any suggestions, other than going to speak to the boys' parents—which might create more problems." He glanced at her. "I thought you might have a solution."

Mim nearly smiled. It was typical of Danny to look for a diplomatic way to solve a problem. "I think he needs to make a friend of Jesse and Luke," she said after some thought.

"Jesse Stoltzfus?" He looked skeptical. Very, very skeptical. "And your brother Luke?"

"He's as smart as a whip, that Jesse. Luke could be too, if he ever set his mind to anything."

"Why not with Sammy? They're closer in age."

"Mose is gentle. He doesn't need another gentle friend like Sammy. He needs an ally."

"How do I encourage Jesse to be a friend to Mose? Or Luke?"

"Maybe put them on a project together. Make them stay after class to help you, so they get to know each other without the other big boys interfering."

Danny pushed his glasses up on the bridge of his nose. "I'll give it some thought. Thanks, Mim. I knew you'd have some good advice."

When Danny thanked her, it almost brought tears to her eyes. It was so easy to solve a little problem for someone else when they asked, and so hard to sort out your own. She gave him a smile, a real smile this time, which she hadn't done in months, and she wondered what Danny would think if he knew she was Mrs. Miracle.

All at once, Danny turned. His face was shadowed, but she could see his eyes—very, very blue eyes—watching her, waiting. "Mim," he started hesitantly, "it won't be long until—"

Who knew what might have happened next? She would never know, because in the next second Jesse and Levi came soaring down the Stoltzfuses' driveway on their scooters, screaming like banshees, and Mim and Danny had to scatter to get out of the way so they wouldn't get plowed over.

The moment was over, it might never come again.

Danny and Mim looked at each other, pretended they hadn't, and went home.

Brooke sat across from Jon Hoeffner at the Sweet Tooth Bakery. A cinnamon roll and a coffee—with two dollops of cream, just the way she liked it—were waiting for her at her place.

Today was the second time Jon had ordered for her and the first time he had paid for her. Things were definitely progressing between them. He was adept at conversation and peppered her with questions about her work, her family, her upbringing, her plans for the future . . . of which she had none.

"Aren't you planning to go back to the museum?"

She stirred her coffee. Could she tell him? Should she? "I was . . . let go."

"Ah . . . the pain of downsizing."

"Not exactly. There was a . . . ," she paused, brushing her hand in the air as if to shoo a fly, ". . . tiny misunderstanding."

Jon's eyes went soft and she melted. There was just something about his eyes. Mesmerizing. "Do you want to talk about it?"

Actually, she would. She wanted to vent to someone safe, someone outside of the art world, and Jon was the ideal person. She didn't have anyone else to talk to about the injustice, the humiliation of getting fired. She told him the whole story, starting with her credit card debt, and the meeting with the art dealer who told her about a client, a man who was a devoted lover of Jean-Baptiste-Camille Corot plein air studies.

Jon interrupted, a quizzical look on his face. "Forgive my ignorance, but who is Jean-Baptiste-Camille Corot?"

Brooke tried to mask the shock she felt. Who didn't know the work of Jean-Baptiste-Camille Corot? "He's an artist from the nineteenth century who was, and is, enormously popular in America. He was an innovator. He bridged the gap between Neoclassical painters and Romantic painters and inspired the Impressionists."

She was afraid she might sound too know-it-all-ish and would scare him off the way she intimidated other men, but Jon seemed fascinated. "Go on," he said encouragingly.

"The Neoclassical painters felt that landscape should have a serious, moralizing purpose. Romantic painters felt the role of nature was to transport the viewer to imaginary places. Corot allowed for both. He responded to nature with his emotions, yet he also was astutely accurate in how he depicted nature—capturing specific weather conditions or the way that light transformed color."

She pulled out her iPhone and googled a few Corot paintings

to show Jon. "Do you recognize any of these?" She scrolled through them, but he didn't seem to know the artist. "Corot has a signature brushwork. It starts bold, then matures into a feathery, light touch."

"I don't know much about art, but I'd like to know more. Meeting you makes me all the more determined to learn."

Was he flirting with her? Brooke's heart started to pound. He reached out and took her phone, brushing her fingers with his. He was definitely flirting with her.

"So which of these paintings did you reproduce?"

"None that were well known. When Corot died, it was a surprise to collectors to find over 300 paintings and plein air sketches in his studio. Those sketches became the inspiration for the large, formal works that eventually hung in the Paris salons." She described how she painstakingly practiced Jean-Baptist-Camille Corot's soft brushwork, studied the majority of his paintings, honed his light-drenched palette of colors. She paused. "It hadn't occurred to me before, but I think his landscapes are one of the reasons I feel so intrigued by Lancaster County. The hazy fog we had this morning, the radiance of light—it reminds me of his nature scenes. The topography is light-drenched, luminous . . ." Her voice drifted off. She really needed to start sketching the landscape. It had completely slipped her mind.

"So . . . ," Jon said politely, in a tone to remind her she had veered off topic. "So . . . you reproduced a painting of Corot and sold it to the art dealer."

"That's what was supposed to happen. What actually happened was that the dealer sold it to a collector as an original. When it was discovered, the art dealer had vanished, and even though I wasn't legally implicated, I lost my job."

Jon tilted his head. "There must be a little part of you that feels somewhat pleased you had pulled a fast one on the art world."

Brooke shrugged. It did, indeed.

"And you had absolutely no idea that the art dealer was going to pawn your painting off as the real thing."

"No."

"Come on, Brooke. Really?" Jon leaned forward, eyes twinkling, and gave her a charming rascal smile. "No idea at all?"

She had never admitted such a thing to anyone. Not a living soul. "Well, maybe just a teeny, tiny hunch."

11

As Mim swung along the village road after leaving the Sisters' House, good feelings tumbled about inside her. Even if she were soaked in a downpour, nothing could dampen her spirits today. Just moments ago, Ella had greeted her at the door with a big smile. "Welcome back, Mim. I've missed you."

"Isn't Bethany here?"

"Yes, she was here, but she is not you. People are not as replaceable as . . . a pair of boots."

Ella had missed her! Mim smiled inside and out with pleasure.

Sylvia came to the door behind Ella with a message from Bethany to meet her at the Bent N' Dent. Mim needed to hand off her finished Mrs. Miracle letters to Bethany to be dropped off at the *Stoney Ridge Times*. After finding inspiration in her conversation with Jimmy Fisher, she labored long and hard over the right wording in Mrs. Miracle's response to that vegetarian who didn't want to work in his father's butcher shop:

Dear Animal Lover,

Naturally, I believe in showing respect to parents. It sounds as if you do have respect for your father. Due to these unique circumstances, I think you are going to have to follow your own path.

Sincerely,

Mrs. Miracle

Mim felt a sudden chill as a car drove past her and her happy feelings slipped away. It might sound certifiably crazy, but she thought she had noticed that car a couple of times now, driving slowly and then zooming past her. She felt she was being watched. But maybe it just reminded her of today's breakfast conversation with her grandmother.

As she was spooning out oatmeal into dishes this morning, Mammi Vera had told Luke and Sammy that the devil was roaming the earth, looking for victims, eyes going to and fro. "Do not succumb to the devil's attempts to lead you into sin," she had warned them as she handed them each a bowl.

Luke said he had never actually seen the devil so he wasn't fearful of him, but he was curious about what he looked like. That comment horrified Mammi Vera; she clutched her chest and went to find her Bible.

Sammy's eyes grew wide and thoughtful as he pondered Mammi Vera's warning about the devil. Mim, less sensitive than Sammy but more sensitive than Luke, tried to dismiss her grandmother's caution, but thoughts of the devil stood hovering in the air over her head.

What had happened to the good feelings that were just tumbling about inside her? They were gone.

Mim cut through a field, near where there was a ditch for water irrigation. A strange eerie sound floated up from inside the ditch—the devil himself, perhaps—so she hurried her steps.

The devil was calling, "Is anyone there? Anyone at all?"

Mim sped up. Then stopped. The devil sounded suspiciously similar to the monstrous Jesse Stoltzfus.

"Are you a demon?" she called.

"Mim, is that you?"

She hesitated. "Maybe."

"Mim, I need your help! The cow fell into the ditch and I can't get her out. Come and help me."

She walked slowly toward the ditch and peered into it. There was Jesse Stoltzfus, with his sticky-up hair, pushing the backside of a cow, who refused to budge.

He looked up at her. "I need your help."

She pushed her glasses up on her nose. "What should I do?"

"Do you think we could use your apron as a kind of rope?"

Her favorite apron! Used as a cow rope. She unpinned her apron and threw it down to him.

"You pull, I'll push."

That would mean she would have to get down near that dirty, smelly ditch water. She frowned and he noticed.

"Mim, there isn't time to be prissy. I need to get this cow out of this ditch and get her to the barn before milking time. Come down here and help me. You don't have to get into the water—just stay on the edge. Or go get my dad. He's at home."

She had just come from home and didn't want to go all the way back again. Besides, Bethany was waiting for her at the Bent N' Dent. She sighed; her happy feelings had thoroughly dissolved. She hid the manila envelope of Mrs. Miracle letters behind a rock, then climbed down carefully into the disgusting ditch. Jesse wrapped the apron around the cow's neck and twisted the ends, then handed it to Mim who was standing on the edge.

"When I count to three, pull with all your might." He steadied his legs behind the cow and prepared to push. "One, two . . ."

Mim started to pull as Jesse pushed and the cow stood her ground, bawling an unhappy cow sound. She thought she might go deaf.

"Are you pulling?" Jesse shouted.

"Yes!"

With that, the cow decided she had enough of getting pushed and pulled and she threw her head, knocking Mim into the water before charging up the side of the ditch. The cow stood on the edge, peering down at Mim and Jesse, batting her big black eyelashes, as if to ask what they were doing in a dirty ditch.

Jesse waded over and offered Mim a hand, which she reluctantly took. She smelled disgusting!

"I'll help you up the side of the ditch."

"No," she growled. "I'll get myself up."

"Suit yourself." He grabbed the abandoned apron-turned-rope, squeezed it out, and scrambled up the ditch. "No one would ever accuse you of being a garrulous girl."

Garrulous? What did that mean? It bothered Mim to not know a word. She collected words. She even read the dictionary. Words were her hobby.

Jesse and the cow peered down at her. He looked at Mim as if she had braved a lion in a den. "You have pluck, Mim."

He tipped his hat. "Mim is no name for a lass who rescues a lad and his cow in distress. What's your real name?"

"Miriam."

"You have pluck, Miriam." He grinned. "And I will never forget your act of selfless charity during my time of need. Just another charming quality to add to your long list of charmingness. You will make any man proud to call you his wife one day." He bowed, then bobbed up. "And I will be first in line to try to win your hand."

Wife? Win her hand? Was he *crazy*?! "I would never, ever marry you, Jesse Stoltzfus!"

He grinned, saluted her, and turned away, leading the cow with Mim's apron-turned-rope. She tried to scramble up the ditch as fast as Jesse had done, but it took her a couple of tries. By the time she had reached the top, he was halfway across the field.

"I suppose someone will marry you eventually," she shouted. "But it'll have to be someone who is stone-deaf so she doesn't have to listen to your nonsense!"

He waved cheerfully and kept pulling the cow with the rope-apron to keep her moving forward.

She watched him move the cow along until he disappeared beneath a hill. She looked down at her sopping, dripping dress and tried to wring it out. It was very hard to get the last word in with someone as verbose as Jesse. That Jesse Stoltzfus thought he had the world sorted out.

She remembered the manila envelope filled with letters from Mrs. Miracle and ran to the rock where she had hidden it.

It was gone.

—⟨◊⟩—

Things between Galen and Rose were not as easy as they had been before Paisley arrived. They'd even had sharp words one afternoon, something that had never happened before, when Rose had complained to him that she still hadn't heard back from Tobe, though he must have received her letter by now. She was anxious to know how he would want her to handle this Paisley person. Should she ask her to leave? Could she do that? Because Paisley was surely not telling the truth about Tobe being the father of her baby.

"Maybe there's a reason he hasn't responded quickly," Galen said.

She frowned at him, knowing what he was thinking. "You've made up your mind ahead of the facts."

"The facts are the facts," Galen said bluntly. "Paisley is pregnant and Tobe Schrock is to blame."

Rose was furious! And she was just about to tell him so when she heard someone call her name. It was her new neighbor, David Stoltzfus, walking up the driveway of Eagle Hill with the rope of a milk cow in his hand.

She wanted to finish this conversation with Galen, but what could she do? She went to greet David. With a big grin, he deposited the rope in her arms. "Your boys told me your cow didn't give much milk. Growing boys need milk."

"That's true. But that's because they forgot to milk her for a few days and she started to dry up. So now milking the cow is Mim's job. Thank you, David." Though to be truthful, Rose didn't want another cow. Milk cows were a heap of trouble. She would have been just as happy to have a bit of extra buttermilk now and then.

But she took the rope from David and watched dumbly as Galen shook his hand, turned to her, and said, "I'd better get back." Left, without another word, without a backward glance.

"Do I smell coffee?" David said, looking up at the kitchen.

"Of course. Go on inside. I just started a fresh pot. My mother-in-law Vera is in the kitchen. There's some cherry cobbler from last night's dinner."

David grinned. "I'll cross many a hill for a good cobbler."

She smiled. David Stoltzfus was a fine man, even if Mim couldn't abide his son Jesse. Luke, on the other hand, couldn't get enough of Jesse. He was even starting to talk like him. "I'll take the cow in the barn and be right in to join you."

"My youngest named her Fireball."

"What?!"

He laughed. "She just liked the name." He patted the cow on her big head. "She's gentle. Most times."

The cow seemed as docile as could be, but Rose had been fooled before. "Um, well. Fireball it is. Thank you again, David."

Before she went down to the barn, she turned back and saw Galen at the privet hole, his eyes resting on David with a slightly puzzled look.

Paisley asked more questions than Rose had answers for. She was certainly interested in anything that had to do with making money, particularly how much Eagle Hill was worth. Finally, it got so that whenever Paisley would open her mouth to start to ask another question, Rose would cut her off and talk about something completely mundane, like exactly what was her baby's due date and when had she last seen a doctor? Any mention of the impending delivery of Paisley's baby would cause her to frown and soon she would disappear from the room. It seemed as if Paisley was ignoring the fact that she was about to become a mother.

Vera did not like the way Rose interacted with Paisley and told her so, more than once. "Don't you understand why she is asking so many questions about the farm? She is planning for her future with Tobe. And you're making her feel as if it's wrong to ask."

Rose frowned. "Doesn't it seem that a soon-to-be mother should be asking questions about baby care and getting a layette put together? She hasn't given the baby's arrival a second thought."

"She's anxious about it, that's all."

There could be some truth in that. Rose could remember how unsettled she felt before each of her own babies' births. She should keep trying to withhold her opinion about Paisley until she heard something from Tobe—which should be any day now. At least, she hoped so. She couldn't silence Galen's remark that Tobe wasn't responding because he didn't want them to know the truth. She still felt annoyed with Galen, but she couldn't dismiss the notion that he might be right. She loved Tobe, but she knew his tendency to avoid difficulties.

And yet, she told herself, wasn't Tobe serving a prison sentence because he was willing to face a consequence for withholding evidence? Wasn't that a sign of maturity? It was. Why couldn't Galen see that? Why couldn't he be more of . . . a partner, helping her raise children to reach their fullest potential?

It occurred to her that she'd never had a helpmate, a partner. She thought of Fern and Amos Lapp, who worked together on their farm. Or Bishop Elmo and his wife, Dee, who ran a quilt shop together. Two become one. She'd heard it said dozens of times in marriage ceremonies. She and Dean had promised it, but it had never happened.

What if Galen were more like Dean than she had thought? A man who couldn't change his mind or listen to a woman's good sense . . . why, that behavior *was* just like Dean's. Maybe that's what all men were like, deep down. Stubborn and prideful.

One thing she had discovered about Dean, early on—he refused to change. After thirteen years of marriage, they were struggling with the same tangled issues: Dean's pie-in-the-sky dreams, his big promises, and his appallingly poor judgment. He felt she didn't support him, didn't respect him, didn't cheerlead for him. But how could you show support to someone who made terrible decisions, one after the other?

She hated to admit it, even to herself, but Dean's death brought some relief. Sorrow for what might have been, lost hope that things might have improved in time, pressure for all that fell alone on her shoulders now. But a measure of relief. She cringed. Wasn't that a terrible way to think about your dead husband?

She remembered the Christmas when Dean told her that he was going to start his own investment business. No more working for others who took all the profit.

"Why do we need it?" Rose had asked.

"What's need?" He put his arms on her shoulders and looked into her eyes.

"Haven't we enough?" she asked, trying to rephrase the same question.

"It'll be a gold mine. It's made for us." He looked so eager. He said he would love the challenge.

He convinced her that he was right, that the opportunity was made for him and the time was now. But she couldn't ignore the feeling that he was taking on that kind of a career risk just to be a significant man. Just for show. To show some anonymous people who didn't even care.

When Schrock Investments started to flounder, Rose wasn't at all surprised. In fact, she was expecting it. In that way, she had to admit, she wasn't much of a partner to Dean either.

Maybe she was too independent for her own good. Dean had often said so. Maybe she was better off alone.

Certainly, Galen needed someone who could give him babies, not grandbabies. Earlier today, her heart missed a beat when Paisley called her a grandmother-to-be. It hadn't occurred to her that this baby could be her grandchild. Why, she was barely thirty-seven years old!

Rose couldn't get past the disquieting notion that she was missing something important about Paisley. It dangled in front of her, a ripe apple on a tree that she couldn't quite reach.

So many unanswered questions.

She didn't know what to do. She just had no idea what to do.

"Rose, doesn't something seem odd about that Paisley girl?"

Rose looked up from watering the garden to find Bethany, standing with hands on her hips in that defiant way she had. Rose smiled. She didn't know where to begin with all the red flags that had been waving at her since she had met Paisley, but she didn't want to share those worries with Bethany. "What do you mean?"

"She's supposed to be head over heels in love with Tobe,

but anytime she's anywhere near Jimmy Fisher, she finds a way to be right next to him, like she's a cat and he's a scratching post."

Rose bit on her lip to hold back a laugh. She turned off the hose. "Tobe will be able to shed light on this topic. Until then, your grandmother is right. We need to be hospitable."

Later that night, as Rose got ready for bed, she took off her apron and stored the pins in the apron belt. She untied the stiff strings of her prayer cap and twisted her head from side to side, stretching the ache of a long day out of her neck. She put the cap on the top of her dresser and her eye caught Allen Turner's SEC business card that she had tucked into the mirror frame. Should she ask him to contact Tobe and find out who Paisley was? But she couldn't even imagine how to frame the request: A girlfriend from Tobe's past has shown up, out of the blue, about to deliver his baby. Would you ask him if he remembers her? She could just imagine the long pause as solemn Allen Turner took in that news, wondering how he got so involved with an Amish family and their trivial woes.

She changed into her nightgown and climbed into bed, its springs squeaking softly as she slipped under the covers. She reached over and opened her Bible, silently reading the words of Psalm 139, lips moving to each word. She needed to be reminded to dwell in the knowledge that God knew all there was to know. Everything.

"O Lord, Thou hast searched me and known me. Thou dost know when I sit down and when I rise up; Thou dost understand my thought from afar . . ."

She read it through twice before turning off the flashlight.

"Dear Lord," she prayed, "please give me answers. Soon. Now. Amen."

Slowly, slowly, she let herself relax into the darkness, closing her eyes, letting the words of Scripture move through her.

The barn was redolent with the familiar musty smell of hay and horses. Mim set her stool at Molly's flank and the pail beneath her speckled udder. Her mother had warned everyone to stay clear of the new cow, to let Galen do the first few milkings. There must be a reason she was named Fireball, she warned Mim. As she started to milk Molly, the plink of the milk in the pail drummed a steady beat. Outside, strutting along the roof of the hen house, Harold the rooster was crowing. She heard horses nickering to each other in the pastures as her brother wheeled hay out to them in the old blue wheelbarrow. How could it be an ordinary day?

Mim pressed her forehead against Molly's warm belly. She wondered idly if cows were ever scared—really scared. She had seen Molly jitter away from Micky the dog, but that was different. A yapping pup at your heels was an immediate threat, but the difference between her and Molly was that when there was no dog in sight, Molly was perfectly content, rhythmically chewing her cud. She wasn't wondering and worrying, while anxiety ate holes through all her stomachs.

Mim closed her eyes and her hands stilled as she wondered how this week had gone so terribly awry. The insufferable Jesse Stoltzfus had stolen her envelope full of Mrs. Miracle letters, and for some reason and without saying so much as a word to her, he had delivered them to the newspaper. They were in yesterday's edition.

Molly shifted her big back hip and Mim snapped to

attention. Maybe everything would turn out all right. Maybe Jesse had the decency to deliver them to the *Stoney Ridge Times* newspaper office without opening the envelope. The address was on the front of the envelope and it was sealed. Mim made sure of that because she didn't want Bethany poking through them. Yes. It was entirely possible that she was worrying for naught.

Her father used to say that the perfect state of mind was halfway between Luke and Mim; Luke never saw worries or responsibilities even if he was surrounded by them. But Mim, he would add, always faced a thousand worries long before one appeared on the horizon.

She smiled at her silly fears, at the woolgathering she'd been doing, and lifted her forehead from Molly's warm hide to set to work, making the milk pail ring.

Brooke Snyder hurried to the Sweet Tooth Bakery and was disappointed to see that the store was crowded and that Jon Hoeffner wasn't sitting at their usual table. In fact, he wasn't even in the bakery. Brooke asked the woman who sat at their special table if she was going to be there very long. The woman glanced at the wall clock. "Maybe just a few more minutes and then it's all yours." She motioned to Brooke to go ahead and sit down. "I'm Penny Williams. I work as the receptionist over at the *Stoney Ridge Times*."

"Nice to meet you. I'm Brooke Snyder."

Penny Williams wore pointy glasses and her hair in a tight doughnut bun on the top of her head. "I haven't seen you around. Are you new to Stoney Ridge?"

"I'm staying out at Eagle Hill for an extended vacation.

I'm . . . in between jobs." Brooke took a sip of coffee. "I've been reading your newspaper." She leaned across the table. "I would love to have an introduction to Mrs. Miracle."

Penny smiled. "Join the crowd. So would everyone. The features editor, especially. He's been wanting to talk to her for weeks now. But no one knows her true identity."

Intriguing!

Penny lowered her voice. "Just between you and me—that column is the reason most people buy this paper. About six months ago, it was on its last legs—it was only getting published a few times a week. But Mrs. Miracle has changed all that. It's back to being a daily newspaper. The editor said he's got an offer to syndicate. That's why he's trying to track her down." She rubbed the tips of her fingers together. "Syndication means big bucks."

Brooke leaned back in her seat. "You're telling me that the paper's livelihood is dependent on someone no one has ever met?"

Offended, Penny stiffened. "I said no such thing. Any paper's livelihood is dependent on advertisers. What I did say was that Mrs. Miracle's column has boosted circulation. Considerably. And that makes advertisers very happy. Which makes the publisher and editors happy too."

"What makes Mrs. Miracle's column so unique?" Brooke added cream to her coffee and stirred. "There are plenty of advice columns."

"Mrs. Miracle sees things in a different way. And she has a knack for pointing people back to the most important things in life. The column used to be once a week, now it's twice a week, and the editor wants it to go to three times a week."

"What *do* you know about Mrs. Miracle?"

Penny shrugged. "Nothing, really. An Amish girl drops off the column and picks up her paycheck and she won't reveal the identity of Mrs. Miracle. I've tried."

Brooke's mouth dropped open. "Are you telling me that Mrs. Miracle is an Amish girl?"

"I said no such thing." Penny's feathers ruffled again. "Absolutely not. Not a chance. Around here, a lot of Amish girls work for the non-Amish—doing errands and housecleaning, that sort of thing. My guess is Mrs. Miracle is a well-to-do woman in her sixties. She's seen it all." She looked at the clock. "I'd better get back to the office. Nice to meet you, Brittany."

"Brooke. Brooke Snyder." But Penny was already out the door and hurrying down the street.

All afternoon, as Brooke strolled through the little Main Street shops, hoping to bump into Jon, she pondered the secret identity of Mrs. Miracle. Could she be Amish? These Plain people kept surprising her. She stopped and picked up a copy of today's newspaper and sat on a sidewalk bench in the sun to read it. Automatically, she turned to the Mrs. Miracle column. As she started to read, she sat up. *There* was her letter to Mrs. Miracle!

So what advice would Mrs. Miracle have for her predicament?

Dear Borrower,

Rather than try to change yourself or copy others, why not try to accept the person you're intended to be? The thing about looking for a new identity is that, when all is said and done, you're still you. Wherever you go, there you'll be.

Sincerely,
Mrs. Miracle

Wait. *What?* Brooke had heard that same thing before, but where? Where, where, where? Slowly, awareness dawned on her. Could it be? Could it possibly be?

Fourteen-year-old Mim Schrock *was* Mrs. Miracle.

12

Later that afternoon, Rose was down in the barn. She clipped a lead line to the mare and led her out to the pasture, her little foal trotting behind. Her mother-in-law Vera met her out in the yard as she closed the gate. "Rose, what did you say to Paisley to get her all . . . jittery?"

"What do you mean?"

"She's in there pacing around the house like a caged tiger."

Rose rolled her eyes. "An apt description. She seems a little like a tiger."

"You shouldn't be aggravating her so."

Rose stopped in her tracks. "Do you honestly believe her story? You think she's Tobe's girlfriend? Tobe might have sowed some wild oats, but does she seem like the kind of girl he would be interested in?"

"Tobe has been under a great deal of stress. People aren't themselves when they're stressed." Vera bristled. "And he would do the right thing by her."

"Vera, a girl like Paisley could never become Amish. You must see that, don't you? She would only keep him from the church."

"If you would just show a little kindness, she might be interested in joining our people. You're not even giving her a chance."

Rose was astounded. Vera found fault with nearly everyone—all but Dean, her son, and Tobe and Bethany, her favorite grandchildren. And now Paisley was added to the brief list. Paisley, of all people? "That girl came here out of the blue. What do we know about her?"

"She says she's carrying Tobe's baby. What else do we need to know?"

"I won't believe that until I hear it from Tobe."

"You have to be in control of everybody and everything, don't you?"

Rose flinched. Just as she was about to open her mouth to say something she was sure she would regret, Luke and Sammy burst out of the house and ran to meet Rose in the yard. "Paisley said to come quick! She's having her baby! Right now! Right on the kitchen floor!"

—ᘒ ◊ ᘓ—

Six hours later, a baby girl was born to Paisley at the Lancaster County Hospital. Rose stayed by Paisley's side as she labored. She wiped her forehead with a cool cloth and fed her ice chips, all the while realizing that Paisley was completely, thoroughly unprepared for bringing a newborn into the world. When the contractions rolled over her, overwhelming her, she screamed out in pain and insisted she didn't want to be a mother.

Paisley took in a breath and blew it out slowly. "I'm not qualified."

"Every new mother feels that way. I certainly did."

"Please," Paisley pleaded, clinging to Rose's hand. "Get it out. Whatever you have to do, just get it out."

"You're doing it," Rose said, with a calm she didn't feel. "There's only one way to get through this. You're the only one who can get this baby out . . . and you're doing it."

A long, moaning wail emerged out of Paisley. Her body was finally surrendering; she stopped fighting, and the baby began to move, slowly, down the birth canal and into the doctor's waiting arms.

The room went still. A time that was usually so joyful, buzzing with activity, but no one spoke. The obstetrician and nurses had serious looks on their faces as the pediatrician examined the baby. There was a flurry of whispering, then the baby was briefly shown to Paisley before getting whisked away.

Paisley grabbed Rose's arm. "Something's wrong with it."

Rose looked to the nurse to answer.

The nurse was checking Paisley's blood pressure and kept her eyes fixed on the blood pressure monitor. "The baby's being looked after right now. The doctor will talk to you soon." She unwrapped the blood pressure cuff from Paisley's arms. Then, more kindly, she said, "You must be exhausted. After we get you cleaned up, you should try to sleep." She nodded in Rose's direction. "You too."

As soon as Paisley drifted to sleep, Rose went back to Eagle Hill to get a few hours' sleep, then returned around noon.

Paisley was curled up in the hospital bed, facing the window, away from the baby in the bassinet next to her.

"How are you feeling?" Rose asked her, before bending to kiss the sleeping baby's forehead.

Paisley didn't want to talk. She wasn't interested in seeing the baby, holding it, nursing it. Rose was appalled; she kept encouraging her to look at the baby, but the nurse assured her that wasn't entirely unusual, under the circumstances.

The nurse motioned to Rose to meet her in the hallway. "The doctor wants to talk to you." She pointed to the pediatrician standing in scrubs by the nurses' station, filling out paperwork.

The doctor sat down with Rose and told her what she already knew after seeing the epicanthic folds around the baby's eyes last night before she was whisked away. She had seen it before. She had known it the moment she saw the baby. This was a special child. One with Down syndrome.

"We ran a number of tests last night and the baby seems to be very healthy," the doctor explained. "Sometimes, these babies have heart defects."

Rose let out a deep sigh. "I assume you've already told this to Paisley?"

He nodded. "She's still in shock. She had no idea the baby would have an issue. Nowadays, an anatomical ultrasound would pick up markers that give indication of chromosomal defects. She said she never had one. I don't see this kind of case very often, where a mother doesn't realize she's going to have a baby with Down's."

"I don't think she had any prenatal care."

He put the pen back in his shirt pocket. "In this day and age, there's a lot of counseling available to help. Most T-21 kids grow up to be loving, caring individuals. As the baby develops, everything will take longer, each new skill will be a huge hurdle, but your granddaughter should have a full and happy life. She'll just need extra time for everything." He patted Rose's arm. "I can't deny it gives me peace of mind to think this child will be raised in an Amish home. I know your people perceive handicapped children differently than the non-Amish."

"Special children," Rose said in a distracted way.

"Pardon?"

"That's what we call them. Not handicapped."

Pleased, he bobbed his head. "That's just what I meant. Exactly that."

His pager went off and he excused himself, so Rose went to sit by Paisley's bed. "Did you notice the baby's ten little fingers and ten toes, Paisley? Perfect."

"She's *not* perfect."

Rose reached out and patted Paisley's bent knee. "Everything will be all right. You'll see." She tried hard to stop her voice from sounding like Paisley's mother or her schoolteacher.

"I've heard that line before." Paisley yanked her knee away and turned her head. "Nothing ever works out the way it should for me."

Rose tried several times to get Paisley interested in the baby, but with no success. Paisley didn't want anything to do with the baby; she just wanted to leave the hospital. The baby had weak muscle tone for sucking, which might make nursing difficult, so the nurse provided a bottle with a specially designed nipple that the baby accepted. Once the baby started to take the bottle consistently, the doctor agreed to let them go home, as long as the baby was brought back for a follow-up physical in two days.

"I think Paisley might adjust to the baby a little better at home than here," he said to Rose as he signed the release papers.

Rose hoped he was right, but knew otherwise.

The last thing Paisley needed to do before she could be released from the hospital was to fill out the birth certificate. She said she didn't care what Rose called the baby so she chose the name Sarah, after a favorite cousin who had Down's. All Paisley cared about was that Tobias Schrock was named as the baby's father on the birth certificate.

"The name you put on that birth certificate has to be legal. Tobe will have to sign the birth certificate to admit to being the father of your child."

Paisley blinked, then scribbled Tobe's name on the line. "And why would he not?"

Well, for one, Rose thought, he might not be the baby's father. She didn't say it aloud, though, because she actually felt a little sorry for Paisley. She couldn't imagine how she would feel if she were in Paisley's shoes right now and so she didn't even try. She thought it would be best to try to support her as she stepped into motherhood. Was it possible for a woman to simply not have a capacity to mother her own child?

With a jolt, she thought of Dean's first wife, Tobe and Bethany's mother, whom she knew little about. Dean rarely mentioned her, nor did Vera. All that Rose knew of Mary Miller Schrock was that she abandoned her young children, divorced Dean, and left someone else to pick up the pieces of a shattered family. Two years later, Rose became that someone.

She cringed, feeling an odd foreboding.

Whoever that fourteenth cousin twice removed thought he was, he still needed to have his sheets changed and wastebasket emptied. The day came when Bethany was fed up waiting for him to show himself. She found a screwdriver and pins and jimmied the lock open to the second-floor guestroom. She turned the knob and cautiously opened the door. She couldn't believe it. She walked slowly into the room. From the unmade bed to the clothes that littered the floor, the room was in complete chaos. Candy wrappers, gum wrappers, old newspapers, soda cans, crumpled dinner napkins, tin foil, cookies, and crackers.

Clothing lay in a soiled heap in the corner. The bed was full of crumbs. The remains of a sandwich lay on the pillow, and an open bag of potato chips had been shoved under the blanket. Nothing had been washed or cleaned since the day the old sisters' fourteenth cousin twice removed had arrived.

Well, she thought, as she stripped the bed, if she had any doubts about his connection to the sisters before today, the condition of this room squelched them. The fourteenth cousin twice removed fit right in with his elderly relatives.

Mim arrived at the schoolhouse early one morning and put her books in her desk. On top of her desk was her "What Pennsylvania Means to Me" essay that she had labored over, graded and returned: B- in big fat red ink.

She slunk into her seat, disappointed and frustrated, angry with Danny Riehl, who thought he was so smart. She opened her desk and was startled to find a red rose—the first of the season, lying on top of her neatly folded and freshly laundered apron-turned-rope that saved the cow in the ditch. There was a card attached:

A boy met a girl as sweet as caramel,
Of all the girls, he thought she was the pinnacle,

But she thought he was quite unbearable.
To win her hand, he would need help from . . . Mrs. Miracle.

Mim gasped! Then . . . cringed. Trust Jesse Stoltzfus to make this into a big, big deal. She *knew* he was going to torture her over the identity of Mrs. Miracle. She ripped up the note and scrunched up the rose and stomped to the garbage to throw them away. That Jesse Stoltzfus! He was a loathsome creature. When she turned around, Danny was peering at her with a curious look on his face. "Everything all right, Mim?"

"No! It's not all right. My paper should be an A." She cringed again. Did she really just say that?

He was very Teacher Danny now, sitting at his desk, peering down at her. "I gave you a B- because I believe you can do better."

A few children came into the classroom and put their lunch boxes on the shelf that lined the back wall. Danny glanced at them and lowered his voice. "We can talk about your essay after school, if you like."

She didn't like. She felt just as mad at him as she did at Jesse Stoltzfus. Even madder. Her essay was excellent. Just excellent. He was being intentionally hard on her and she didn't know why.

When Jesse came into the classroom, she purposefully ignored him, though she doubted he noticed. He was too busy crowing to Luke and Mose over the A+ on his stupid essay. When he passed by her desk, he whispered, "B minus?" turned, and wiggled his eyebrows at her. She snapped her head away from his goofy face.

Why couldn't there be another girl in her grade? Or seventh grade. Sixth, even. She was surrounded by horrible, terrible, abominable boys.

On the way home from school that day, she stopped at a horse trough in the field of the nearly-falling-down barn and leaned over to look at her face in the water. "This face," she said, "belongs to someone who can write well enough to have her own advice column in a newspaper, despite what Teacher Danny seems to think. And she has pluck. And this is me, Mim." She stopped. Jesse was right. Mim was no name for someone who could write as well as she could. "Miriam."

What a day. She had been given her first rose, was humiliated by Danny Riehl and mortified by Jesse Stoltzfus. *What a day.*

───◇───

Rose, Paisley, and the baby returned to Eagle Hill that evening, barely twenty-four hours after the baby had been born. The house was quiet; Vera, Mim, and the boys had gone to bed, Bethany was out with Jimmy Fisher, and Rose was thankful for a quiet entry. There would be time tomorrow for everyone to ooh and aah over the baby.

Paisley went straight upstairs to bed. Rose hadn't heard anyone come into the kitchen but suddenly looked up and found Naomi standing by the doorjamb, looking at the tiny baby sleeping in the Moses basket in the corner. In her arms was a small pink baby quilt she had just completed.

"I had a feeling the baby was a girl," she said, a shy smile on her face.

Somehow, that didn't surprise Rose. Naomi was known for those kinds of presentiments. Rose wasn't sure if she had a unique gift or if she just listened to her intuition better than most. "The baby quilt is her first gift, Naomi." She took the quilt from her and laid it on the table. One-inch squares of pink fabrics in varying shades were perfectly cut, sewn, and quilted with Naomi's precise stitches. "What a treasure you've given her."

But Naomi wasn't even listening. She was transfixed by the baby. That intense look she had on her face—well, for the first time, Rose noticed how she and Galen resembled each other. Naomi's hair was coffee-brown, like his was, her face was angular like his, though their eyes were a different color, and her features were far less classically attractive than her brother's. She wasn't beautiful, but she was. She had the beauty of happiness.

"Can I pick the baby up?" Naomi whispered softly, as if she were standing on hallowed ground.

"Of course," Rose told her. "Her name is Sarah."

She watched as Naomi lifted the tiny baby nervously, almost shyly, and held her to her chest. She said nothing, just walked around the downstairs in a big loop. She mumbled something soft, a prayer or a poem or a tuneless lullaby— Rose couldn't make it out. Naomi's hold on the baby was sure, her love obvious.

After Naomi left, Rose went into Paisley's room with the baby. Seeing that Paisley's eyes were open, Rose started to take the baby to her, but she turned away to face the wall. Rose took the baby to her own room to lie down for a while. She was afraid to trust Sarah with her mother yet.

She dozed lightly, wakened by the baby whimpering, and went downstairs to warm a bottle for her before Sarah started to cry. She sat in the rocker and held the baby against her, reminded of those exhausting days with her own babies: of Mim and of Luke and Sammy. How had she survived them? She remembered feeling too tired to rise.

When the baby had taken all she would from the bottle, Rose wrapped her tightly in a swaddle, the way babies like best, and sat down to rock her to sleep. The moon was full, sending streaming beams of light into the living room.

Little Sarah fell sound asleep, tucked against her breast. She stroked the baby's wispy tuft of dark hair. Was it her imagination or did the baby look more helpless and alone than any other child? As if she knew she was motherless and fatherless from the moment she had come on earth. "You could be worse off," Rose whispered. "Your mother's a fool not to want you, but maybe she was smart to wait until she got to people who would look after you."

But it wasn't really smarts, Rose feared—Paisley just didn't care.

13

The full moon flooded Naomi's bedroom with yellow light, as bright as day. She wasn't asleep. She couldn't sleep tonight. She hadn't been able to stop thinking about the baby at Eagle Hill Farm. There was something about her that deeply touched her.

When she held the baby for the first time, she had gazed down into Sarah's little face, and Sarah gazed back at her, her eyes large and shiny. Trusting.

A silent communication had passed between them in that moment, deep and heartfelt.

Naomi had breathed in deeply that sweet newborn smell. Sarah's neck was so small and fragile looking. Her skin was soft and she smelled better than any human being Naomi had ever been near. Unexpected pleasure stole over her. She understood, suddenly, why everything that mothers went through—the long nights, the endless crying, the daily weariness—was worth the sacrifice to them.

Naomi's thoughts drifted to her own mother, long gone, knowing that her mother must have held her in the same way. Her throat swelled and tears rushed to her eyes, but she kept up the gentle motion she had watched Rose use with Sarah to rock her to sleep. Back and forth. Back and forth.

The baby's eyes held innocence and a sort of uncanny wisdom. They continued to look at each other for a long stretch, then Sarah's lids grew heavy and fluttered shut. Rose told Naomi to set the baby in her basket to sleep, but she couldn't bring herself to let her go. She had ended up staying in that rocker for hours.

An owl hooted once, then twice. Naomi should try to sleep. She rolled onto her side to face the wall, away from the bright window. A faint sense that she had forgotten something needled the back of her mind. What was it? Something definitely was missing. Had she left something over at Eagle Hill?

And then it hit her. The thing that had disappeared? Her anxiety. Gone, like a wisp of steam from a teacup. Vanished into thin air.

Her stomach? Settled. Headache? None. Nerves? Steady. Heartbeat? Normal. Breathing? Calm and relaxed.

Astonished, she thought of Sarah, sleeping peacefully in her arms this evening. *She'd* done this, she realized. This tiny gift of a baby had stilled the roiling inside of her. This little person she scarcely knew and already loved.

"I'm going to help you, Sarah," she whispered aloud, as if the baby were still in her arms and could understand her words. "Your mother brought you to us, for whatever reason, and it's the right place for you. I'm going to help you. You're safe here."

Naomi released a deep sigh, and fell asleep.

The next morning, Rose sat on the porch swing, holding the baby in the morning sunlight. The nurse had suggested that the baby get some sun each day to help combat jaundice.

"Hey there."

She looked up to see Galen, a gentle smile lighting his eyes. "Well, hello." She lifted her arms slightly. "Meet our newest houseguest."

He came up on the porch and moved some papers to sit beside her on the swing. He held out a finger for the baby to grab on to. "A special baby."

"Yes. A special child." She smiled at the way Galen was gazing at the baby. He was such a masculine man, all angles, no nonsense—but his face was now soft and tender. To see the baby's little hand grasping his strong finger touched her heart.

He glanced at the papers on the porch swing. "Hospital bills?"

The baby closed her eyes, drifted to sleep. "Yes," Rose said. "Paisley had them all billed to me."

"Well, don't worry about them now," Galen said. "Have a little faith."

Rose wanted to have that kind of faith. She truly believed anything was possible with God. "I think it will take a miracle to get those bills paid."

"We could have a benefit to raise money."

"I can't ask Bishop Elmo for yet another benefit for the Schrock family."

"Sure you can. That's what we do for each other." He nudged her. "You would do it for anyone else."

True, but somehow, it was always easier to give than receive. "Naomi's been a wonderful help. Yesterday she was here all evening, then again this morning."

"She likes babies."

The baby startled awake and Rose transferred her to her shoulder. "Naomi is so remarkably mature." She was like her brother in that way. Mature beyond her years. She glanced at Galen. "I can't imagine what must be running through her mind about Tobe." The moment the words left her mouth, she wished them back.

He flashed her a look of impatience. "You're looking for something that isn't there. Naomi has never even mentioned Tobe. Probably doesn't even think twice about him."

Annoyed, she rose to her feet. "Galen, you're the only one who doesn't think twice about Tobe." She passed the baby to him. "I need to go get a bottle ready. Hold her for a moment, will you?"

"Me?" His voice sounded almost . . . frightened.

She smiled and her irritation with him dissolved. Imagine that. Galen King was intimidated by a little six-pound baby.

Bethany came outside to feed the hens and was startled to see Galen King on the porch swing, holding the baby as if she were made of spun sugar. He looked up when he heard the door open, a shy, embarrassed smile cracking his face, as if he'd been caught.

"I have some news about Lodestar," he said, quickly passing the baby to her.

Bethany couldn't read anything in his demeanor. Galen was such a steady man that good and bad news would probably sound the same, something to be dealt with either way. She sat down on the porch swing to hear what he had to say, awkwardly shifting the baby into her other arm as the baby started making mewling sounds. She wasn't accustomed to newborn babies and had only met this one an hour ago. Where was Rose with that bottle, anyway?

"A farrier knew of a horse that was being used as a mini-backyard breeding factory. The farrier was called out to keep his hooves trimmed on a regular basis. He didn't know the owner and was concerned he might not get paid if no one was around during the shoeing, so he asked to be paid in advance."

"What makes you think it could be Lodestar?"

"He described the horse's unusual looks—that long flaxen mane, the golden coat—from the sound of it, it resembled Lodestar. But I can't be sure."

Bethany sat up in the porch swing. "Let's go find out."

"Now, hold on. There's more to the story. The horse has been kept in a pasture with an electric fence surrounding it. The farrier said the first time he trimmed his hooves, everything was in order. But the second time, the horse looked thinner, dirty and unkempt, like no one was taking care of him. And this last time, the farrier found him in really bad shape. Ribs showing, living in filth, bad water in the rain bucket. Hoof rot too, so he wasn't able to shoe him."

Her heart was beating fast. "Galen, we need to rescue him!"

"It's more complicated than just going and getting him. I'm not even positive it is Lodestar. Besides, the farrier is involved. He said he called Equine Rescue and they're going out this week to check on the horse."

"Could we ask the farrier to take us out to see the horse? Just to see if this horse might be Lodestar?"

"I suppose we could." He took off his hat. "On one condition. I didn't tell the farrier the whole story—about Jimmy Fisher and Jake Hertzler. I just want to take things one step at a time. If it's not Lodestar, we just leave the situation alone and let Equine Rescue handle it. We don't get involved." He looked right at her. "Is that understood?"

"But what if it is Lodestar?" The baby's face scrunched up in distress and Bethany glanced at the kitchen window. Where was Rose?

Galen gave her a warning look. "We'll still take things one step at a time."

"Okay."

He put his hat back on. "You realize we might be walking into trouble, don't you?"

Bethany grinned, even as the baby started to howl. "I do. But to quote Jimmy Fisher, some things are worth a little trouble."

Mim discovered something new about herself: she did not like babies. In fact, she thought babies were revolting and couldn't understand why her mother and Naomi practically stumbled over each other as they went to pick Sarah up and soothe her when she started to howl. Babies might not know how to do much, but they sure knew how to scream. And when the baby wasn't screaming, her mouth was always open and drooling. And those vile diapers! How could anyone so very small need to be changed ten times a day?

Nothing felt normal since Paisley had come to Eagle Hill.

Bethany was preoccupied, her mind seemed a million miles away. Luke was continually in a bad mood and would argue with Sammy at the drop of a hat. Her mother would get upset and send them to their room; she was tired every evening and had no time to talk about school or anything.

Mammi Vera, usually bleak and mournful, was actually acting a tiny bit happy at having a squawling baby in the house. That, too, wasn't normal. She was *never* happy. But Mim noticed that Mammi Vera didn't offer to change Sarah's vile-smelling diapers or wipe the drool off her little pink cheeks.

Mim choked down another bite of oatmeal and wondered if Mammi Vera would notice if she added more sugar. It could be she had already forgotten the first four spoonfuls, but you never knew with Mammi Vera. Some things she forgot right off and others she remembered. Like what someone died from. Old people were always trying to figure out what people died from, or how many sisters and brothers they had and what they died from. That made up half the conversations Mim had to sit through when she helped Bethany at the Sisters' House.

She put down her spoon and stared at her oatmeal, thinking of how huffy her mother became a few minutes ago when Mim shared the suspicions and whispers that were buzzing around the school playground about the fatherless baby at Eagle Hill.

"Suspicions and whispers? That's the most ridiculous thing I've ever heard. What kinds of friends do you think we have?" Her mother's voice shook with anger and Mim was instantly sorry she had brought the subject up. "Three neighbors dropped everything and brought over baby clothes and a crib. Mattie Riehl made a diaper bag and filled it with pacifiers, tiny T-shirts and socks, diapers, bottles, and formula. Galen chopped all that wood for us. Naomi has rocked this baby for hours. Fern Lapp brought supper, and David Stoltzfus offered to do chores as if we'd been friends all our lives."

"I thought you might want to know what other people are thinking," Mim admitted in a quiet voice.

Her mother drew in a deep breath. "Such neighbors wouldn't tell tales and gossip. Love thinks well of others, and the people here have poured out that very kind of godly love and friendship. You worry what they'd think? Down deep in my heart, I know they consider us blessed."

Mim couldn't look her mother in the eye as she stammered, "Those are only some of the neighbors."

"For once your mother is right," Mammi Vera said as she came into the kitchen. "We are blessed by this child."

Mim was shocked. The world was turning upside down. She was astounded that her grandmother wasn't more upset. One of her grandmother's favorite sayings was: Aaegebrenndi Supp riecht welt. *You can smell scorched soup from afar.* Scandals spread like wildfire, she would warn, wagging a finger at them. "I guess I mean, you're supposed to get married and then have babies, right?"

"That's the best way." Mammi Vera peered at the baby, sleeping in a borrowed Moses basket, tucked in a corner by the window where the morning sun streamed through and kept her warm. She tucked a blanket around Sarah's little pink toes. "But things don't always happen in the best way, and once some things have happened, we can't go back and change them to the best way." She looked at Mim. "But it's my belief that every child the Lord sends is a gift, and even when things aren't as they should be, God can make a way out of no way."

"Is that in the Bible?"

"Many times in many stories. Remember how the angel Gabriel told Mary, 'With God nothing shall be impossible'?"

Mammi Vera straightened and peered out the window. "Soon, Tobe will be home. You'll see. All will turn out well when Tobe finally comes home."

The farrier drove Galen and Bethany out to look at the horse later in the week. In the corner of a dirty pasture was a muddy, broken-down horse. His head hung low, eyes lifeless, and his ribs stuck out. The saddest discovery of all was that his back feet were buckled together in leather hobbles. "He's in even worse condition than he was a few days ago."

The Equine Rescue truck pulled up at the same time. Two men climbed out and walked to the pasture with grim looks on their face as they saw the condition the horse was in. "There's an electric fence," the farrier pointed out. "I'll turn it off and then we can go in."

Bethany watched him click off a small handle. He tapped the fence with his gloved finger and declared it safe. "The juice is cut off. Go on in."

As they walked in the pasture, through the mud and muck toward the horse, Bethany wasn't at all sure it was Jimmy's Lodestar. This horse was covered in ticks, its eyes had a beaten down look, its ears were flattened back, its mane wasn't flaxen but brown, dirty, and matted. She looked at Galen to see what he was thinking. He was walking around the horse, running a hand down its girth, over the joints in its legs. There was no way this horse could be Lodestar. No chance at all.

Galen looked up at her. "It's him."

"What?! Are you sure? He doesn't look the same."

"It's him." He sounded certain.

The farrier and the men from the Equine Rescue were

discussing how to proceed as Bethany tipped over the dirt-filled pan of rainwater and went to go look for fresh water for the horse. Galen had brought a hay bale in the back of the farrier's truck and took it out to Lodestar, who lunged for it. Galen pulled a hoof pick out of one pocket, a bottle of apple cider vinegar and a brush out of the other. With a practiced hand, he unbuckled the hobbles. While Lodestar ate, Galen lifted each foot and cleaned the hoof, then painted vinegar over the frog. An old remedy for hoof rot.

"What happens now?" Bethany asked the men.

"We'll post a warning on the door to the house. If we don't hear from the owner in a few days, we'll return and post another."

She turned to the farrier. "What do you know about the owner?"

"I only met him one time, when he asked me to come shoe the horse every eight weeks. There was something odd about him."

Galen's head snapped up. "What was it that struck you as odd?"

"He only carried a one-hundred-dollar bill. Wanted me to break the change for him, and when I couldn't, he said he would have to pay me next time. I've been on the wrong end of that before, so I told him I only work if I'm paid in advance. It made him mad, but he ended up paying me for two shoeings."

"Do you remember what he looked like?" Bethany said.

"Thirty or so. Nice looking. Clean shaven. Seemed to care about the horse." His lips hardened as he glanced around the paddock. "Nothing like this."

"Was the man pleasant? Charming?" She wanted to know.

"Very. The kind of guy who could charm the spots off a leopard."

It *had* to be Jake Hertzler. It had to be! But Bethany could see the run-down house was empty, deserted. Jake must have left awhile ago, abandoning Lodestar. "What happens if you don't hear back from the owner in a few days? If he never does come back?"

"Then we'll return with law enforcement and confiscate the horse."

Galen's gaze was fixed on Lodestar. "What'll happen to the horse?"

"He'll be taken to a rescue center and rehabilitated. Then he'll be put up for adoption."

"How long could that take?" Bethany said.

"Six months. Maybe a year."

Bethany couldn't bear the thought of this pathetic beast left in this filthy pasture without food and water for another week. And hobbled! One of the men from the Equine Rescue apologized to Galen but told him he would have to put the hobbles back on so they could photograph the condition the horse was in, while the other one wrote up a warning and posted it on the door. Galen looked sadly at the hobbles in his hand and gently replaced them on Lodestar's back legs. The horse turned his head from the hay to stare at Galen, as if betrayed.

As they left the pasture, they reminded the farrier to turn the electric fence back on. "By law, we have to leave everything just the way we found it."

Bethany sidled up to Galen to whisper to him. "We can't leave him hobbled. At the very least . . . not hobbled."

He gave her a slight nod. "Distract them as they walk to their cars," he whispered.

Bethany put herself in front of the men, walking backward, asking them every question she could think of about their work. Behind them, she saw Galen quickly unbuckle the horse's hobbles and hurry across the pasture to join them before they reached the gate and the farrier flipped on the switch to the electric fence.

As they climbed back in the farrier's truck, Bethany said, "Wait! I dropped something by the pasture." She jumped out of the truck and hurried over to the gate. She dropped her handkerchief and leaned over with one hand to pick it up, waving to the farrier and Galen to show them she found it. With the other hand, she flipped the electric fence power switch off. The horse looked at her with sorrowful but mildly curious eyes, munching on the hay. "Okay, Lodestar. I'm giving you a chance. Don't disappoint me."

No one said much on the ride home. They were almost back to Eagle Hill before the farrier broke the silence. "I don't know if that horse will ever be the same."

Bethany looked to Galen for that answer.

"He's young," Galen said reassuringly. "It's amazing how quickly an animal can heal once he's got good food, good shelter, and a little loving care."

With all the excitement of the baby's birth, no one had remembered to check phone messages or pick up the mail. While Naomi was feeding the baby her bottle, Rose walked to the mailbox and pulled out three days' worth of mail. Three days! She shook her head. Then she stopped by the phone shanty and listened to messages.

She hunted for a pen to write down names and numbers

as she listened to three different messages from guests who wanted to book reservations in April and May. Her pen fell on the floor, and as she bent to get it, she almost missed the last message. "Rose, this is Tobe. I'm sorry I haven't gotten back to you but there's a reason—I'm getting released this week. I'll be home on Friday. I'll explain about, well, about everything, when I get home."

The first thought that ran through her mind was: Tobe was coming home! Alleluia! And then: Friday? Friday! That's tomorrow! And of course, so like Tobe, he didn't say how he would be returning, or what time. But the important thing— Tobe was finally coming home.

14

Bethany hurried over to Naomi's. They were planning to go to the Sisters' Bee at Edith Fisher's and she was running late, as usual. As she slipped through the privet, something caught her eye. Outside the far fence, near the road, she noticed a loose horse, unbridled, grazing on shoots of new spring grass. She looked in the barn for Galen but couldn't find him, so she grabbed a handful of hay, tucked a rope under her arm, and walked slowly, slowly toward the horse.

The horse shied but was too weary, too thin, to bolt. "Don't tell me . . . can it really be . . . is it you?" She held the hay out to the horse and gently slipped a rope around his neck. She reached out and rested her hand on the horse's nose. The horse bumped her with his nose, a sign of recognition. "I know someone who is going to be pretty excited to see you."

Bethany rubbed the horse's long neck, looking him over for injuries. The horse seemed completely calm. Ears in the upright position.

She ran her hand down each leg, the way she'd seen Galen do, looking for swelling or bruising or cuts. Then she led the horse into Galen's barn and into a large box stall, customized with extra latches especially for a certain horse who liked to escape, but she had a feeling that wouldn't be a problem any longer.

Jimmy Fisher's Lodestar had come home.

As soon as Bethany arrived at the Fishers' farm for the Sisters' Bee, she made a beeline to find Jimmy in the pullet barn. It was ten times as large as the henhouse at Eagle Hill. She had never been in it before and cringed at the loud sound of the hens, cackling and clucking in their nesting boxes. The air was pungent, fusty and sour, nearly overwhelming her, though it was a well-kept barn with plenty of ventilation. One or two of the hens flapped their wings and pecked at her as she walked down the narrow aisle.

No wonder Jimmy couldn't stand being a chicken boss! These birds were downright ornery.

She found him cutting up apples at a workbench in the center of the barn, tossing the apple slices in a bucket to feed to the hens. When he saw her, he startled. "Bethany, what are you doing here?"

"Jimmy, I found him! Well, Galen helped too."

"Who?"

She paused, unable to hold back a grin. "Lodestar."

He cocked his head and looked at her as if she might be sun touched. "Bethany, are you feeling all right?"

She laughed. "It's really him. Lodestar!"

Jimmy didn't move for a moment, didn't breathe. Then he threw the apple knife down on the workbench so hard it stuck upright, point in the wood. "Where?" His voice made a funny, choking sound. "Where is he?"

"He's not in great shape. He's been mistreated pretty badly. He's lost a lot of muscle mass. But Galen thinks that with good food, good care, love, and kindness, he'll be as good as new." She bit her bottom lip. "Hopefully."

He took a step closer to her, impatience on his face. "Bethany, where is he?"

"In Galen's barn, of course."

Jimmy tossed his worn leather gloves on the ground and blew past her, leaving her alone in the stinky chicken barn.

⸺ ❦ ⸺

Micky was getting too old for all the silly games he played like a puppy, but he didn't know it, which was why Rose ignored him when he woke her in the middle of the night with his cold nose on her hand. He hunkered down on the ground and made a whimpering sound, then he ran around and around in a tight circle, jumped up on the bed, jumped off, only to do it all over again. Something was up, so Rose got out of bed. She heard a sound outside and went to the window, just in time to see Paisley's car start up, cough, and sputter down the driveway.

Rose flew into action and bolted down the stairs. "Stop her, stop her! She's leaving! Paisley's leaving!"

Bethany burst out of her bedroom, down the stairs, and ran past Rose to go outside, waving, trying to catch up with the car. At the end of the driveway she gave up and walked back to Rose, furious. "I can't believe she actually left before Tobe got home. I can't believe it!"

All kinds of feelings ping-ponged in Rose's head. Relief that Paisley was gone, that the family would no longer need to walk on a knife-edge of anxiety, that Tobe wasn't home yet to be caught in a quandary about whether to go with her or not.

Then, panic! The baby. The baby was gone! How dare Paisley take that baby away! Rose felt devastated. She was already falling in love with little Sarah.

Suddenly a familiar wail floated down the steps.

Bethany looked at Rose, puzzled. "Paisley didn't take the baby with her?"

The baby's wail grew louder.

"Apparently . . . not," Rose said in a thin, unsteady voice.

In the morning, Rose told Vera that Paisley had vanished. Vera's face suddenly grew gray and wrinkled, as if she had turned a hundred years old.

"The less said about that Parsley woman, the better. The English are very unreliable." Vera's face was in that sharp straight line again. There would be no more said.

When Naomi received Tobe's call that he was coming home, asking her to meet him at the bus stop at three o'clock and to come alone so they could have time to talk, she found herself deliberating over which dress to wear to make her look most appealing—the rose or the teal green—then she pulled herself up sharply and was ashamed to realize how vain she sounded, even to herself. But she wore the teal green one that gave her more color and didn't make her look wishy-washy. She could barely wait to see Tobe. No day had ever seemed longer.

It was nearly time. The bus would be in at three p.m., he said. Only four hours to go. Three. Two. It was time.

Today, fortune was in her favor. Mr. Kurtz was due to arrive at the house at two o'clock during the exact time when Galen happened to have gone to town to buy supplies.

No lies were told and none were needed. By three o'clock, Naomi was waiting at the crowded and noisy bus station in Lancaster—so crowded she felt like a hen being crated off to market, so noisy she couldn't hear herself think. She tried to push her way to the front of the crowd as she watched Tobe's bus pull in and stop. She felt a nervous quiver in her belly and unconsciously smoothed her apron again and again.

At the top of the bus steps, his hand clutching the door handle, Tobe paused and his eyes roamed the crowd. The sight of him filled Naomi's eyes with tears. He was so . . . beautiful. Tall, broad, handsome, and he was hers.

She could tell, from the frown on his face, he couldn't find her in the crowd. He stepped down from the bus and started to make his way through the cluster of people. She hurried to catch him and pulled at his sleeve.

"Tobe?" she said, almost hesitatingly.

Tobe spun around.

Their eyes met immediately, but neither of them moved. It was as if words and greetings and reactions had been blown out of them like air after a kick in the stomach. Then words tumbled out.

"I was afraid you weren't coming—"

"How could I not—"

"For hundreds of reasons," he said. Then he gave a quick scan around the bus station to see if he recognized anyone, and satisfied there was no one, he reached out to engulf her in a hug. They left the station with arms linked together and went across the street to a coffee shop to talk. The discreet Mr. Kurtz said he had an errand to run and would return in an hour.

Over coffee, Naomi told Tobe about the baby's arrival, and then about Paisley's midnight disappearance.

He was speechless at the turn of events. Delighted, even. "It proves it, then, doesn't it? I'm not the father. She couldn't face me."

"Maybe. Maybe not. She didn't seem the same after the baby was born. I'm not exactly sure why. Bethany thinks it's because the baby is a special child. Rose thinks Paisley was under the impression that you came from a well-off family and was not happy to find out that wasn't exactly so—"

"No kidding." He made a scoffing sound. "So why do you think she left?"

"I truly don't know. I hardly traded more than a few words with her while she was at Eagle Hill. After the baby was born, she stayed in bed. She just seemed unhappy and disappointed."

They stopped talking while the waitress brought two mugs, one of coffee, one of tea, and set them on the table.

Tobe poured cream into his coffee and stirred it. "Naomi, I hope you can forgive me." His eyes probed hers as though looking for answers to unasked questions. "Do you?"

She was careful to answer as honestly as possible. "I don't believe that all things that happen are good, but I do believe the Lord can make good come from even the worst things."

He kept his eyes on the brim of his coffee cup. "Even Paisley? Even leaving a baby without a mother? Is there any good in that?"

"A new baby is always a blessing. God wants us to celebrate that."

"I don't know what Paisley told you." She saw his muscles tense as he said the woman's name. "It doesn't matter. No one knows the truth about Paisley. Not even me, but I'll tell you what I do know. Then you'll have to decide who to believe."

She met his gaze. "That decision has already been made."

"Some decisions have to be made over and over." He pulled his eyes away from hers and stared at a bee buzzing against the window of the coffee shop.

Naomi waited for him to elaborate, her hands in her lap, twisting and turning the paper napkin.

"I had met Paisley, years ago. She had worked as a waitress at a restaurant near the office of Schrock Investments. Jake and I used to grab lunch there. During that year when I took off, I stayed at her apartment a few nights while I was trying to find work. Now and then . . . well, we would have too much to drink and get carried away."

Naomi's cheeks reddened, but her grip on the napkin loosened.

With great tenderness he lifted her face up. "Naomi, nine months ago, if I had known what was waiting for me with you . . . I never would've . . . I never imagined I'd fall in love with an Amish girl who lived next door to my grandmother. I never dreamed of the consequences, that I would be hurting someone I loved." She started to say something, but he put his fingers softly on her lips. "Do you have regrets?"

She didn't hesitate. "Nothing could ever change the way I feel about you, Tobe. Or that we belong together."

Tobe's mouth began quivering and his face crumpled as tears filled his eyes. He brushed the back of his hand across his eyes and drew in a shaky breath before he was able to go on. "Truly? No regrets? Because now is the time to say so." He asked with a kind of stillness in his eyes as if her answer was especially important.

She smiled, feeling light-headed all of a sudden. Feeling lighthearted. "None. Not a one."

Rose kept glancing at the kitchen clock—it was after five— then looked out the window. The table had been laid with more than usual care. All of Tobe's favorite foods had been prepared.

She had wanted to be sure that everything was perfect to welcome Tobe home. Instead, it was chaos. Rain had started and was now pummeling the farm. Baby Sarah seemed particularly fussy this afternoon, Luke was teasing Sammy, something was bothering Mim and she wouldn't say what—she had the energy of a trapped bird. Mammi Vera truculent, Bethany in a mood . . . this would be no way to start a new life. She sighed. If only it would stop raining.

Her thoughts drifted to Paisley's whereabouts. She teetered between relief that the girl was gone and concern that she would come back. What irked her more than anything was that Paisley had left with nothing settled. Nothing!

Rose glanced out the kitchen window again. And suddenly, there was Tobe, walking up the driveway with a satchel in his hand, rain running off the brim of his hat. Her big, handsome, restless son. His smile was tired. Her heart skipped with worry about him, as it so often did. A loud whoop sailed down from the upstairs, then a beat of footsteps clamored down the stairs as Luke and Sammy tried to beat each other out the door to greet their brother. They all rushed out to welcome home the prodigal and soon the farmhouse of Eagle Hill was filled with a happy chaos.

Tobe paid special attention to Mammi Vera, which made

her glow with happiness. After supper, which was wonderful and noisy, he admired all the improvements to the farm and said the blueberry cobbler was the best thing he'd eaten in years. But he never held the baby, Rose noticed, nor glanced in the baby's direction when she fussed.

Before turning in, Tobe went to the barn to check on the animals and was gone for quite a while. When he came inside, he had such a pensive look on his face that Vera asked him what he was thinking. "It's so quiet here—I'd forgotten what silence sounds like in the countryside."

"That's why we live here," Mammi Vera said, delighted.

"That's why we live here," Tobe said flatly.

Mim had never felt so at sea. She shifted on the cot to try to get more comfortable. It had seemed to her when she went to bed that she could forget all her worries, that she could sleep and everything was going to be all right, but she awoke in the middle of the night with the horrible realization that two additional people knew she was Mrs. Miracle. Bethany and Ella didn't worry her, they weren't loose cannons. But these two . . . there was no telling what could happen. She tried to push that worry out of her head, but crazy thoughts kept shooting through her mind. Maybe she could go ask Bethany right now. Shake her awake and say, "That lady with the spiky blonde hair in the guest flat found out I'm Mrs. Miracle. Tell me what to do."

Earlier this morning, she had delivered breakfast to the guest flat, like she usually did. Brooke Snyder had a strange look on her face, pinched and pleased. Mim asked if she were feeling well, and she answered her with, "Very well, thank you." She pointed to the newspaper. "So . . . perhaps you'd like to compose a Mrs. Miracle letter while you're here?"

Mim gasped, too surprised to deny she wrote the letters. "You won't tell, will you?"

Brooke turned to Mim, a smile as brittle as toffee fixed to her face. "Why would I tell?"

Mim squeezed her eyes shut and tried to think of something else, or of nothing, but her mind kept circling back to the fact: two people knew she was Mrs. Miracle. She wasn't sure whom she was more worried about: Jesse, whose father was a minister, or Brooke Snyder, who seemed oddly pleased to hold Mim's secret. She got out of bed and looked at her face in the mirror. It was gray-white and there were shadows under her frightened eyes. The room grew gradually lighter, although no warmer. She was doomed.

The disturbing black cloud that came on the horizon for Galen and Rose with the arrival of Paisley was something that they danced around, carefully avoided, and tried to pretend wasn't a problem between them. But when Tobe arrived at Eagle Hill, another storm came and settled on them. This gulf between them was growing huge.

Rose wanted to clear the atmosphere between them. When she discovered the woodpile had been chopped and stacked, she was touched beyond words. She had been so busy lately that she'd hardly had time for Galen. And yet . . . he had chopped a cord of wood for her. And she had forgotten to thank him! She hurried over to catch him when she saw him lead a horse from his barn to the round training pen.

He seemed to be thinking along the same lines of wanting

to clear the air. He put the horse in the pen and turned toward her with an eager look on his face.

"I heard Lodestar is back. How's he doing?"

"Well, he's not lacking for attention, I'll tell you that much. Jimmy's in the barn with him now, brushing and preening him like a mother hen fussing over a chick."

"Think Lodestar will make a full recovery?"

"In time. God designed his creatures to heal."

They fell silent then, and a full thirty seconds passed while their gazes held, the only sound was the horse shuffling around in the pen. At last, reaching for her hands, Galen said in a voice so low it was barely audible, "Rose, I want things between us to go back the way they were."

Her face broke into a radiant smile. "I wanted to thank you for chopping all that wood. I . . . can't tell you how . . . I hardly know what to say. It might seem like a small chore to you, but it meant so much to me."

Galen stiffened. In a voice she hardly recognized, he said, "I didn't chop wood for you."

─ ⌀ ⌀ ─

Feeding little Sarah a bottle took nearly an hour, but Naomi didn't mind. The feedings gave her time to study her face, to memorize her row of stubby eyelashes, to watch her temples beating. When the baby's eyes flitted open, she studied the dark gray, looking for signs of the brown or blue or green they would become.

Edith Fisher was, as usual, practical about the baby. "Don't grow too fond of the child," she warned Naomi at the quilting bee the next afternoon. "That unfeeling lout of a mother will be back for her the day it suits her."

What did people mean . . . don't grow too fond of the child? The very first time Naomi had held the baby, a wave of protectiveness almost overwhelmed her. This poor, helpless baby had no one else in the world. How could anyone put a limit to the love she felt for this little girl with the big dark eyes, the head of fuzzy brown hair, the endearing habit of holding her little hands clasped together as if she were praying? It was as if baby Sarah had made her life complete.

Nobody had told Naomi how much she would love this baby because nobody could have known. "I'll do my best for you, little one," she promised to her in a whisper, and she could have sworn Sarah smiled.

—⟋ ◊ ⟍—

The thought that Paisley might have a change of heart and return for her daughter was never far from Rose's mind. It would be awful to have to give Sarah up. She told herself if the mother didn't want her bad enough to come and get her, then she was too foolish to have her.

She knew she had already grown dangerously attached to the baby. She liked to lie in bed with her and watch her try to work her small hands, the tiny, perfect little fists with their miniscule nails. Sarah would peer at her for long stretches, frowning, as if trying to figure life out. But when Rose laughed at her and gave her a finger to hold, she would stop frowning and settle happily.

The morning after Tobe's return, Rose intended to let Tobe sleep in as late as he wanted and was surprised to see him come into the kitchen at dawn as she prepared Sarah's bottle. "What are you doing up?"

He sat on the bench by the kitchen door to get his boots on.

"The warden raised poultry. When he found out I was raised Amish, he assumed I know all about chickens, which I didn't. But there was a surfeit of spare time in prison, so I read all I could and the warden let me take care of his chickens." He shrugged. "Better than doing laundry." He pulled out a boot from under the bench. "I heard Harold the rooster crowing, so I thought I'd get up and feed your hens. Mim told me that the old hens were waiting for an opportunity to peck her eyes out." He stuck his foot in one boot. "I used oregano powder in the chicken feed. Made them healthier. Antimicrobial and antibacterial. Mind if I try it?"

Odd, Rose thought, that prison life would be the thing to make a farmer out of Tobe.

"Bethany said you were due to host church soon. I'm sure there's a lot to be done to get ready. I want to help out as long as I'm here."

Her breath caught. Was he already thinking of leaving? He'd only been home one night. "Tobe, I'm going to ask you a question and I want an honest answer." She motioned to Sarah, tucked in her arm. "Is there any chance this baby is yours?"

Tobe dropped his boot and looked up sharply. A long moment passed, then another. "Yes. A small one, a very small chance, but there is."

Rose went cold inside. A hope she had kept burning, sure that he would say he had never known Paisley, extinguished.

"I met Paisley a couple of years ago. She was a waitress at a coffee shop. In fact, Jake introduced us. Then when I was gone that year, working odd jobs, I didn't have a place to stay one night and she let me stay at her place . . . " He hesitated and glanced at Rose.

She lifted her free hand in the air. "I think I can fill in the blanks."

"Rose, Paisley was friendly with a lot of guys. It was never a thing between us."

She glanced down at the sleeping baby. Never a *thing*? "Paisley had a different opinion about that. She said you were planning to marry her as soon as you were released."

"We never, *ever* made plans like that. I haven't even seen her since that . . . those few nights when I stayed at her apartment."

"Why would she claim you're the baby's father if you weren't?"

"I have absolutely no idea. She told a pack of lies and is trying to palm her child off on me."

"She seemed to think you were going to inherit Eagle Hill."

He scratched his chin. "Maybe I said something like that once. Mammi Vera always makes it sound like I will."

"She also seemed upset when she found out that your grandmother wasn't knocking at death's door."

"Is that why she left?" He picked up the boot and jammed his stocking foot into it.

"I don't know. When I told her you were coming home, she became agitated. A few hours later, she vanished. Obviously, she didn't want to see you."

"Well, doesn't that prove to you that I'm not the father of that baby?"

"Sarah. Her name is Sarah. And no—Paisley's disappearance only proved to me that she wasn't a fit mother." She wiped some drops of formula off Sarah's cheek. "The bishop wants to have a talk with you."

Tobe shook his head forcefully. "Oh nooooooo. No, no,

no. I'm not baptized. I am *not* about to sit on the sinner's bench over something like this."

"I asked him to come. He's the leader of our church. Stoney Ridge is a small, tight-knit community. A baby has been born who bears your name on her birth certificate—"

Tobe winced.

"—and there needs to be some discussion about what to do with baby Sarah. We need some guidance. All of us." She was trying her best.

Tobe looked down at a spot on the floor for a long moment. Then he lifted his head. "When is he coming?"

"Around eleven this morning, he said. The deacon will be with him."

He slapped his hands on his knees and rose to his feet. "Good. Mim and the boys will be over at Windmill Farm for the afternoon and Bethany will be at the Sisters' House. I want Galen and Naomi to be here. Mammi Vera too." He was sliding away without answering.

"Why?"

"Rose, if you don't mind, I'd rather explain everything when you're all together."

Elmo and Abraham drove up in the deacon's buggy right at eleven o'clock on the dot. Rose was struck by how elderly and frail the bishop appeared as he climbed out of the buggy. He was shaped like an S hook, bending or straightening as he spoke to each person. She knew he played an increasingly smaller part in the events of the church and that most things were done by Abraham, his bustling, energetic deacon.

They all gathered in the living room—Rose, Galen, Tobe, Naomi, Mammi Vera, Bishop Elmo, and Deacon Abraham.

Sarah slept in her Moses basket, wedged in between Rose's and Naomi's chairs.

Tobe looked so uneasy that Rose almost felt sorry for him. He had the helpless expression of a man who knew he was looking at disaster but couldn't figure out how to stop it. "This whole situation is very complicated," he said.

"Simplify it so we can understand," Galen said in a sharp tone.

"Galen," Rose said. Her voice sounded a warning note, but he didn't meet her eyes.

Abraham steepled his fingers together. "Tobe, people make mistakes, and once the mistake's been made, you have to move on and figure out what to do next while you try not to make a bigger mistake."

"I don't disagree about making mistakes," Tobe said. "I've made plenty. But I don't believe I'm the father of Paisley's child. I'm going to get a DNA test to prove that and clear up any lingering suspicion."

Elmo was about to say something when Tobe lifted his hand to stop him. "There's something else. Another reason I need to prove to you that I'm not the baby's father because . . ." He glanced at Naomi. She gave him a nervous but encouraging smile. He reached over, took her hand, and breathed a deep breath. "Last fall, Naomi and I were married in a civil ceremony while I was in custody in Philadelphia, right before I was sent to FCI Schuykill."

His words fell like a stone into the room. Everyone went entirely still. The only movement came from Mammi Vera, who started clutching her chest.

"You must be joking," Galen said.

Naomi was looking at her brother calmly, her honest eyes fixed on his.

"It's not a joke, Galen," Tobe said. "It's a fact. It was the best way to ensure that Naomi could have visitation rights at the prison. As my wife, she could be on the preapproved visitor's list and visit as often as she could. If she wasn't a family member, she'd have had to get special permission through the warden. We knew we wanted to marry. Circumstances caused us to speed it up."

Galen went white with the news; he was still white. "Naomi, you visited him at the prison? In Minersville?"

"Yes," she said in a quiet but steady voice. "Often."

"I was only allowed a certain amount of visitor points a month," Tobe said. "Rose, that's why I discouraged you from visiting."

Ah. Things were starting to make sense to Rose.

"Why did you never tell me this, Naomi?" Galen's voice was full of emotion.

"What would you have said? What would you have done?"

There was something so bleak and honest in Naomi's tone that Rose could see Galen's fury diminish. Had Galen known, he would have had to inform the church leadership, and most likely, she would have been put under the ban.

Rose wished she could reach out and hold Galen's hand, to let him know that she was there beside him while he absorbed the blow. She knew it was a terrible discovery to him. By contrast, she felt a sweeping relief. She had sensed that Tobe and Naomi had a significant connection and she was actually pleased to think that Naomi stood by him while he was away. She was glad Tobe had someone else in his corner, someone who saw the best in him, someone who cared for him no matter what.

"Well," Galen said and stopped. "This is surprising news," he said, rather stiffly, coldness in his voice.

"We haven't, uh, um, consummated the marriage. We intend to wait until we could have a church wedding." Tobe looked at Naomi, whose cheeks flamed rosy red. "We still intend to wait for that . . . official ceremony."

The bishop let out a deep sigh of relief. "Well, now, this might all work out in the end."

"Not so fast," Galen said. "There's a baby in the middle of this. And a woman who says Tobe is the father of her child."

Tobe nodded. "The DNA test will take care of that."

A trace of stubbornness appeared in Galen's jaw. "And if the baby is yours?"

Irritation crossed Tobe's face. "We'll cross that bridge when we come to it."

The bishop cleared his throat. "Tobe and Naomi, would you give us a few moments to talk?"

Tobe and Naomi left the room and went out to the front porch. Rose heard the faint creak of the porch swing as they sat on it.

Galen glanced at Elmo. "So what do you have to say?"

The bishop and the deacon murmured together for a few moments. Then Elmo leaned back in his chair, a satisfied look covering his face. "What's important is that Tobe and Naomi are going to remain in the Amish church. Naomi has already been baptized. Tobe will need to go through instruction classes to become baptized. We can speed up the classes for him. And then they can be married. Truly married in the eyes of God." His eyes rested on Galen. "And that will be that."

Vera clasped her hands together in delight. "Well, I've always said things have a way of working out."

Galen's face remained stony. "That's your final word?"

Elmo nodded. "It is."

Abraham agreed that it should be done as speedily as possible.

"The important thing," Elmo said, leaning forward, wagging a finger at Galen, "is that they will remain in . . . the . . . church!"

Rose would always remember the way that Elmo's thick round glasses seemed to sparkle as he was telling Galen that. She didn't know if there were tears behind them, or if it was only a trick of the light.

Elmo looked around the room, at each person, then pinned Galen with a stare. "We're all in agreement?"

Rose watched Galen's profile. It was hard and unsmiling. "Yes. Yes, of course." His voice sounded false and Rose knew it.

15

While Elmo and Abraham spoke to Tobe and Naomi inside the house, Galen was pacing the front porch like an animal in a cage. As soon as Rose closed the door, he turned around, his lips hardened in a straight line. "The bishop and deacon are only concerned about having Tobe and Naomi remain Amish. You know as well as I do that they'll bend over backwards to keep people in the church."

"God has an interest in this situation too, Galen. We want them to make a meaningful decision for their future. Isn't that what you want for Naomi?"

"Yes. Of course I do. Yes. But not like this."

"Like what, Galen? They fell in love. They wanted to be able to see each other while he was away. They found a solution to that problem. Maybe if . . ." Her voice drizzled off as she wondered if she should say more.

"Maybe if what?"

"Maybe if you hadn't made it so clear that you were against Tobe, that you didn't want him around Naomi . . . maybe they wouldn't have felt the need to keep it a secret."

Galen was still in a temper. "Oh, sure. It's all my doing.

It has nothing to do with Tobe's lifelong habit of avoiding difficult things."

"But don't you see? He's not avoiding anything now. Just the opposite. Galen," she said, "a man's past is his past. It's what he contributes to the present that matters. And didn't you hear? He said they were going to be married in the church."

He looked at her as if he couldn't believe she was so naive. "Tobe never said he was going to stay in the Amish church. Yes, he said they were planning to have a wedding in the church. He *never* said an Amish church wedding. There's a very big difference. He's already made his decision to leave." He strode forward a few steps, then spun around. "He's doing the same thing he's always done! He married Naomi secretly, out of nowhere a woman appeared, bore his child, disappeared, and he wants life to carry on, business as usual." He crossed his arms, annoyed. "No consequences."

She felt a raw disappointment in Galen and hoped it didn't show in her face. She tried to keep her voice calm and conciliatory. "Whenever I watch you with your new horses, it seems as if you have a vision of what that horse will be like, once it's trained. Why can't you have that kind of vision with people?"

"Because," he said, searching for the right words, "people are far more complicated than horses."

"But it shouldn't be that way! David Stoltzfus says the word 'worldly' means that you only see what's right before you. We can be worldly when we don't see eternal significance in others."

A confused look swept Galen's face. "David Stoltzfus? The new minister?"

"Yes. He said that very thing."

"That it's worldly to be realistic and objective? To face facts?"

She frowned. "That's not what I meant!" She clenched her fists, a sign she was running out of patience. "Why can't you try and understand Tobe's perspective? Why must you always judge him?"

"Why can't you try to see Tobe clearly?"

"Because . . . with Dean gone, I'm all Tobe has."

"That's not true. He has an entire family to lean on. He has a church, if he wants it." He backed off, rubbing his hands on his thighs self-consciously. After a long pause, he took his hat off and walked closer to her. "Rose, this is starting to divide us."

"This?" Rose said, her anger rising. "You mean, the welfare of my son?"

"We have differing views on this subject. Why can't we just set it aside? Agree to disagree."

"Tobe's situation is serious, but there will be other situations with Bethany, Mim, and the boys—we can't always be on opposite sides of the fence about the children."

"That's the problem, right there. Tobe isn't a child anymore. He's a man. By now, he should be. You're going to hobble Tobe from manhood by raising this baby for him." In an uncharacteristic burst of emotion, he nearly shouted, "He will never have to grow up!"

"What do you know about raising children?" Rose flared back.

Galen swallowed. His shoulders stiffened and the wary look returned to his face. His voice came reluctantly, but firmly. "I know enough to see that you try to fix problems that belong to your children, especially Tobe and Luke. Problems that they should find solutions to. Just like you've tried to do with Schrock Investments." He jammed his hat back on his head. "Rose, you keep tethering yourself to the past." He spun on his heels and went down the porch steps.

It was the longest speech that Galen had ever made and it only made her furious. She watched him cross the yard and head to his farm, as if she was watching a stranger.

After the bishop and deacon left, Naomi held and fed the baby so Rose could get some chores taken care of. It took time to get to know a baby—to interpret her cries and figure out how she liked best to be held or cuddled. She had the time to give to Sarah.

"I haven't seen Tobe in the last hour," Rose said as she came into the kitchen, a basket of fresh dry sheets in her arms. "Mim and the boys will be home from school soon. They'll be looking for him."

"He had some thinking to do," Naomi said, "so he took a walk over to Blue Lake Pond."

Rose set the basket on the kitchen table. "Naomi, do you think Tobe will agree to the bishop's plan to join the church?"

Naomi kept her eyes down. "It sounds as if you don't think he will."

"Galen seems to think he won't. I'm not so sure."

Sarah had fallen asleep, so Naomi gently laid her in the Moses basket and covered her with the pink quilt. "Leave Tobe to me."

"And Galen? Think he'll come around?"

"Leave him to me too." But Naomi fingered her pocket to make sure she hadn't forgotten her Tums.

An hour later, Naomi found Tobe at their favorite place—their log at Blue Lake Pond—with his head in his hands. She could see he was troubled. He looked up, startled, when he saw her approach but made room on the big tree log for her to sit down.

"We need to leave Stoney Ridge, Naomi. I'd hoped, I'd thought . . . we were on the same page about this." There was agony and misery mixing in his eyes. "I just wish that your brother—that you—that I—" He gathered her fiercely into a tight embrace, and when he released her, he drew back, holding up a hand to stop her as she was about to say something. "I hope you realize that, by leaving, I'm trying to do the right thing for us."

She was trying to do the right thing too. After all, there was a baby to think of. "And you think that means we need to leave the Amish?"

"I do. You see that too, don't you? You must realize that a lot of your attitudes come from the Amish. You've said yourself that everyone lives in the shadow of the church."

It was true that she had said that, but she meant it in an enveloping, comforting way. Not in the dark, smothering way Tobe interpreted it.

They shifted to sit on the ground, resting their backs against the log, with Tobe's arms wrapped around Naomi, watching the still lake. She listened to everything he had to say, every argument about why they should leave the church. "There's no choices, Naomi. No freedom. You get up in the morning and put on the clothes of your grandparents, you listen to preaching and sing the hymns they once sang, and their faith is your faith and will be the faith of your children's children. Nothing ever changes."

That was exactly what Naomi loved about the Plain life. The slow and steady sureness of time passing, life measured by meaningful customs.

"And where did these old traditions come from? They go so far back no one can even remember why they were important in the first place." He pointed to her blue dress, the one he liked best. "Things like a dress held together by pins and celery at weddings and no screens on the windows. Ridiculous things that make no sense. And people hold on to them as if they were pulled straight out of the Bible."

But this was her life. The sameness, the familiar. Sundays full of old hymns that echoed off the barn rafters, uplifting messages from the preachers, the sharing of the fellowship meal afterward. With weekday mornings full of tossing hay to Galen's horses, afternoons of quilting by the soft light of her favorite window, with keeping house for her brother, with baking bread and gardening vegetables. All the days and nights full of work and prayer and being together. This was the backbone of her life. It was the Plain way and in it she felt safe. She felt loved. *In my heart I am Plain.*

"God gave us a brain and expects us to use it. Instead, everyone just follows the Ordnung like a flock of sheep."

She didn't interrupt Tobe. She let him talk it all out—how few choices they would have, how narrow a life, the way he bristled against conformity, how questions could never be asked, and mostly, the feeling that he would never get free from the clinging disaster of Schrock Investments. She didn't object. She didn't plead. She had always been quick to recognize when something seemed impossible. And a look at Tobe's face told her that this was now the case.

When he was spent of words, she turned to face him. "Tell me again what that year was like for you, after you left home."

"I've told you about it."

"I want to hear more. Where did you work? What friends did you have?"

"I had trouble finding work—I could get some day jobs here and there, working construction or landscaping, but nothing that lasted." He stopped, raising an eyebrow. "I see where you're going. I've thought this out—I'll need to take some classes at a junior college so I can find better work. A real career."

"What about friends?"

He shrugged. "I didn't have many. None, I guess. When Schrock Investments went under, it caused bitter feelings among those I had thought were friends." Then he was silent. "We'll make friends. Eventually. We'll find a church where no one has heard of Schrock Investments."

"And what was missing in that year?"

He looked confused. "I'm not following you."

"After all you've been through, haven't you learned about the most important things?"

He threw up his hands. "How can you say that? I met God in the prison."

"And hasn't that taught you about the most important things?"

He watched her, his expression drawn with concern. "Next to God, you're the most important thing to me, Naomi."

She could see how much he loved her, could see it in the deep softness of his gaze as he looked at her. "Tobe, you must know how important family is to me. Frankly, how important it is to you too. Think of what that year was like without your family."

He looked away.

"I want you to listen to me and not dismiss what I have to say or act like I'm setting out snares to trap you." He opened his mouth to object and she cut him off. "I see it in your eyes, so don't think I don't know what's running through your head. You're underestimating what it would be like for us to live without family. Without our church family too."

She looked down at their hands, twined together. "We would have more to lose than we would have to gain. Being cut off from our family, from our church. We would be sheep without a fold. Look at what the church has done for Rose—they've provided donations to pay back the investors who lost money in Schrock Investments. They've paid off your grandmother's medical bills. They've embraced Sarah without questions or judgments."

"We can find that outside the Amish church too."

She shook her head. "Not easily, Tobe. Our experience would be much like yours—out of work and lonely, cut off from those we love."

He didn't speak for a long while. "Do you think your brother would shun you?"

"Yes." She looked up at him. "And it would break his heart to do it."

A shadow of indecision passed over Tobe's face. "What you're really saying is that you love the Plain life, don't you?"

What I'm trying to say is, in my heart I am Plain. "I love my Plain family, and you love yours—maybe more than you know."

"And that's reason enough for you to stay?"

Absolute certainty and conviction welled up inside her and spilled out in one word: "Yes."

Taut silence traveled between them. She could sense him hovering on the edge of decision. In an oddly detached way, she empathized with him. She had hovered on the edge of decision herself after she had learned about Paisley—to remain with Tobe or let him go. It had been a turning-point moment for her, just as this was for him.

He walked toward the edge of the pond, bent down, picked up a rock, and skipped it along the surface of the glassy lake.

She waited, on edge.

Finally, he looked upward, sighed deeply, and turned his full attention to her. "What kind of a husband would I be if I asked you to give up the life you love?"

She walked down the pond's edge toward him. "Are you sure? Absolutely, positively sure? You won't wake up one day and regret this choice?"

"I'd regret hurting you far more."

He leaned forward, holding his hands out to her, and said, "Whatever it would take—I just can't live another moment without you by my side."

She reached out for him and let him pull her toward him, kissing him directly on the lips. She felt his arms tighten around her and they stood locked like this for a time. She pulled back, forehead to forehead, and they looked at each other for a long moment before she spoke. "Tobe, I want you to want it too."

"You've given me everything I've ever wanted."

"I haven't begun to give you anything."

"But you have, believe me. Without you I'd be nothing. You've given me encouragement, and faith, and hope that things will work out, in the end. You've given me the courage to return to Stoney Ridge. And now . . . to stay." He took her hands in his and held them close to his heart. "Now you must give me one more thing . . . you must believe in me. You must believe I'm trying to do the right thing."

"About what?"

"About . . . other things that are still . . . unfinished."

She didn't believe him. Not entirely. It wasn't that she didn't fully trust him, because she did. There was something he wasn't telling her, something he didn't want her to know. And even if he was telling her everything, there was still Sarah to consider. Still, her instinct told her to wait for him—that he would tell her everything when he was ready.

She reached up on her tiptoes to kiss him her answer, feeling a bone-deep happiness she didn't know was possible to feel, this side of heaven, as his arms wrapped around her waist to pull her against his chest. It was a perfect moment.

Soon . . . she would have to face her brother. She reached one hand down to her pocket and patted it. Good. Tums were still there.

By the time Naomi and Tobe arrived back at Eagle Hill, the sun had almost disappeared and the air had thickened with hazy twilight. She said goodbye to him at the hole in the privet, slipped through it, and slowed her walk to a crawl. She was dreading this moment, had been dreading it for months now. She took two Tums and chewed them fast and hard.

In the house, she took her cape and bonnet off, hung them on the wall peg by the back door, and walked into the living room to talk to Galen. He was writing bills at his desk. Naomi noticed his tense jaw and how he was clenching his pen. The guilt she felt about keeping something so important from her brother brought her an instant headache. Where had all her bravery gone?

She tested a please-don't-be-mad-at-me smile that usually worked on Galen, but he didn't look up, didn't acknowledge her presence in any way. "I . . . I wanted to say that I'm sorry."

He radiated a stony silence. This was worse than she thought it would be. Maybe she should just wait until he was ready to talk. As she turned to go to the kitchen, she heard him say, "The worst thing is how deceitful you've been."

She stopped and turned around. "I never lied to you."

"You never told me the truth, either."

Her heart fell. Gone was the warmth and affection that usually flowed between them. She hated that she had done this—brought this kind of hurt to her brother. He had never been anything but kind and caring toward her; she couldn't even remember a time when he'd been angry with her. Glancing down, she noticed that her hands had curled themselves into fists. Finger by finger, she relaxed. "Please, let me explain," she began, hoping he would hear her out.

"There's no need. Tobe Schrock has a strong influence on you."

A protective anger over Tobe buoyed her strength. "What about my influence on him, Galen?" Her chin went up a notch. "Have you considered that?"

He turned back to the bill he was writing.

"We're staying in the church. We're not leaving. It's decided."

Galen's hand stilled. Slowly, he turned to stare at her in wonder. She nearly smiled at his stunned look. Nearly.

"It's true. We just discussed it. Tomorrow we'll go to the bishop and set the date. Tobe has to be baptized first." She walked over to him. "I'm so sorry to have kept this from you. Truly, truly sorry."

Relief and disbelief flooded his face. "I only want what's best for you." His eyes softened and his voice grew shaky. "That's all I've ever wanted."

As he said that, as soon as she heard his voice wobble, tears lodged in her throat. Galen dipped his head. "Rose said . . . she thought I was partly to blame. She said I caused you to feel you had to keep it secret."

"Maybe a little." Naomi smiled, wiping away a tear that was rolling down her cheek. "Maybe a lot. But I don't regret my choice. Getting married the way Tobe and I did—it wasn't meant to hurt you, Galen. It's just that . . . it's just . . ."

When Galen looked up, his eyes were shiny with moisture. "You fell in love."

He said it so softly she wondered if it was more his thought than his voice she'd heard. Maybe she'd only hoped he would say it. "I fell in love. And love does extraordinary things to people."

The next morning, Rose stood by the kitchen window and watched Tobe and Naomi walk together from the buggy after returning from the bishop's home, where they had gone to set a date for a wedding. What a mystery love was: the small figure of this strange strong girl, the tall figure of her own stepson, who seemed even taller since he had fallen in love with Naomi.

They stopped and turned when they saw David Stoltzfus striding up the driveway of Eagle Hill. David dropped by Eagle Hill every other day to check on Molly, he said, though he always accepted the invitation of a cup of coffee in the kitchen with Rose and Vera. On this day, Rose saw Naomi hurry back through the privet and Tobe remain outside with David for a long while.

The two walked together to the porch, then sat on the steps, deep in conversation. Bethany had left the window open to air out the kitchen after burning a pan of granola in the oven. Rose crossed the room to close it and stopped abruptly as she heard Tobe mention the name of Jake Hertzler.

"Why does God allow innocent people to get hurt? My father wasn't a bad man. He was a good man who was trying to help people with their money. God let him die for it. It's like God has no sense of fair play."

Rose held her breath. She wondered how David Stoltzfus might respond to a comment like that. If anyone but Tobe said it, Vera would have called it blasphemous. But David Stoltzfus didn't seem at all shocked or put off. In fact, he asked a few questions to encourage Tobe to keep talking.

Tobe wondered why a loving God could be so unjust to allow Jake Hertzler to have the freedom he seemed to experience. David Stoltzfus had an answer for that. He said it was God's plan to test men's love and goodness for each other. "It's easy to love God," David said. "Nobody has any problem in loving our heavenly Father. The problem is to love people who have sinned against us."

Tobe didn't respond and Rose backed away from the window. Would this ever go away? she wondered. Jake Hertzler's hold on her family went on and on. No one seemed to be able to move forward—not Bethany, not Tobe. Maybe . . . herself too. She had tried so hard to not allow vengeance to take hold of her heart.

A little later, when David came into the kitchen and sat at the table for a cup of coffee, Rose couldn't help but notice how easy it was to talk to him. They had so much in common: their spouses had passed, they were trying to fill the roles of both mother and father to their children. He liked to talk and he was never in a hurry, unlike Galen, who wasn't much of a talker and was always on to the next thing. At first, she felt a little nervous to see David stroll up the driveway of Eagle Hill; she knew he must be busy with the Bent N' Dent and settling his family into the farm. But soon she realized he liked people, he liked visiting, talking. It was nice to be around someone who thought the way she thought, felt the way she felt, understood what she was experiencing. She shouldn't compare David to Galen, but she wondered if she and Galen would ever be able to see eye to eye about children. About Tobe.

During recess one morning, a crowd of children surrounded Jesse Stoltzfus as he sat on the ground and began to unravel one of his socks. Mim sidled a little closer, trying to figure out what he was up to. Whistling through the gap in his front teeth, Jesse wrapped the yarn from his sock around a dried-up old apple. He kept winding and winding, and after a few minutes, he had made a ball.

What was it about boys and balls? If there was snow or a stone or an apple and a sock, there was a ball. And if there was a ball, there was a game. She knew this because of her brothers, Sammy and Luke, who turned any and every thing into a ball. Eggs from the henhouse, pillows from their beds, socks from their sock drawer.

When Jesse had tied a knot to finish off the ball, the children ran to the bases. He looked over at her, standing near the tree where the children carved their initials at the end of each school term, and he waved to her. "Come on and play with us, Mim. Put away your notebook."

She shook her head. She had absolutely no talent for hitting or catching a ball and had given up, humiliated long ago.

He tossed the ball to Luke so the game could get underway, slipped his bare foot into his shoe, and walked toward her.

She ignored him when he stood in front of her. "I have work to do, and you distract me."

"The Mrs. Miracle column?"

"Yes." Mim squinted at Jesse. "And don't you dare say a word."

"Not me." He plopped himself on the ground next to her. "Your secrets are safe with me. Half the time, I don't even listen."

That she believed.

"I don't mean that. Actually, I do. I always mean what I say. I just don't always mean to say it out loud."

"Jesse, why don't you just go play softball with your sock apple ball?"

He didn't budge. "Why don't you ever play softball?"

"I can't hit."

"You're going to have to play in the end-of-year game. Eighth graders versus the sixth and seventh graders. Teacher Danny is playing for them to even out the teams. 'Cuz of me, due to my athletic prowess."

She rolled her eyes. "I can't. I really can't hit."

"We need every player. We have to win." He frowned. "Can you catch?"

"Nope." She shook her head. "But sometimes, I can throw a ball and get it pretty close to where it's supposed to be."

"You mean, pitch?"

She nodded.

"Risky," he said. "I like that in a girl." He looked up at the budding leaves on the tree for a moment. "Miriam, my lovely lass. Have you ever heard of a knuckleball?"

She sensed a trap.

16

Brooke Snyder was naturally nosy and Eagle Hill was turning out to be a place of high drama—always a compelling curiosity to her. Something big had happened the other day but she couldn't tell what and not knowing was driving her crazy. Midday, a buggy had arrived with two very serious and grim-looking Amish men. An hour or so later, Brooke watched from the guest flat window as the two climbed back into their buggy, laughing and smiling and joshing each other.

But all afternoon, she noticed that the Schrock family looked serious and grim. Even those two little boys seemed to sense something was awry when they came home from school. Normally hooting and howling, they went about their chores on the farm subdued, unnaturally quiet.

Brooke would have liked to question Mim Schrock about what earthshaking news those two Amish men might have delivered, but the girl was studiously avoiding her after she had uncovered Mrs. Miracle's true identity and revealed it to her. Perhaps . . . she should have waited for the big reveal. She hadn't meant to alienate Mim and cut off her information source. She was just so pleased with herself for figuring it out!

And she couldn't stop dwelling on the unfolding drama in that farmhouse. She figured it must have something to do with the boy who returned from jail and the baby. How fascinating! Better than a reality TV show.

This morning, before a cup of coffee—which should have been a waving red flag to Brooke, but she was never good at noticing red flags—she blurted out a question to Vera Schrock as the older woman delivered a breakfast tray to the guest flat. "So, Mrs. Schrock, what do you think the chances are that the missing mother will show up and reclaim the baby?"

Vera froze, set the tray on the kitchen table with a decided bang, and turned to Brooke with an icy stare. "What I think is . . . ," she lifted a hand and pointed a finger directly at her, ". . . that you are a girl who needs more on her mind."

Weather permitting, Jesse organized the eighth graders to stay after school to practice their softball game. On the pitcher's mound, Jesse worked with Mim to show her how to throw a knuckleball.

"It doesn't look very hard to hit," she said. "It looks slow and easy."

"If it works, batters can't hit it."

"And if it doesn't work?"

"If it doesn't, even the pitcher doesn't know where it's going."

That made it sound easier to her. "How does it work?"

"It's a mystery. A small flip of the fingers and wrist, and the ball is thrown with zero spin."

He threw the ball. It seemed to go slowly, and Mose Blank,

who was in a younger grade but liked to hang around Jesse, cocked the bat and swung. And missed.

The children, especially the boys, howled with laughter.

Then Mim threw the knuckleball, just the way Jesse had taught her. It went slowly, like his did, and it even got close to the batter, but it didn't have zero spin on it. Mose Blank, who normally struck out, hit the ball over the school fence and into the cornfield next door.

Again, the boys laughed long, unrestrained. From the schoolhouse window, she saw Danny watching. Mim was mortified.

"Well," Jesse said philosophically, "this might require a little more practice than I had anticipated."

On the way home from school, Mim leaned over a horse trough at the farm with the huge falling-down barn and examined her face in the still water. Curly hair surrounding a thin little face with a pointed chin. Gray eyes that were hidden by big, clunky glasses.

Out of nowhere, Jesse Stoltzfus was leaning over her shoulder, peering at her face. His lean face was ruddy from the wind. "Pretty terrific looking, I'd say."

She snapped up and scowled at him. *That* boy really thought he was somebody. She could only imagine what her grandmother would have to say to a boy who complimented his own image.

"I was talking about you."

Mim stood perfectly still. "Don't make fun of me."

"But you must know that." Jesse said this as if it was as obvious as the day is from night.

"How would I know? No one ever told me."

"I'm telling you."

"Well," she said, at a loss for words. She felt her face and neck redden at the praise. Mim Schrock hadn't known a compliment from a boy before. She put her hand up to her face so Jesse wouldn't see her flush, but his attention had already moved on to the eagles, circling above the creek that ran along the border of Eagle Hill. They weren't far from the eagles' aerie.

"Luke says there are three eggs this year."

"He would know," Mim said, her voice still shaky from the unexpected compliment.

Jesse's eyes were glued on the eagles as they walked down the road. "I think one of them just caught a fish. Look what's in its talons."

Whenever Mim was nervous, she started to spout off facts. "Did you know that bald eagles can lift about four pounds? And that's one-third of their weight. They have hollow bones and about eight thousand feathers. And they can swim too, unless the water is extremely cold and they get overcome by hypothermia." She knew she should stop, but her mouth just kept going and going. "They have excellent eyesight too. They're at the top of the food chain. The very top." She paused, exhausted of eagle facts.

Jesse was grinning at her.

She eyed him suspiciously. "You already knew those facts about eagles, didn't you?"

"Pretty much, but it gave me a chance for a quick nap." He stroked his chin. "But I think you're slightly off on the eight thousand feathers. There are only seven thousand . . . give or take a few during molting season."

So much for showing off her knowledge.

As they reached their driveways, he turned to her. "About

the knuckleball, I have no doubt that you'll come through with waving colors."

"Flying colors."

"I only made a mistake to make you feel superior." He swept his hat off his head and bent over at the waist in an exaggerated bow. "I bid you adieu, my lovely lass." Then he turned and ran up the driveway.

Lovely lass? She felt a smile pull at her mouth but fought it back. She barely made it home and up the stairs on shaking legs as she hurried to her bedroom. There she found Luke and Sammy staring up guiltily from the bed where they had been reading her diary.

"I thought you stayed after school," Luke said, flying immediately to the attack.

"We hadn't gotten to anything really private," Sammy said, far more frightened. "Not yet." He handed her the diary like it was a hot potato.

Miriam Schrock, who was considered a lovely lass, a terrific-looking girl, by one of the most intriguing boys in Stoney Ridge (and there were only two), drew herself up to her full height.

"You can explain all that later," she said. "To Mom and Mammi Vera."

"Don't tell Mammi Vera!" Sammy pleaded. "She'll give us a lecture that will last for a month of Sundays."

"Mom won't like what you've been up to," Luke threatened.

Mim's stomach clenched. In that diary were all the thoughts and questions she had about Mrs. Miracle and Danny Riehl and Jesse Stoltzfus. How far had he read?

When she told her mother what the boys had done, they were grounded for a week. "A person must be allowed to have her private life," her mother told the two sulking boys. "It's a terrible thing to invade someone's privacy."

"But there was nothing in it!" Sammy said.

Mim's mother frowned at him. "To say that is making it worse still."

Mim felt as if she was having trouble breathing. She had no idea how much the boys had read by the time she found them. She wasn't worried about Sammy. He was very young and didn't really understand anything at all.

But Luke . . . he was a continual worry to Mim. Luke was nearly thirteen and thought he knew everything.

If he read the part about Mrs. Miracle and figured it out, that meant that two more people now knew her secret identity. *Two more people!*

It felt like she was falling down a hill. She couldn't stop and she couldn't change direction and she was bound to get hurt.

Bethany looked at Tobe thoughtfully across her coffee. She had made the mistake of politely asking him how the new henhouse was going and he assumed she was actually interested in the answer. He explained in meticulous detail the concerns he had about the timing of the new henhouse coinciding with the annual moulting of the chickens. They might get stressed, he said, and that wasn't good for their health. She was just about to tell him that boring a person to death about chicken feathers could create stress too . . . when suddenly she saw a solution to everything.

Tobe would be the perfect answer.

Later that morning, Bethany gathered Jimmy and Tobe

and Naomi to share her idea. A brilliant idea, she thought. "Tobe, you need a job and Jimmy needs a manager for his mother's egg farm."

Tobe tilted his head. "I thought Jimmy was the manager."

"I am," Jimmy said. "But I hate chickens. Despise them. I want to get back to my horse breeding business now that Lodestar has come home." He gave Bethany a wink and a nudge. "Thanks to your sister."

"I don't mind chickens," Tobe said, looking a little embarrassed. "In fact, I sorta like them."

Naomi was almost glowing. "Jimmy, what would your mother think of that arrangement?"

"I don't know for sure," Jimmy said, "but it's worth asking."

"Naomi should be the one to ask her," Bethany said. "She adores Naomi."

Jimmy nodded. "That she does. Still, I can't imagine she'd be agreeable. You know my mother."

"What do you mean?" Tobe said. "I don't know your mother."

"Well," Bethany started, "let's just say that Edith Fisher is considered by all to be a woman whom it might be easy to annoy."

Tobe's eyebrows lifted.

The following day, Edith hammered Tobe with questions about poultry when they stopped by her house. He answered every one correctly, then turned the tables and asked her a few questions. "Have you considered speckled Sussex hens? They're less aggressive than the Old English games you've got. The ones you've got might be good layers, but they're mean birds."

Edith glared at Jimmy.

Jimmy glared back. "How was I supposed to know that? I thought all chickens were mean and evil spirited."

"Sussex are friendly, curious birds. Fine layers too." Tobe folded his arms against his chest. "Though if I were going into the market, I'd go for heirloom hens."

Edith gave him a suspicious look. "What are those?"

"They're heirloom breeds of hens—Ameraucana and Marans. They lay brown and white eggs. Their yolks have a bright color, a rich flavor. Taste better than commercial eggs."

"Do tell." Edith stroked her big cheek. "Like heirloom tomatoes?"

Tobe's dark eyes took on a hint of amusement. "Yeah, I guess. Except that these hens are bred to produce more eggs and eat less chicken feed."

Now he was speaking Edith Fisher's language. Saving money.

"Why not sell chicks to small-flock poultry farmers? And what about expanding to raise and sell meat birds? You've got the space for it and there's a market for local birds. It's called the locovore movement."

That brought a whoop out of Edith. "A movement? We call it the Amish way of life."

Tobe grinned. "English folks want food produced locally and are willing to pay top dollar."

He had Edith in the palm of his hand, but he didn't stop there. "We'll have to make a few adjustments—the best results come from having the brooders in field houses that can be moved from pasture to pasture. The more greens they can eat, the better."

Edith frowned. "We've got hawks here."

"Better netting would solve that," Tobe said.

Edith gave Jimmy a look as if to ask why he had never thought of any of this. She decided that having Tobe manage the chicken and egg business would be an excellent idea. *Fallen straight into their laps* was the way she described it.

"I'll arrive early and stay late," Tobe said.

Edith speared Tobe and Naomi with an unblinking stare. She had always been able to apply pressure with a glance. "Nonsense. After you're *officially* married, you'll live here. You can have Jimmy's room. It's the biggest."

Jimmy's eyebrows shot up. "But . . . what about me?"

"You can move into Paul's old room. Oh, wait. I've turned that into my sewing room." Edith dismissed that worry. "Well, we'll find a place somewhere."

"It's high time for you to move on anyway," Bethany whispered to Jimmy. He looked less certain.

"But . . . what about Galen?" Naomi said. "I can't leave him alone."

Edith waved that concern away with a flick of her wrist. "He's a grown man. It's time he found a wife." She pointed an accusing finger at Naomi. "You're the reason some sweet gal hasn't been able to nab him."

Naomi's eyes went wide. "I just thought he didn't want to be nabbed."

Edith snorted. "Fat chance. He's kept his life on hold for your sake."

A confused look covered Naomi's sweet face. Had that truly never occurred to her? Everyone knew that.

Edith jutted out her big jaw. "That's the only way this will work out. My chickens need twenty-four-hour-a-day care."

Naomi straightened her back. "We'll stay, but we're going to live in the Grossdawdi Haus. We need our own home."

Everyone turned to look at Naomi, shocked by her boldness. Edith Fisher was a bear of a woman. A year ago Naomi wouldn't have raised her glance to her, let alone her voice.

Tobe grinned at Naomi. "If that sounds suitable to you, Edith, then it's a deal. As soon as we marry, we'll move in and I'll take over the chicken business. Jimmy can get back to his horses."

Edith grazed her chicken-hating son with a look. "Fine."

Jimmy Fisher beamed. He positively beamed.

Bethany could have floated away on a cloud of happiness. Everything was finally coming together for her!

But a few days later, Bethany found herself moaning to Geena Spencer about her Jimmy Fisher situation over coffee and gingersnap cookies at Eagle Hill. "Thanks to me, the horse has been returned. And thanks to me again, Jimmy can leave the chicken and egg business and resume horse breeding and training. There's nothing stopping Jimmy from asking me to marry him." She rested her chin on her palms. "Except that he can't seem to get around to it." She sighed. "I think he takes me for granted."

"Most men have no idea what they want," Geena said with the voice of authority. "They are much more simple than women think, but more confused as well."

Bethany looked at her. "What else can I do?"

"You need to tell Jimmy Fisher the truth."

"I have been! I've been telling him that I want to get married."

"Not *that* truth. The truth that you are perfectly happy, that you have no wish to change your life from the way it was. Assure him you are more than satisfied with the way things were. There's nothing that drives men as crazy as that, nothing that makes a woman more attractive to a man than realizing she is content the way she is, not scheming and not conniving to drag him to the altar."

"But that's not exactly true," Bethany said. "I'm not totally content the way I am. I *want* to drag him to the altar."

Geena smiled. "You want Jimmy to think—to *know*—you are a prize he had hardly dared to hope for." She reached over and squeezed Bethany's hand. "Because you are. Don't ever forget there are plenty of young bucks in the woods."

"I wish Jimmy realized that."

"Here's a thought for you: Happiness is an inside job. You can't wait for happiness and contentment to arrive. It's up to you to find it."

Bethany mulled that thought over between bites of a gingersnap cookie. "How'd you get so smart about men?"

Geena swallowed her cookie and shrugged. "It's one of the perks of being a youth pastor. You get to observe hundreds of teenagers who are constantly doing a courting dance."

Bethany jabbed her gently with her elbow. "And what about Allen Turner? From what I hear, he's doing a courting dance of his own."

Geena's cheeks flamed and she hopped up to go. "I'm sure I don't know what you mean."

Mammi Vera marched Luke and Sammy inside, clutching their shirt collars so the boys hung like union suits on a clothesline, a stormy look on her face. Mim wasn't sure what had just happened, but it was bad. Even Luke looked contrite. She ducked into the pantry so she could eavesdrop while her grandmother told her mother what the boys had done.

"The Stoltzfuses have gotten a new refrigerator," Mammi Vera told Rose. "The old one was put by the side of the road with a sign that said 'Free.' As I went to get the mail, I noticed the refrigerator and thought I'd take a look—after all, the one we have is on its last legs. So I opened the refrigerator, and there was *that* one. He fell straight out, stiff as cardboard. I nearly had a heart attack."

Luke, she meant. Mim didn't even need to hear her say it.

"Luke!" her mother said. "You know better than to get inside of a refrigerator. That was so dangerous! You could have suffocated if Mammi Vera hadn't come along when she did."

Luke was strangely silent.

"Oh, he knew exactly what he was doing," Mammi Vera said. "He was waiting for some unsuspecting soul to come along and think there was a dead body in the refrigerator."

"What?" her mother said. "Luke, what were you thinking?"

"It wasn't my idea!" Luke said. "Jesse had it all figured out. He took the back off so there was an air vent."

"But you were playing tricks on people?" Her mother sounded incredulous. "A horrible trick like that?"

In a small and puny voice, Luke confessed. "We didn't figure that Mammi Vera would be the first person to come along. Jesse had it timed for when Mim came out to get the mail."

More silence. Mim wondered what kind of punishment would have an impact on Luke.

"Upstairs," her mother said. "You're not to spend time after school with Jesse Stoltzfus for the rest of the week."

Horrified silence followed. Then Luke and Sammy squealed like pigs stuck under a fence. "Unfair!"

"Go." Her mother sounded hopping mad.

Mim waited a few more minutes after hearing the heavy

footfall of the disappointed boys on the stairs, until she could be sure the kitchen was empty and the coast was clear. Her heart sank when she heard the scrape of a kitchen chair along the floor and its creak as her grandmother sat down. "You were right to keep them away from Jesse Stoltzfus. He's the root of the problem. He's the one who starts it all. He has a powerful influence on those boys. Powerful. Luke especially. He admires Jesse far too much. Mim is absolutely right. Jesse Stoltzfus is abominable."

Mim sat down in the corner to wait. It would be a long wait. Once her grandmother settled into a chair, she didn't budge. But Mim didn't mind waiting, not so much. Her grandmother had just given her a near-compliment. First time, ever.

The recent rains softened the soil in the vegetable garden, and Rose planned to spend some time, as soon as Sarah slept, turning the soil around the strawberry plants, then adding straw as mulch to keep the bugs away. Come June and July, these berries would end up in jars of jam, glistening like rubies.

The steady beat of a hammer distracted her for a moment. Tobe had finished building the new henhouse and was now enlarging the yard for the chickens. He said they laid more eggs if they had more room outdoors to peck for insects and have dust baths and generally do what chickens loved best.

Rose turned her attention back to the garden. She was spreading straw down one row, then another, when she looked up and saw Galen, slipping through the privet.

Now. Tell him now.

"So you were right, after all," he said, his eyes hidden by the brim of his hat. "About Tobe and Naomi staying in the church."

She took a pitchful of straw out of the wheelbarrow and scattered it around a strawberry plant. "It's wonderful news. Vera is lit up like a child on Christmas Day." She set down the pitchfork. "Naomi said you gave them your blessing."

He looked up and his Adam's apple bobbed once. "Rose, I'm sorry about the other day. About our argument."

"So am I." She set down the pitchfork against the wheelbarrow and walked over to him, taking his hand in hers. *Now. Tell him now.* "We can't do this, Galen. There are too many things between us. We need to cancel our plans to wed." Her voice was gentle, apologetic.

Galen was stunned—for a moment he was unable to speak. Just a few feet from the porch, he leaned his back against the railing very suddenly. "Did I do something?"

"No. It's not that simple. We're just at very different stages of life."

"We're only a few years apart."

Her gaze fell to her lap. She put a pleat in her apron with her fingers, then smoothed it out with her palm. "You're so young. It keeps coming back to me, no matter how much I try to put it from my mind."

"Count the love between us, Rose, the happiness. Not the years."

"I don't mean age in a literal way. I mean . . . the way life has gone for us. The paths we've taken. They've been radically different. For heaven's sake, I'm a grandmother now. We're too vastly different ever to spend a lifetime together."

He was gazing at her intensely but sadly. "No. No, that's not what's troubling you. This is because of Tobe."

She sighed. "I suppose you're right. But I'm right too. It seems as if this situation between Naomi and Tobe has shown us the kind of people we are." The sound of a baby's cry came from the kitchen and Rose pulled off her gloves to head inside, responding without thinking.

He straightened, muscle by muscle, and blew out a shaky breath. "If that's what you want, Rose, then so be it." He looked at her as if he wanted to say more, but he didn't.

A hard, tight knot stuck in her throat. She wanted to tell him that this wasn't what she wanted . . . it wasn't at all what she *wanted* . . . but it was for the best. "I hope we can remain friends. Good friends, like we've been to each other."

Galen looked away so that she wouldn't see his eyes fill up with tears. But she saw all the same.

Jimmy Fisher appeared at Eagle Hill one fine May evening, pleased when Bethany opened the door to his knock. "I came to ask if you'd like to go for a walk."

Bethany said thank you but no. She had plans for the evening.

What? He felt surprisingly put out by this. "Don't tell me you've got plans with someone else?" he asked, only half teasing.

"Goodness no. I'm just helping Naomi work on wedding plans."

Jimmy was at a loss for words. That seemed like something that could be easily rearranged. He waited a moment, assuming Bethany might offer to do just that. But she didn't.

His usual smart joke or casual response deserted him.

_ஃ ◊ ௨_

Brooke Snyder was getting a little tired of cinnamon rolls. Why didn't Jon Hoeffner invite her out on a real date? Maybe she'd gotten it wrong. Her man radar had always been a little off-kilter, like a crooked weathervane. It was possible that she'd misread him. He might not like her romantically at all.

But then again, he always seemed eager to see her. His face brightened and he was fascinated by what she did with her days—which wasn't all *that* fascinating. She had bought a sketchbook and planned to draw some landscape settings around the area, but she hadn't quite got around to it yet. What had happened to her objective to create a new life while she was staying at Eagle Hill? It seemed to have been pushed aside by her consuming preoccupation with Jon Hoeffner. She spent the morning planning what she would wear when she saw him at the bakery. She spent the afternoons fixing her hair to look just so.

She didn't believe in love at first sight or any such foolishness, but there was something that drew her to Jon. She couldn't say what it was. For all she knew, it was the pull of the moon on the Amish countryside. The only thing she was certain of was that she felt sad when the bakery closed and their coffee and cinnamon roll accidentally-on-purpose dates were over. She counted the hours until she would see him again. Those were the thoughts that spun around in her mind as she sat across from Jon at their special table at the Sweet Tooth Bakery.

"What's going on at Eagle Hill?" he asked.

"Too much, if you ask me. I wanted peace and quiet and, instead, it's been as busy as a weekday at Grand Central

Station. The family is going to hold church Sunday soon, so there's a lot of sprucing up going on. Tons of people in and out, painting and hammering and the like. Frankly, the place looks much better." She smiled. "Maybe other churches should do the same thing—threaten to hold church at your home so you'd clean it up now and then. Imagine how many home improvement projects would get finished if you thought you were hosting church for two hundred people."

"I think you mentioned a baby?"

She nodded. "Now that's something interesting. Didn't I tell you? I thought for sure I'd told you all about it. The mother of the baby disappeared. Left the baby and vanished into thin air. I heard her car sputter off in the middle of the night and then the oldest girl—Bethany—yelled for her to come back."

Jon looked shocked. Then he quickly arranged his face in its normal, slightly quizzical, casually interested expression. "Any idea where she might have gone?"

"None."

"Think she'll be back?"

Brooke shrugged. "She wasn't much of a mother type, if you ask me. Seemed very young and immature. Maybe it's for the best, now that the boy is back from jail."

Again, Jon's eyes went wide but just for a split second. "You didn't tell me that, either."

"Didn't I?" *So what?* Why would it matter?

"Sounds more like a soap opera than a quiet Amish farm."

Brooke laughed. "You're right. It does."

And then the subject changed as Jon wanted to know what her plans were for the next week. "Nothing!" she replied, too quickly, too wide-eyed. Then, dropping her head, "Well, nothing that couldn't be rearranged."

He swept a slow glance across the bakery and she studied his profile: those beautiful deep-set eyes, the crisp, straight nose, the dimple in his cheek, that thick, wavy hair. "Maybe it's time to make some plans," he said, offering up that dazzling smile that made her stomach do cartwheels. Their eyes met and she heard her own pulse drumming in her ears.

She was sure, just sure, that he was going to ask her out soon.

17

Outdoors it was unmistakably May. Lilacs bloomed, fields were velvet green, purple martins swooped around white birdhouses on tall poles, and Eagle Hill had never looked better. Every member of the family, along with friends and neighbors, had spent days cleaning and sprucing up the farmhouse. The windows had been washed, the floors rewaxed, every cupboard and bureau drawer was swept out and reorganized. Even the barn had been tidied so that you wouldn't recognize it. Not a single spiderweb remained.

"I think the farm was perfectly all right," Vera grumbled as Rose finished preparing the food for tomorrow's fellowship lunch. She looked around her transformed home and saw nothing different.

Tomorrow, church would be held at the farm and Bethany and Tobe would be baptized. Rose wished that Dean could know how well his family was doing. She hoped he did.

The kitchen was a hive of activity and Rose looked on in amazement. Chickens boiled in a huge pot, bacon sizzled in another. Fern Lapp had brought over a large pot of bean soup, Bethany and Naomi had baked loaves of bread and dozens of cookies and brownies, other neighbors would bring additional food.

Bethany put the finishing touches on a tray of brownies and swatted away Luke's hand as he tried to snatch one.

"It isn't fair if we don't get to eat them," he said, a whiny twang to his voice.

"There's bound to be leftovers," Bethany told him.

The next morning, there wasn't a hair out of place, a dirty chin, or a bare foot to be seen. Luke and Sammy looked like little angels, Rose thought. It was always a great surprise to her—the difference a little cleaning and polishing could make.

She had barely rinsed out her coffee mug when she heard the wheels of the first buggy crunching onto Eagle Hill's long driveway. Soon, bearded and bonneted neighbors spilled from their buggies and crossed the yard to gather quietly and shake hands. Children, with freshly polished shoes already coated in dust, darted behind their mothers' skirts and around their fathers' legs. The sheep and goat's pasture had become a temporary holding spot for the many horses that had transported families to church. Galen had brought over a few wheelbarrows filled with hay to act as temporary food troughs.

By 7:45 a.m., a crowd of almost two hundred people milled around the yard. Some of the men leaned against the fences or walls, stiff and stern in their dark Mutza coats, discussing weather and crops. The women gathered together in clumps, their black bonnets nodding as they chatted about canning or gardening or children.

Furniture had been moved out of the downstairs to make room for the long, backless church benches, which arrived by wagon and could be transported from home to home.

The benches were placed in every spare inch so that nearly everyone could see the center of the house from his or her seat—the center being where the ministers would preach.

Shortly before eight, as if drawn by a silent bell, the women organized themselves into a loose line and filed into the house. The young single women walked at the front of the line, the older ones at the back.

Rose half listened while Elmo preached a message, her attention focused more on keeping an eye on Luke, seated on the other side of the room from her. Normally she followed every word of the sermon, but this morning she wished the ministers would finish early. She was eager to get to the baptisms of Tobe and Bethany and felt very distracted.

A small plate of graham crackers was making its way around the room for parents who had little ones curled beside them. Rose saw Luke reaching out to grab one and she sent him an arched eyebrow look, straight across the room. Luke's hand hovered over the plate, sensing his mother's message without acknowledging eye contact. His shoulders shrugged in a big sigh and he passed the plate along, untouched. Down the row on the women's side, a little girl was making a hand-kerchief mouse to amuse her toddler sister. She glanced over at Sarah, sleeping in Naomi's arms.

Mim nudged her with an elbow. "Mom, who is that?"

"Where?"

"Sitting next to the insufferable Jesse Stoltzfus." Who, Mim tried to ignore, was flashing her one of his sweet-rascal smiles.

"It's Jesse's cousin, visiting from Ohio. Why?"

"He can't stop staring at Bethany. And Jimmy Fisher keeps noticing that very thing."

To be sure, Jimmy was scowling at Jesse's cousin, who was

staring dreamily in Bethany's direction. She was oblivious, Rose realized, her mind a million miles away.

Mim was glaring at Jesse's cousin, not saying a word, of course, but then, she didn't have to. Rose knew just what her daughter was trying to communicate; it was something Vera would do and she had to stifle a smile. Church, Mim was saying with her pointed stare, was not the place to make eyes at a girl.

The silence lay heavy and warm over the house. Bethany relaxed, they were nearly there. Only a few more moments and the baptism would begin. She breathed in the Sunday smells of laundry starch and shoe blacking and coffee percolating. So familiar, yet on this sunny spring morning, she felt as if she were experiencing church for the first time.

Bethany and Tobe had four crammed sessions with David Stoltzfus studying the Dordrecht Confessions. Usually, a minister spent nine sessions of instruction classes to go through all the Articles, but the bishop was eager to get Tobe baptized. Most likely, Bethany reasoned, he wanted to hurry before Tobe changed his mind.

Bethany expected the instruction classes to be boring, and they mostly were, but her brother made them surprisingly enjoyable. He peppered David Stoltzfus with all kinds of bold and audacious questions that the minister didn't seem to mind at all. In fact, he enjoyed Tobe's inquisitive mind and encouraged questions. It was a pity Jimmy Fisher declined to take part in the classes, Bethany mulled for the umpteenth time, because she knew he would've enjoyed the spirited and lively debates.

Earlier this morning, before church began, Jimmy had sidled close to her and asked if Tobe had smooth talked her into getting baptized with him. It wasn't just smooth talk; Tobe had badgered her into taking the classes with him, but Jimmy didn't need to know that. She gave him a benign smile.

"I just can't understand why you'd want to go ahead with it now. I thought we'd wait and do it . . . you know . . . later."

She tipped an eyebrow his way. "Oh? What's later to you?"

"Well, what's the rush to you?"

"It's hard to explain. But it's a real thing, you know, baptism opening the floodgates of grace."

His mouth formed an O, but the word never made it past his lips. He gave her a strange look, before she moved to the porch where the women were gathering.

When the time came for the baptisms, Bethany looked out at the congregation, all those she knew and loved. Her face grew hot and her voice trembled and she felt herself perspire, but she didn't waiver. Bishop Elmo asked her and Tobe questions: Did they still desire to be baptized? Were they ready to say goodbye to the world and to rebuke the devil? Would they stay in the church until the day they died?

Tobe gulped at that last one, took a long time answering, so long that everyone leaned forward on their benches, straining to hear him. He turned and held Naomi's gaze for a moment. In a loud voice, he said, "Yes. Yes, I will," and there was a sigh of relief among the benches.

Then the bishop turned to the congregation and asked questions of affirmation. He motioned to Tobe and Bethany to kneel for a prayer. A prayer so long that Bethany was sure her knees had sailed past hurting and had gone completely numb. The bishop's wife unpinned Bethany's prayer covering as Elmo took a pitcher of water and poured three trickles of water over Bethany—one for the Father, one for the Son, and one for the Holy Ghost—and she felt the water stream down her face. Then she was up, dripping and wet and cold, and she felt new.

The tables groaned with food. Oval platters offered up sandwiches of peanut butter and marshmallow cream mixed together, slathered on homemade bread. A simple bowl of cut apple wedges sat at each table's end. There were trays of bologna and cheese, dishes of pickles and red beets. Coffee, tea, and containers of unsweetened grape juice—a lively purple from Amos Lapp's own vineyard.

Rose set out a pitcher of hot coffee on the table and noticed Galen standing by the doorjamb. There was something about the set line of his mouth that made Rose decide to go and see what might be wrong. She followed him into the kitchen to find Bethany, Mim, and Vera, standing frozen in a tableau, their faces expressing different degrees of horror.

"Mom, you won't believe it!" Mim said, barely able to speak. She held up a tray of half-moon apple pies with the corners nibbled away. "Every single one!"

"And my brownies!" Bethany gasped, white as a sheet. Teeth marks dented the corners of the brownies. Each one.

"It's the same with the apple snitzes!" Mim's tears were now openly flowing down her cheeks. "Luke. It was Luke. I know it was him."

"No—the one to blame is Jesse Stoltzfus! Ee fauler Appel schteckt der anner aa." *One rotten apple corrupts all those that lie near it.* Vera stood with her shoulders pulled back and her bosom lifted high, her nose wrinkled and her mouth puckered. "And now Jesse Stoltzfus has added sweet Mose Blank into his gang. Mose has been following him like a shadow lately and Nancy Blank is beside herself with worry. She blames Teacher Danny. She said it was his idea to get Mose friendly with that awful Jesse. She didn't want her baby to be bullied and now he's turned into a bully. Leroy Blank is talking of getting Danny turned out as a teacher."

Mim gasped and Rose noticed that she looked both horrified and guilty, all at the same time. Mim fled the room and banged out the door of the house.

Mammi Vera's face was working itself into a terrible anger. "When did that ruffian get into this house?"

"Jesse said he'd help the men with the benches," Bethany said. "I told him I had counted all those brownies before he came in. I saw him eyeing the brownies."

"If only they could have just eaten a few," Rose said.

"It's all ruined," Mammi Vera said. "Entirely ruined. How easily the young can be seduced by the devil." Her voice held that familiar high tinge of hysteria that meant a lecture about the devil was on its way. She got very excited when things were emotional.

Rose had to take action. "Of course it's not all ruined, Vera. Bethany, take the coffee out. Vera, hand me a knife. I'll cut up the brownies and put out a smaller selection."

Galen assembled the criminals together in the kitchen: Jesse, Luke, Mose, and Sammy. "Correct me if I have made an error in identifying you four as the ones who ate bites from the desserts."

The boys looked around the room like rabbits caught in a trap.

"Well?" Galen's voice thundered.

"Sammy wasn't in on it," Luke said.

"I did have a few bites, though," Sammy said, his voice full of regret.

"Do you realize what you did? Bishop Elmo and Deacon Abraham are very interested to hear why you felt you had the right to ruin the desserts that Rose and Bethany and Mim made for today's fellowship lunch. Ruin!" Galen roared the last word.

The boys jumped back in fright.

"But I told them I would handle it," Galen said in his cool, slow way. "I told them you had all volunteered to wash every dish and plate and cup and glass. That it was your contribution. Tomorrow, right after school, you'll put the benches back in the wagon and then return the furniture to the rooms. Then you would come to report to me when it is all completed."

The boys looked at each other in dismay. That would take them all afternoon and evening.

Jimmy Fisher wandered into the kitchen, curious about what was going on.

"What about Jimmy Fisher? Would he like to help—?" Luke began.

"No, Luke, he wouldn't want to," Galen said, "and people like Jimmy Fisher will be delighted to know that you volunteered to put away the benches so they don't have to come back tomorrow to do it."

There was a beat of silence.

"This day will never be forgotten," Galen said. "I want you boys to know that. Every time I see you, this will be at the forefront of my mind."

Sammy's eyes began to fill with tears.

"NOW." Galen glared at the boys. "Get started this minute."

The boys rushed outside to start gathering dirty dishes.

David Stoltzfus stood by the door. "Galen," he said, in a voice of warning. "I think you might have frightened them."

"Good."

"Perhaps you could have just asked me or Anna to handle it. They are our children, after all."

Rose looked at David. "Anna?"

He looked puzzled, then gave his head a shake. "I'm sorry. That was my wife's name. I meant Rose. I meant you should have let Rose and me handle it."

"But you weren't handling it, David," Galen said in a patient voice. "You were outside talking to people, completely oblivious to the mischief that your son had stirred up. I saw what you couldn't—or wouldn't—see."

Rose looked across the room at Galen and their eyes locked. There was a message in those words. David opened his mouth to object and Rose cut him off. "He's right, David. He saw something you didn't see."

The boys hurried into the kitchen, tail between their legs as they walked past Galen, their arms full of dirty dishes.

Rose looked once more at the criminals as they filled the sink with hot water and stirred soap into it. It was probably the first time they had ever washed a dish . . . and they would be washing hundreds today. Because her heart was big and the desserts hadn't been entirely ruined, she gave them half a smile.

As Mim helped Elmo locate his buggy in a long row of buggies standing upright against the barn, the bishop kept exclaiming that it was amazing the way time raced by. It was already midafternoon, he said, astonished by that fact. It was extraordinary how old people thought time raced by. Mim found it went very slowly indeed.

A blue car drove into the driveway. Everyone stopped to watch a portly man get out of the car and look over the crowd, milling about, some moseying over to the pasture thick with horses to hitch them to buggies.

"Where is she?" the man said. "Where's Mrs. Miracle?"

Dread pooled in Mim's stomach.

Bethany sidled closer to Mim. "*That's* the features editor of the *Stoney Ridge Times*." She gave her a look of abject pity. "You are in so much trouble."

And didn't Mim just know it.

The buzz of conversation died down, a silence almost like the respectful hush of church came over the crowd.

Elmo walked up to the editor. "How can I help you?"

"Someone in your church writes the Mrs. Miracle column." He gazed around the yard as Bethany ducked into the house. "Some Amish gal drops off the copy and picks up the paycheck every week. I don't remember who she is, but I know she's here."

Elmo looked thoroughly confused. "I don't understand. What do you want?"

"Mrs. Miracle is ruining me, that's what! Her advice is losing advertisers for the paper. She wrote a letter telling people if they'd just stop buying televisions, they'd end up saving their marriages."

The bishop's spiky gray eyebrows drew together, as if tugged by complicated thoughts. "Well now, there could be some truth to that."

"Not when your biggest advertiser is the Stoney Ridge Electronics." His red face grew redder. "Then she told the butcher's kid to not go into the family business. The Stoney Ridge Butcher Shop just canceled a year's worth of advertising!"

Silence. No one said a word. Bishop Elmo turned and looked around those who remained. "Does anyone know who this man is talking about?"

The editor waved a paper in the air. "I can't make out the sloppy signature, but the name of the person who signed the W-4 form starts with a *B*. Last name starts with an *S*. Now . . . where is she? Who is she?"

BS for Bethany Schrock, who had signed the paper because Mim was underage. Mim thought she might faint dead away, right in front of the entire church and her family. Her lungs felt like they were on fire and she knew everyone was looking right at her, boring their eyes into her soul.

"I'm the one you're looking for. I'm Mrs. Miracle."

Heads whipped around to see who had spoken. It was the woman from the guest flat, standing about ten yards from the editor. "I'm Brooke Snyder. Also known as Mrs. Miracle." She smiled widely at him. "I've been meaning to get back to you about syndicating the column. Would you like to come in and talk about it over coffee?"

Mim watched the editor follow Brooke into the guest flat. She was stunned, completely and utterly flabbergasted. There was a burning behind her eyes, a hard place forming in her throat.

Jesse Stoltzfus, who seemed to materialize whenever any drama unfolded, spoke up. "Well, wonders never cease!" he said in a very loud voice. "Mrs. Miracle was right here, under our very noses."

Everyone started talking, and the sound swirled around Mim like the clucking of a flock of chickens. She was wordless. A girl who loved words was thoroughly wordless.

Jesse slipped up behind her, his arms full of dishes. In a voice so low Mim had to strain to hear, he whispered, "Stop shaking and trembling. It may turn out all right. If you're smart, you'll realize you just dodged a bullet."

Mim flashed Jesse a grateful look. But he wasn't looking at her. He was gazing at Rose, standing on the porch, talking to his father.

"You've got a lovely mother," he said. "She's strong but kind."

Mim shrugged. "I suppose."

"I guess people don't ever appreciate their own mothers properly, until it's too late." He kept his gaze on Mim's mother. "She reminds me of my own mother."

She didn't know anything about Jesse's mother, other than she had passed recently. She thought about asking him about her, but he darted away, off to the kitchen with another armful of dirty dishes.

She had always thought Jesse Stoltzfus was nothing but a joker, as happy as a fly in pie. But now she wondered if all his jokes were meant to cover up his sadness.

⸻ ◊ ⸻

Vera sat at the kitchen table, rehashing the day, the church service, and the dessert disaster.

"Still, all in all, it was a wonderful day," Rose said, as she brought Vera a cup of tea.

To Rose's surprise, Vera's eyes filled with tears. "If only Dean could have been here. If only he could have seen Bethany and Tobe baptized."

But Dean Schrock was in the Amish graveyard a few miles away.

Rose sat very still. As she gazed steadily at her mother-in-law, she realized dark circles had gathered in the hollows beneath Vera's eyes. And lines had been pressed into her cheeks. When had she gotten so old? And why hadn't she noticed before?

"You should have insisted on an autopsy," Vera said. Every few weeks, she brought up this topic with Rose, probing it like a sore tooth. "You should have had more presence of mind. Even now, two years later, I know people are whispering. I know what they think about us. About Dean. They all think he took his own life. You missed your chance to clear his name once and for all." She wiped her eyes with her sleeve. "And now it's too late."

Vera liked to believe that she knew everything. But Vera was wrong. As hectic as that day of Dean's drowning was, Rose had had enough presence of mind to know she couldn't allow the unthinkable. She told the police no autopsy.

If it had turned out that Dean had done himself in, then he would have been buried outside the walls of the cemetery, where the goats and sheep and cows would walk over the graves of those who had not been allowed to have a Christian burial. Life wasn't yours to take, it was a gift from God and those who threw it back in his face had no place being mourned by the faithful.

Because there was no autopsy to confirm or deny the means of death, Dean was buried with honor and the family could give him a good farewell. It was better, she felt; it gave the family a sort of peace. But she knew, even now, that there was a shadow over how and why Dean had died.

After Vera had gone to bed, Rose fed a bottle to Sarah and rocked her in a chair next to the woodstove. She tried to dwell on the day, on the moment of baptism for Tobe and Bethany, a holy moment. But one thing kept interrupting her thoughts and that was Galen's pointed remark to David Stoltzfus: he had seen something David hadn't seen. He was absolutely right. David was often preoccupied with lofty theology discussions while his son Jesse stirred up all kinds of trouble.

But that wasn't all Galen was insinuating, in his quiet way. She knew that. She and Galen may have their differences, but she could count on him to tell her the truth.

Luke wandered downstairs and came over to look at the baby, then walked around the room. Something was on his mind.

"If Dad's in heaven, he could see us now," Luke said, looking at the ceiling.

Dean seemed to be on everyone's mind tonight. But then, she wasn't surprised. Some days were harder than others, and days of significance, like today, were the hardest days of all. "Of course he's in heaven," Rose said, pushing aside the fear that bubbled up to the surface.

"He wouldn't be in hell, would he?" he asked hesitantly. "Suffering torture for all eternity?"

Rose put down Sarah's bottle and looked at Luke in amazement. "Why would you think that?"

"Mammi Vera said that suicide is a sin that can't be forgiven. She said it's giving up hope." He turned and looked right at her. "Do you know what really happened?"

"Luke," she said softly, "what makes you think that your father took his own life?"

"I remember how upset and angry he was. I remember that he couldn't sleep at night. He was unhappy for a long time."

Now Rose was firm. "It's true, he was under a great deal of stress. But I refuse to believe that your father would have done such a thing."

"But—"

"No buts, Luke," Rose said, with a pain in her chest that she felt would never go away.

Sarah had fallen asleep so she tucked her into the Moses basket and covered her up with a blanket. Then she turned to face Luke. There was something he wanted to say, and she could tell he was trying to put it into words.

"Would it have been terrible . . . drowning? Would it have felt like he was choking?"

Rose gave the matter some thought. "No, I think it would have been very peaceful, you know, like the feeling you get when you're falling asleep and you can't stay awake. You feel as if you're being pulled away. I don't think it would have been very frightening."

"Do you think he thought of us . . . of Sammy and me . . . as he was dying?" Luke's voice was shaking.

"I think he would have been hoping that you'd all be all right, that you'd carry on, that we'd be strong as a family and appreciate days like today, when Bethany and Tobe became baptized."

And then, for the first time in front of her since he was a small boy, Luke let himself go and wept.

18

Monday dawned beautiful, warm, and springlike. After Mim and the boys set off to school, Rose fed the baby her bottle on the porch swing. Sarah was already changing—gaining weight, stretching out her spindly arms and legs so she seemed less and less like a tightly coiled newborn. The baby waved a tiny fist in the air and Rose offered her finger for her to grab. Such miniature fingers! So fragile, so perfect. Rose wondered where her mother Paisley was and if she even thought about her. When Tobe crossed the yard from the barn, she stopped him.

He held up a hammer. "I'm finishing up a few things with the henhouse."

A wave of irritation about Tobe came over Rose. Those hens were going to end up with a castle. "Not right now."

His head snapped up, surprised by the tone in her voice. "You sound angry."

"I think it's time you take a look at this child," Rose said. "Really look at her. She might be your daughter, she might not. But she might be the making of you. She might make you into the kind of person you need to be." She walked down the porch steps and handed the baby to him.

"I don't know anything about babies," he said. The baby stared at Tobe with wide eyes, evidently as surprised as he was. "What if I do something wrong with it?"

"Her. Not an it. She's a person. Her name is Sarah. A real live human being."

"She's so very small." Just then the baby began to cry, squirming in his hands. Tobe looked helplessly at Rose, but she made no effort to take the baby. "How can anyone know what a baby wants?"

"The more time you spend with her, the more you start to learn her language. Right now, she's telling you she doesn't like the way you're holding her."

He said he was afraid he might drop the child, who started to twist in his hands like a trapped rabbit. She whimpered, then cried, then yelled so loud she turned red as a beet.

"Put her against your shoulder," Rose said. "You don't have to hold her like that—she isn't a bag of flour."

He dropped the hammer and shifted the baby against his shoulder. "Do you think she might be sick?"

"No, she's fine," Rose said. With that she turned and walked up the porch steps, intending to leave him with the baby, who at once began to cry even harder. But, as abruptly as she had started, the baby stopped crying. She whimpered a time or two, stuck her fist in her mouth, and then quieted. He looked so relieved that he scarcely moved. The baby had wet his shirt with drool, but at least she wasn't crying.

"Talk to her a little," Rose said. She stood at the doorjamb.

"What should I say?"

She made a snort of disgust. "Introduce yourself, if you

can't think of anything else," she said. "Or sing her a song. She's sociable. She likes to be talked to."

Tobe looked at her blankly. "I don't know if I'll be able . . . I mean, I'm pretty clumsy."

"All new parents are clumsy," Rose reassured him. "You'll get better at it."

He looked at her sharply. "Why should I have to do this at all? The DNA test will—"

"I don't care about a DNA test. You'll do this because this child needs you. You'll do it because you're a decent man. And if that's not good enough"—she bore down on him—"you'll do it because I'm telling you to."

She felt a little heartless, but she knew he had to learn to do it without her.

Naomi tried not to smile as she listened to Tobe's complaints. Rose had insisted that the family, including Naomi, hand over the bulk of responsibility of the baby to him. They were allowed to give him fifteen-minute breaks now and then, so that he could shower or change clothes, but no help with nighttime feedings or walking the baby back to sleep. She was adamant about that.

After two days of being Sarah's primary caretaker, Tobe was near to weeping with fatigue. There were dark circles under his eyes; he looked as if he hadn't slept in days. He walked the hallways with Sarah in the night, trying to burp her after her third feed of the night. He said he found himself stumbling against furniture, almost incapable of remaining upright.

"How can anyone learn to identify what kind of crying

means hunger, discomfort, or pain?" he said. "All crying sounds the same—and it all wakes you up from the deepest sleep. No one ever told me how exhausting it is to be up three, four times every night, night after night. This is awful." He was tired all the time.

It didn't occur to him that Rose and Bethany had been doing that very thing for weeks now, ever since the baby was born. Or that Naomi had cared for the baby during the day.

Then, to his obvious relief, Naomi took the baby from him. "I'm going to grab a nap," he said.

"I'll wake you in fifteen minutes," she said, and his smile faded.

There wasn't much Brooke Snyder wouldn't do for Jon Hoeffner. At times, she wondered if she was falling in love with him. Imagine that! Over cinnamon rolls in a little Amish town. So when he asked her for a small favor, she was elated. "How can I help?"

Jon looked at her squarely, kindly. His lips curved up a little on one side, showing off a dimple in his cheek. He seemed a little sheepish to have to ask her for help, but his boyish embarrassment only melted her. "I have a safety deposit box that I share with my sister. It was something our parents set up before they passed on to glory. My sister and I both have to sign to get into it. I need to get into the safety deposit box because I'm trying to sell my car. I've got to get the title." He blew out a puff of air. "My sister is Old Order Amish and frowns on the life I've chosen—driving a car and using electricity and all that. She refuses to talk to me. It's something called shunning. Kind of like excommunication."

"I've heard of that! I saw a reality TV show about the Amish." Then, after thoughtful consideration, "How awful for you."

Jon nodded. "It's been difficult. I'm left out of every family gathering. It's been . . . well, lonely."

Brooke reached out and covered his hand. "How can I help, Jon?"

"Would you mind posing as my sister at the bank to help me get the pink slip out of the safety deposit box? You'd need to sign in as her, but you could do that, couldn't you? You duplicated my signature perfectly."

A tiny alarm bell pinged inside Brooke's head, but she ignored it. "I suppose the signature part wouldn't be difficult. But what about the ID?"

He smiled. "Not a problem. I've got that covered. My sister doesn't have a photo ID, being Amish, so it's just a matter of getting her Social Security card."

"How would you get it?"

He looked embarrassed. "To be entirely truthful, I saw her Social Security card on the counter awhile ago when I asked her if she'd go with me to the bank. When she refused to go with me, well, I'm not proud of it, but I slipped the card into my pocket. I'll put it back as soon as I get this pink slip taken care of."

She thought about it for a while, stirring her coffee. It didn't feel wrong, but didn't feel quite right, either. *Ping, ping* went the alarm in her head. "You promise you'll return your sister's Social Security card as soon as you get the pink slip?"

"Absolutely! I just couldn't think of any other way . . . not until I thought about how easily you copied my signature.

Then I realized, well, you were heaven sent." He squeezed her hands and she melted.

"Okay. When?"

The bakery clerk stood by the door, an irritated look on her face. Brooke suddenly realized it was past five and they were the only customers left in the bakery. They hurried outside so the clerk could lock up.

"I'll let you know when I have the deal completed with the car buyer." He closed the distance between them and pressed a kiss to her cheek. "You're a peach, Brooke. I'm so glad we've met." Jon lifted her chin and kissed her lightly on the lips. He smiled, then walked around the corner and disappeared.

Brooke leaned against the bakery door, feeling like she might explode with happiness. *Ping, ping, ping!* That stupid alarm bell kept going off in her head, so she tried to wipe her mind clean of it and closed her eyes to concentrate on the sweet goodbye kiss Jon had just given her.

Tobe handed baby Sarah to Vera and took the pan of spring peas onto his lap. Rose had to smile. He would rather shell peas than hold a baby, but at least he wasn't shirking his duties with Sarah like she thought he might.

"Where do you suppose that Paisley went off to?" Vera asked him.

"I have no idea," he said. "I called the restaurant where she worked and they haven't seen her in months. They said they fired her because she was helping herself to the cash register."

"Did you try calling the manager of her apartment?"

"I did. They said she was evicted about that same time." He rubbed the underside of his nose with his forearm.

Vera looked up. "But then why was she looking for the key to the apartment?"

Tobe's chin jerked up. "Key? What key?"

"She told me she had lost the key to her apartment and thought you had the only spare. She said it would cost her a fortune to get a locksmith out there, so she really needed to find it."

Tobe's face went white. Slowly, he sat up, his spine poker-straight. The spring pea pan crashed to the floor, and peas bounced all over the kitchen. He didn't even realize what he'd done as he turned to Rose. "Call Allen Turner. Tell him to get out here as fast as he can."

Tobe and Naomi sat on the porch swing, waiting for Allen Turner. Every fifteen minutes, Mim went out to check the phone shanty to see if any messages were waiting from the lawyer. Bethany thought they should take turns waiting at the phone, but Rose said no, that they had plenty to do and staring at a phone didn't make it ring. But no one could get much done.

By the time Allen Turner's car roared up to the house two hours later, Rose breathed a sigh of relief, grateful the boys were still helping Galen feed the horses and weren't in on this. She watched Tobe warily, but color was back in his face.

Allen Turner walked in and sat at the kitchen table, an expectant look on his face. "So. What's the emergency, Tobe?"

"Jake Hertzler is nearby," Tobe said. "I'm sure of it."

Ten seconds of beating silence before Bethany added, "I've had the same thought." Tobe snapped his head to face her. "At least, I know he was here in the last few months."

"Me too," Naomi said.

Mim bit her lip. "Same here."

Allen Turner's head turned from Tobe to Bethany to Naomi to Mim, then back again to Tobe. He seemed thoroughly confused and he was not a man prone to confusion.

Tobe pointed to Bethany. "Is this about the horse?"

She nodded and explained how Galen had found Lodestar, abandoned. She looked at Mim. "What makes you think he's here?"

"There's been a couple of times when a car has driven by me, slowly at first, then it sped up to pass me. The driver was a man, and even though I never saw his face, something about him seemed like Jake."

"That's the same feeling I've had," Naomi said. "I thought I saw someone who looked like him near the post office one day. But it was too dark to tell, for sure."

So far, Allen Turner wasn't impressed by hunches and feelings. He glanced impatiently at his watch and turned to Tobe. Soon, all eyes were on Tobe. He took a deep breath and explained to Allen about Paisley's sudden appearance, about the fact that Paisley had known Jake—quite well, in fact. Much better than he knew her—and then came to the part about the key. "Jake must have sent her here to look for the key."

Allen leaned back in his chair. "Tell me about the key."

"It belongs to a safety deposit box in the York County Savings and Loan. The account is under Dad's and Jake's and Rose's name."

"My name?" Rose said.

Tobe looked at her. "Don't you remember when Dad had you sign some papers to set it up? It was right when Jake started working for Schrock Investments. Jake wanted to put the P&L statements in the box each week. Dad felt it would be wise to have three names on it, so two would always have to go together to sign in."

Rose vaguely remembered when Dean set up the safety deposit box, but she had never used the box. Not once. "Go on," she urged.

"I know Jake and Dad visited the safety deposit box regularly, weekly, but knowing Dad, he would have signed in, spotted someone he knew in the bank, got talking to him, and let Jake go into the vault alone. I found the key in Jake's car on the day—" he glanced at Rose and hesitated—"well, I grabbed it. Along with the ledgers."

"Where is the key?"

"I hid it in a very safe place."

"Where?"

He cut another glance at Rose's direction. "I hid it in my mother's nursing home. In her room."

"What?" Rose said. The word came out as a tiny squeak. "Your mother's . . . *what*? She's . . . *where?*"

Tobe pressed on. "My mother isn't well. She's a paranoid schizophrenic. She lives in a home for mentally ill women."

Vera pinned Tobe with an accusing look. "You're mistaken. Your mother left years ago. She ran away and abandoned the children."

Tobe held her gaze for a moment, then flickered aside. "Bethany knows. She visits our mother once a month."

All eyes turned toward Bethany, but her attention was riveted to a small mark on the tabletop. She was aware that everyone was waiting for an explanation, but she hesitated, taking time to gather her thoughts, before her voice cut into the silence. "That's what my mother wanted everyone to think. She knew that Dad would try to have her come home, and that she wasn't capable of taking care of her children. She checked herself into the facility and had papers drawn up that allowed Dad to divorce her because of abandonment. She planned it all out. She wanted everyone to move on without her."

Rose had often heard of people saying they were rooted to the ground by a shock, and she just realized how apt a description it was. She was not able to move, not able to say a word.

It was almost too huge to grapple with. For years, Rose had felt as if she was picking up the pieces that Dean's first wife had left behind. She was astounded to think Mary Schrock had given her family away to protect them. She felt dizzy, as if she might faint, and she tried to steel herself.

Vera! She glanced over to see how her mother-in-law was taking this revelation. Vera remained as colorless as skim milk. Her lips moved silently, but not a sound came out. One hand was touching her heart.

Allen turned to Tobe. "What do you think is in the safety deposit box?"

He lifted a shoulder in a careless shrug. "Money. What else? Enough to get him out of town and set him up somewhere. I think he was siphoning money off the top, right from the start."

Allen Turner released an exhausted sigh. "Why didn't you tell me about the safety deposit box when you were getting interrogated? You could've saved us a lot of trouble."

Tobe looked away. "I wanted to deal with Jake myself. I couldn't figure out how, but that was my intention. My plan." He looked straight at Naomi. "I know better now."

"So you think Jake sent Paisley here to find the key?" Allen Turner said.

"He might've, but it wasn't here," Tobe said. "I hid it at my mother's."

"Wait." Bethany's eyes were round as silver dollars. "Wait a minute. Tobe, what kind of a key? Mammi Vera said Paisley was looking for a key to her apartment."

"She was lying," he said. "It was a small key for a safety deposit box."

Bethany gasped. "I know that key. But it isn't there. During Christmas, I was visiting Mom and she gave me the key. She told me not to lose it. She said it belonged to a little boy and he needed it. I didn't know what she was talking about, Tobe. She doesn't make sense most of the time. I just thought it was a key she had found."

Allen Turner looked like he was about to jump out of his skin. "So *where* is the key?"

"It's up in my room," Bethany said, already at the stairs. "I'll go get it."

"Oh no," Mammi Vera said, touching her chest again. "Oh no."

Rose blew out a puff of air. "Paisley . . . she stayed in Bethany's room."

Bethany came back down the stairs, her face white. "It's gone."

Allen Turner didn't seem at all surprised.

Tobe was practically out of his chair. "What if he's already gotten to the safety deposit box? What if he's emptied it?"

"It's possible. I'll get someone to check on that. But if he hasn't connected with Paisley to get the key, then there's time to set a trap."

"Why wouldn't he have connected with her already? They were working together."

"Calm down, Tobe. My guess is that Paisley is smart enough and shrewd enough to make him have to find her. She's got something he wants, and she knows it. If my hunch is right, then we need to flush him out." Allen Turner bit on his lip, thinking, tapping a pencil on a paper. Then a light came into his eyes. "I'm going to put a notice in the local papers that the York County Savings & Loan Bank is going to drill into all inactive safety deposit boxes and seize the contents."

"Do they do that?" Tobe asked.

"Banks do it frequently," Allen Turner said. "The contents get auctioned off and the money goes to the state."

"Can you do that?" Tobe said.

"Oh yeah." Allen Turner smiled, a first. "If I can force Jake Hertzler to make his move, I'll be waiting for him." Then his smile faded. "But this part is my job. Not yours. Your job is to wait." He looked right at Tobe as he said it. "To wait."

19

Mim kept bouncing the baby up and down to stop her from crying, but the decibel level was getting higher. The noise was starting to grate on her. She didn't like babies and they didn't like her.

She had agreed to go with Tobe to the doctor for baby Sarah's one-month checkup, but she didn't realize that meant Sarah would be getting a shot. Mim nearly passed out when the nurse brought in that long needle, but she held the baby snugly in her lap and squeezed her eyes shut and wished she had earplugs.

She also didn't realize that Tobe was getting a paternity test. "It's just a swab of the cheek that gets sent off to the laboratory," he told Mim. "No big deal."

"And if it turns out that you are Sarah's father?" Mim had asked. "That seems like a very big deal." Even though she didn't like babies, she did think Sarah was a nice baby, as babies went. Mostly, she had an uncommonly good smell about her. And sometimes the tip of her tongue peeked through her little pink lips. Mim was amazed at the smallness of it, just as she was at her tiny starfish-like hands.

"I'm not."

"But what if you are, Tobe? What then?"

He frowned at her. "I have to know for sure, Mim."

Afterward, as Tobe was paying the receptionist for the paternity test—cash borrowed from Mim with a promise of a high-interest return—and asking how long the results would take, she tried to calm the baby down. She jiggled her, she paced the room, she sang to her, she hummed to her, she bounced her. Nothing worked. Sarah flailed and began to cry loud, unstoppable sobs. Little tears rolled down her cheeks, making Mim feel even more terrible, if that was possible. She wanted to cry herself. Tobe kept glancing back at both, a worried look on his face. Finally, he came over and got the bottle of formula out of the baby's diaper bag and sat down to feed Sarah.

As Tobe fed the baby, almost magically, the crying stopped, the baby calmed down, and peace was restored.

"It's like she knows, Tobe."

"Knows what?" The baby looked up at him solemnly, as though committing his face to memory.

Mim bent down to kiss the baby's forehead. "Sarah knows you are the one she can count on. She trusts you."

"Babies are too little to know about trust."

"I'm not so sure about that. Trust is a big part of life. If Sarah already trusts you, you're halfway there."

As usual, just like Sammy and Luke, Tobe wasn't listening to Mim. His eyes were fixed on a distant wall, lost in his private thoughts, as if something was weighing heavily on his mind.

Having Brooke Snyder stay in the guest flat for a steady few weeks certainly helped Rose pay some basic bills, but there were always unexpected expenses. A lamb that had to be treated for colic, Sammy needed to go to the dentist for an aching tooth, Mim needed new glasses, Sarah needed her newborn checkups. Rose still hadn't brought up Paisley's hospital bills to the deacon. Soon, though.

Rose looked over the vegetable garden, now planted for summer's bounty. She felt a deep satisfaction in watching things grow. As a child, she had worked alongside her mother to prepare seedbeds, till the garden, plant and tend crops, and harvest fruit and vegetables at the optimal time. They harvested more fruit than they could haul to market, and nearly everything on her table came from her family's farm: cheese and sausage, bread and eggs and jam, apples and peaches and corn.

She scooped up a handful of dirt. This was how her mother had started. Year after year, her mother had added to the garden plot, until her father finally gave up on wheat and corn and became a full-time fruit and vegetable farmer. There was always a need for lettuce and carrots and onions and zucchini and pumpkins and strawberries.

She walked past the garden, past the barn, to a neglected section that once housed a pigpen. Perhaps . . . she could do what her mother did. Perhaps . . . *this* might be a potential source of additional income.

If she could turn the pigpen into a garden, she could double the size of her output and start to sell produce at a roadside stand. Or maybe even at the Stoney Ridge Farmers' Market where Bethany used to work.

She should get the pigpen plowed under before spring was too far gone. Tobe could do it, but she wanted him to focus on the baby and not have an excuse to leave her care to others. She thought about asking Galen, but that wouldn't be right. Then she saw David Stoltzfus's buggy drive along the road. "Any time you need any help, just ask," he had told her at church on Sunday. Anytime.

She dropped her handful of dirt and watched it scatter in the wind. Why, now was a time she needed a little extra man's help. She tucked a lock of loose hair back under her prayer cap, straightened her apron, pinched her cheeks, and headed over to David Stoltzfus's.

Jimmy stopped by the Kings' every day to check on Lodestar. When he first saw the horse, the day Bethany had given him the good news, he had been shocked at his weakened appearance. If Jimmy had happened across Jake Hertzler that day, he didn't know what he might have done to him—so severe was Lodestar's neglect. The thought disturbed him, knowing he could harm another man. And yet to see Lodestar's condition was even more disturbing. Another week alone, hobbled, without food or water, and that beautiful animal might have suffered a lonely, painful death.

Galen thought it would be best to keep Lodestar at his barn in a big box stall and Jimmy heartily agreed. Galen's barn was more secure than the small Fisher barn. Though Lodestar didn't seem at all interested in escaping. Just the opposite. He stayed at the back of the stall and only seemed interested in food, not in people. But he was making progress. His ribs were already starting to fill out, his eyes looked brighter, he held his head up again. The vet said it might take months to fully recover, that stress can have a very negative effect on an animal, but he was cautiously optimistic. "He was rescued in the nick of time," the vet told Jimmy, who told Bethany, who said it was meant to be, and that it proved everything happened for a reason. She had a gleam in her eye when she said it too, which made his throat tighten and his palms sweat.

"First things first," he had told her. "Lodestar needs time and attention to mend properly."

At that, she gave him a probing look, one he couldn't read. It set off that panicky feeling deep within him again.

After Jimmy spent time grooming Lodestar, he led him into an outdoor paddock for a little fresh air and sunshine. He stayed nearby, leaning his back against the paddock, boot heel resting on the lowest rung, so he could observe Galen working in the round training pen. Galen was constantly improvising and trying new things, customizing training to the individual needs of the horses. Jimmy didn't want to miss a trick. He was *that* eager for Tobe and Naomi to hurry up and marry so he could retire as a chicken boss and resume his position as Galen's partner in horse training.

On this breezy May afternoon, Galen was in the pen with a newly purchased bay Thoroughbred, a gelding with intelligent eyes. Jimmy walked over to the pen, keeping one eye peeled on Lodestar.

"Want to see my new business card?" He pulled one from his pocket and handed it to Galen.

Galen peered at it. "You're calling yourself a stallion manager?"

"That's what I am. I manage a stallion." He glanced at Lodestar, who was stretching his neck to crop new grass near the paddock gate.

"That title usually indicates a knowledgeable, experienced horseman."

"Exactly."

"Is that so?" Galen handed him back the business card. "So do you have better odds pasture-breeding or with artificial help?"

"Artificial help."

"Wrong." He raised an eyebrow. "A healthy mare can call the shots a lot better than a human can." He flicked the whip to keep the horse loping. "Can you keep stallions together in a pasture?"

Jimmy sneered. "Of course not."

"Wrong again. Horses aren't territorial. As long as there aren't any mares or foals nearby, they don't fight over real estate—only females." He gave Jimmy *the look*—the one that made him feel like he was a dense child. "Maybe you want to hold on to those cards a little longer."

Jimmy tucked the business card into his pocket. "Speaking of being territorial, have you noticed David Stoltzfus hanging around Eagle Hill like a summer cold? Something happen between you and Rose?"

"None of your business."

"He's over there right now, plowing up the old pigpen. Folks say he's got Rose marked off with a red flag."

Galen's whole body drew taut and he eyed Jimmy askance. "I suppose you believe everything you hear?"

Jimmy shrugged. "Pretty much."

Galen had already set his mind on the next task: shaking a plastic milk jug partially filled with gravel at the horse to accustom him to unexpected sounds. Jimmy had always been impressed with Galen's ability to focus. He had never been good at getting his mind to consider two facts at once, much less two big facts. He saw Lodestar mouthing the paddock latch and then unhook it. He ran over to stop him, a big grin on his face. He'd been looking for some sign of bluster from Lodestar, some hint of his uppity nature. His horse was on the way back. Truly back.

Jimmy noticed Bethany across the top of the privet at Eagle Hill, smiled to himself, and reflected that she was a remarkable girl. Against impossible odds, she had found Lodestar. She had thought up a plan to help him get out of the chicken business, which he hated, and back to the horse business, which he loved. He owed a great deal to Bethany.

Yes, she was a truly remarkable girl. She was beautiful, sweet one minute, strong and fiery the next. A fellow would never get bored with a girl like Bethany at his side.

What was he waiting for? He knew she was impatient, eager for him to propose. He decided to bring up the subject soon, maybe the next time he took her for a buggy ride to Blue Lake Pond. He exhaled, a matter decided.

Then he spotted Peter Stoltzfus, cousin to the town menace Jesse Stoltzfus, walk toward the Eagle Hill farmhouse. Bethany met him at the bottom porch step and she laughed at something he said. The sight and sound of it disturbed him, and he was annoyed at himself for being disturbed.

Mim was walking home from the Sisters' House, past the nearly-falling-down barn, when she heard some loud whoops and shouts coming from the barn. She saw three boys climbing on the roof, trying to reach the peak, egging each other on. Boys she recognized. Luke, Mose Blank . . . led by Jesse Stoltzfus.

"First one to the top wins!" Jesse shouted.

One loud crack filled the air, then another sound of creaking timber, and another. Seconds passed. Suddenly the boys disappeared in a blur of motion as the barn roof collapsed. The moment lasted forever. Too scared to move, Mim gave a piercing shriek that rent the afternoon air.

She raced like the wind to get to Eagle Hill, sprinting past the schoolhouse and through Amos Lapp's cornfield and jumping across the creek to reach the shortcut to the farm. The first person she spotted was David Stoltzfus, starting to plow one row of the old pigpen.

"They're dead!" she shouted to him, waving her arms. "Luke and Mose and Jesse! They're all dead!"

David dropped the plow behind the mule and ran to her. "Calm down, Mim, and tell me what happened."

"The nearly-falling-down barn fell down! The boys were trying to climb to the top and it collapsed on them."

Together they ran toward the accident, expecting the worst.

As they arrived at the now-fallen-down barn, Jesse and Luke were climbing out of the debris, dusting off their clothes, grinning and laughing like they were at a Sunday picnic. Mose sat on a rock, holding up his elbow with one hand. His other hand dangled at an odd angle.

It was a fine day for the turning of the sod. Bethany smiled to herself as she saw Amos Lapp and Galen King put their hands together on the shovel and dig into the ground of one of the small garden plots at the Second Chance Gardens behind the Grange Hall. Geena Spencer asked Bishop Elmo if he wanted to say a few words about the results that came from a caring community.

Oh, big mistake! The bishop ended up saying a great many words. He had a habit, when he spoke, of clasping his hands at his spine and rocking back on his heels. When he did, his black shoes would squeak. They squeaked now as he rocked repeatedly, lifting his face to the sky while composing his words.

When Elmo finally wrapped it up, Geena took command, dividing Amish and wayward girls from the Group Home into groups to work together, giving them lists of chores. It was remarkable how much authority a relatively small woman like her could possess, and Bethany admired her tremendously.

All throughout the day, Bethany and Jimmy worked companionably on the garden plots. Toward the end of the day, when normally she might have lingered and ended up going home in Jimmy's buggy—via a stop at Blue Lake Pond—she pondered what to do. Should she stay or leave early? Hard though it was to do, she excused herself and said goodbye.

"You're leaving now?" Jimmy said, surprised and bothered. His disappointment was honey to her soul.

"I have a few things to take care of," she said. And she was gone.

The next day, he was thoroughly put out. "Are you going to keep running away all the time? I was hoping we could plan a picnic."

Big eyes wide, she said that honestly she was sorry . . . she just had a lot of things to do lately. But, of course, she would be delighted to have a meal with him sometime . . .

There was a silence. Jimmy went on to fill it.

"I thought you might arrange it," he said.

In the old days, like every day up to this minute, Bethany would have immediately made plans and offered to prepare a picnic and tell Jimmy what time to pick her up. This time she made no such offer. He reached for her hands, but she pulled them away.

"Oh no, I wouldn't dream of it. If you are asking me to have a picnic, then you must, of course, choose when and where." He was inviting *her*—he must remember that.

Jimmy had, of course, expected Bethany to make the picnic. She realized that the next day as they were sitting on the banks of Blue Lake Pond, eating peanut butter and sardine sandwiches on day-old bread. She nibbled on the corners of the unappetizing sandwich, smiling, pretending it was delicious.

From far away came a faint sound like old nails being pulled from new wood. Over the treetops flew a wedge of Canada geese, squawking and honking, heading toward the pond. They landed on the surface of the pond with such grace that it moved Bethany to a silent reverence.

Jimmy seemed slightly distracted as he took a bruised apple out of the basket and looked for a spot to bite into. His mind was somewhere else. Eventually he got around to what he wanted to say. "Are you seeing Jesse Stoltzfus's cousin?"

"Who? Oh, Peter?"

"He's been hanging around Eagle Hill."

"He's a very nice fellow."

"Bethany, have I annoyed you lately? In a different way than usual?"

"No, of course not." The warm wind kissed her face, fluttered the ends of her capstrings.

"Are you sure?"

"Nothing I can recall. Why do you think you did?"

"I don't know. You're different. You don't stop by Galen's

when I'm over there with Lodestar. You didn't make a picnic today. You don't shoot sparks at me like you usually do. I wondered if you were trying to say something to me . . ."

Her eyes widened innocently. "Like what?"

He looked out at the lake, at two ducks paddling around. "Maybe . . . you're interested in someone else. And I'll admit the thought made me feel like a jellyfish without a backbone."

The face she turned to him wore a polite expression. "You invited me to a picnic and I'm here. And I'm having a lovely time." *Not really.*

He brightened up at once. "A picnic made by my own two hands." He winked at her and threw the sandwich into the lake so the ducks dove for it. "It's just a feeling I've had lately . . ." He took her hands in his. "I wouldn't want to ever lose you, Bethany. In fact, lately I've come to realize how very much you mean to me."

Gone was the lighthearted banter, now he was being serious and caring. For a moment, Bethany swayed. *This* was the moment she'd been waiting for with him, the moment she had hoped for.

"I value you . . . Bethany . . . and I really do appreciate all you did to get Lodestar back and get Tobe set up to work with the chickens."

There was a beat of silence and she looked at him expectantly, not helping him out.

"I think I'm ready to get engaged."

I *value* you? I *think* I'm ready to get engaged? As if he was doing her a big favor? As if she was a broodmare he was thinking about buying? *Shootfire!* Her heart was pounding, a torrent of words was stuck in her throat, but she forced herself not to reply, not to reveal any hint of emotion. She *wanted* to throw the picnic basket at him, jump on the buggy, and gallop home, leaving the dense oaf to walk home. But she remained composed, cucumber calm.

He squeezed her hands. "Well, say something," he said, anxious to know.

"I don't have any words," she said truthfully. None that were ladylike. None that would be found in *A Young Woman's Guide to Virtue*, Mammi Vera's beloved book.

"Yes would do."

She gave him the sweetest smile she could muster, under the circumstances. "I'll need some time to think it over."

Jimmy blinked. "Why is it so hard to answer now?"

"I'm quite happy with things the way they are," she said, and to her surprise—her complete surprise—she truly was. "Marriage is such an important step—I want to make sure it's the right decision." Maybe Geena was right. Men were simple. And she would need to be equally simple in return. She shrugged. "Besides, what's the rush? We have plenty of time."

Gently, she slipped out of his grasp, rose, and walked toward the lake, tossing the peanut butter and sardine sandwich in bits to the hungry ducks, hoping it wouldn't make them sick and die. She felt lighthearted, almost dreamy. Jimmy, she noticed, when she turned to face him, was sitting where she had left him, his thick, dark brows drawn together in a confused frown.

In a little under two weeks, Naomi King would become Mrs. Tobe Schrock. Her sisters were coming soon to help with wedding preparations, and then the quiet life she and Galen had shared would be over.

Tomorrow, Naomi's sisters, both married with families of their own, would slide into the farmhouse and assume control: suggesting, helping, organizing, giving orders and instructions. Naomi felt a sense of overpowering relief that someone was taking charge. After all the waiting she and Tobe had done over the last eight months, their official wedding day was drawing near. Her heart tripped over itself and her skin flushed with excitement. Did every woman who got married go through this must-pinch-myself-to-believe-it stage? She felt so filled with joy and happiness, she could have burst with it.

And yet she felt a tinge of sadness too, knowing this was the last day she would have with her brother Galen. She worried about him, being alone, being lonely. She wasn't sure exactly what had happened to separate Galen and Rose, but she hoped the frost might thaw between them. She wished Galen would talk to her about Rose, but he was a man who kept his business to himself, especially business of the heart.

Naomi was sewing the seams of her blue wedding dress and put it aside when she heard Tobe's special rap on the door. In his arms was Sarah, sound asleep. He bent down to graze Naomi lightly on the lips, one kiss, two kisses, a smile, and then he passed the baby into her arms. He looked into her eyes with a combination of serious intensity and warmth. "Today's the last day."

How sweet! He had realized she was feeling sentimental about her last day she would be living with her brother.

"Today's the last day before the bank is going to drill open the inactive safety deposit boxes."

"Oh . . ." Surprise and deflation colored the single word. "But not really, right?"

"No, but Jake Hertzler doesn't know that." Tobe sat at the table and leaned on his elbows, hands grasped tightly together. "What if he doesn't see the advertisement? He should have shown up by now."

"Maybe he was having trouble locating Paisley and the safety deposit key. She sure did disappear."

"What if he doesn't show up today?"

Naomi sat next to him at the table, shifted Sarah into the crook of her arm, and covered his hands with her free one. "Then we do exactly what we've been doing. We leave Jake Hertzler in God's hands."

When Bethany arrived at the Sisters' House for work on Friday morning, she found the sisters sitting around the dining room table, like they often were, having tea.

"Come in," Sylvia said. "We're all kerfuffled."

"I never liked him," Ella said.

"Who?" Bethany asked, but no one was listening.

"Now, we don't know what the problem was," Lena said.

"Maybe there wasn't a problem," Ada said. "Maybe he finished his work and had to leave."

"Without a goodbye? Without a word to us?" Fannie said, clearly annoyed. "Without a single thank-you for all those weeks of room and board?"

"I never liked him," Ella repeated.

Bethany picked up a pile of newspapers. "Who are you talking about?"

Fannie sighed. "Our fourteenth cousin twice removed. He left this morning."

"Doesn't he go out to do research each day?"

"Not that kind of left. Left, left. He's gone." Ada snapped her fingers. "Just like that."

Bethany stopped and turned. "Why?"

"We don't know. He didn't say a word. Ella heard him packing up before dawn. She went to see what the racket was all about and he just brushed past her, without a word."

Ella nodded. "I never did like him."

"That doesn't make sense," Bethany said. "Are you sure he's really left? Maybe he just had someone he had to see."

"Go see for yourself."

Bethany went up to the second floor. The door to the guest room was wide open. She walked inside and caught a whiff of a familiar scent: Old Spice shaving cream. Unlike the one other time she had been in it, when it was a pigsty, the room was now empty. No garbage in the wastebasket, no clothes on the floor. No sign that anyone had been there. Only the bed was unmade and disheveled. She looked in the closet. Empty. She pulled open the dresser drawers. Empty. She noticed a silver wrapper on the floor and bent down to get it, sniffed it to see how fresh it was: it was unmistakably peppermint gum. Her mind started to race. She could feel her heart start to thump. She spotted something under the bedcovers. She shook out the sheets and a newspaper fell to the ground. She reached down, unfolded the newspaper—the *Stoney Ridge Times*—and felt a shiver run down her spine.

On the front page was the story about the York Savings & Loan, drilling into unclaimed safety deposit boxes and allowing the state to seize the contents. Her hands started to shake as awareness dawned on her. Fighting to control the tremors that shuddered through her, she made her way out of the room on shaky legs, then dropped on the top of the stairs and sat down, holding her head in her hands. Thinking of that man in the same house with those five dear, defenseless sisters, for weeks now, made her feel as if she might throw up.

Jake Hertzler *was* the fourteenth cousin twice removed.

20

Mim took the broom from her mother and began pushing the dirt toward the corner of the porch.

"Are you feeling all right, Mim?"

Mim leaned on the broom with her cheek. Tears were in her eyes. "Mom, I've done something wrong." The terrible sadness she felt nearly choked off her words.

Her mother took the broom from her and propped it against the wall. "Let's sit down."

They sat on the porch swing and, very simply, Mim began to tell the story about Mrs. Miracle. At no stage did her mother's face look anything except sympathetic. It registered no shock, no disbelief. She seemed to take it all in and to realize the enormity without resorting to panic.

Cold shot through Mim's insides. She put her fingertips against her mouth. "You knew, didn't you?"

Her mother nodded. "Well, I've suspected for a while."

"But . . . how?" She had been so careful, so surreptitious.

"It wasn't hard to figure it out."

"Why didn't you say something?"

"I thought it would fizzle out, just like the letters to the inn fizzled after the bishop had you take down the '*Miracula fieri hic*' phrase on the Inn at Eagle Hill sign. I didn't realize the column was having such an impact until just recently. I've been hearing a lot of murmuring about the advice Mrs. Miracle gave out. Good advice." She smiled at Mim. "To be perfectly honest, I could see that you were gaining confidence in yourself and so I let it be. I put that above the rightness or wrongness of the column. I made a mistake, I think."

Mim had never known an occasion when her mother had been wrong or at a loss for a word. Her father, now, he was different, he had always been scratching his head and saying he hadn't a clue about such things. But Mim felt her mother was born knowing all the answers. "Do I have to tell the bishop?"

Her mother gave that some thought. "Is the column truly out of your hands?"

"I don't have any idea what Brooke Snyder plans to do." She bit her lip. "Should I talk to her?"

Her mother gazed down at the guest flat. "She packed up and left this morning. She said she had gotten what she came for and it was time to leave."

"*What?*" Mim asked, shocked. She had avoided Brooke Snyder all week, unsure of how to handle the betrayal, and now it was too late. Mrs. Miracle was truly gone. For her, anyway.

"Mim, if you are asked about the column by the bishop or the deacon, then you must tell the truth."

"I never actually lied about it. Not to you or anyone else."

Her mother's smile faded. "Mim, there are lies you tell with your lips and lies you don't need your lips for. Once people start telling lies, then they become like spiders who weave their web about themselves. They become stuck—caught by the lies all about them. And then they can't get out of the web, no matter how hard they try." Her mother shook her head in regret over these mendacious unfortunates, and then, as an afterthought, added, "That is a fact, Mim. A well-known fact."

Brooke Snyder hated dogs. She would leap in terror when any dog gave a perfectly normal greeting. She was sorry to leave Eagle Hill today but wouldn't miss that big yellow dog that jumped up on her whenever he saw her. Sorry, but ready to go. This time at the inn had been just what she needed. She felt refreshed, reinvigorated, a teensy bit guilty about making off with the Mrs. Miracle brand, but she assured herself she had done Mim Schrock a favor. A syndicated newspaper column would get too big for a naive Amish girl. It was all for the best.

Brooke had come to Eagle Hill to nurse her wounds and find a new life direction. And she was leaving with a new career as a syndicated newspaper columnist—amazing!—and a boyfriend! Jon Hoeffner might not actually be her boyfriend yet, but things between them were moving in that direction. She had never been happier.

Brooke did have a few misgivings about helping Jon with this safety deposit box signature, but each time she voiced them, he reassured her and she felt better. He was very reassuring, very persuasive. This afternoon, she was to meet him at the York County Savings & Loan so he could get the title. "The fellow who wants to buy my car lives in York County. This way, I'll be able to get the car right to him."

"But how will you get back to Stoney Ridge? Do you need me to drive you back?"

"No. I'm actually leaving Stoney Ridge. I've finished the work I came to do. My cousin said she could drive me. It's all set."

She looked at him blankly. "But where will you be? I mean . . . will I see you again?"

Jon slipped his arms around her waist. "Of course. Absolutely. Just try and keep me away." He kissed her then, a kiss that left her breathless. He made her feel so special.

That was the moment when she decided to leave Eagle Hill. There was no reason to be in Stoney Ridge if Jon wasn't there. And she had taken pains to avoid Mim Schrock this week, though she sensed that Mim was avoiding her too. That cranky grandmother was bringing down the breakfast tray each morning.

When she pulled into the bank's parking lot, she waited in her car for Jon to arrive, feeling another spike of concern. Where was he? It dawned on her that she didn't know what kind of car he drove. Not for the first time, she realized how little she knew about him. He fascinated her—she was determined to discover more. She glanced at her cell phone to check the time, then looked up to see Jon getting out of a car that had pulled up in front of the bank. A woman—his cousin?—would be dropping him off.

Brooke grabbed her purse, and as she got out of her car and walked toward him, she heard the woman shrieking, "You said half. HALF! Don't think I don't know what kind of trick you're capable of pulling."

Jon leaned down to say something through the passenger window. The car peeled away and squealed to a stop in a space across the parking lot. Brooke slowed, hesitating, confused. But Jon didn't seem at all upset. As soon as he saw her, his face broke into that smile that made her knees turn into Jell-O.

"Brooke! There you are." He reached his hands out to her, smiling that charming smile. "You look gorgeous, absolutely gorgeous."

Brooke relaxed. The woman in the car was forgotten.

He took her elbow and steered her into the bank. "Thanks again for helping me with this little problem. Shouldn't take more than a few minutes." He sounded as pleased and grateful as if she had offered to walk his dog while he was at work.

That tiny hitch in Brooke's conscience silenced again. This would only take a moment, he had said. Jon went over to the teller and explained that they needed to open a safety deposit box. He gave the teller his driver's license and signed in the book.

While the teller was distracted with another customer, he slipped a Social Security card into Brooke's hand. "Here you are. Just sign on that line under my name and you're good to go."

Brooke glanced at the Social Security card to study the signature while the teller was away. Rose Schrock. Rose Schrock? She glanced up at Jon. "The innkeeper at Eagle Hill? *She's* your sister?"

"Yes."

"But she doesn't seem like the kind of person who wouldn't help you get the title for your car."

Jon glanced at the teller, who was now occupied on the phone. "Trust me."

Something wasn't adding up to Brooke. She looked into his eyes. "Jon, what's going on here? What's really going on? Who was that out in the car—that woman who said she wanted half? Half of what?"

"I don't know what you're talking about." His relaxed façade stripped away as he stabbed the sign-in book with his finger. "Just sign."

She looked at the signature book and saw Jon had signed his name as Jake Hertzler. Who in the world was Jake Hertzler? She felt a bead of perspiration drip down her spine. "And if I don't?" Her words trailed off.

Jon leaned forward to whisper in her ear as his hand latched onto her forearm. "Then I will have to make a discreet call to the FBI to let them know that Brooke Snyder reproduced a Jean-Baptiste-Camille Corot to be sold as an original on the market." His fingers bit into her arm. "That she admitted as much and I have her confession recorded on my iPhone." He gave her his most charming smile. "There's an app for everything."

She was so stunned, she didn't move a muscle.

He had lied to her! There *was* no title for a car. There was *no* Amish sister. This man was doing something deceitful—something to hurt Eagle Hill innkeeper Rose Schrock. A veil dropped suddenly and she saw the true Jon Hoeffner. She could sense the vindictiveness in those cold, pale eyes, something worse than heartlessness. It was a malevolence with which she simply did not know how to deal.

Jon motioned to her that the teller was approaching and he put a pen in her hands. "Sign."

She could sense his vengefulness growing, and her hand shook as she picked up the pen to write out Rose Schrock's name. The teller glanced at their IDs, compared their signatures, and buzzed them into the vault.

Jon smiled benignly at the teller and turned to Brooke. "Rose, there's no need for you to go in with me. You can leave." He flicked his fingers at her. "Go." He walked into the vault, whistling.

What had she done? What had she just done!? Brooke stared after Jon, realizing only now how weak-kneed she was. She sank onto a bench in the bank, hugging her shaky stomach. *Well, he backed you into a corner, so what are you going to do? Sit quaking like a pup with palsy or get out of here?* She walked, practically ran, to the door and exited the bank, gasping in the fresh air. It was over. *Thank God!*

Brooke searched the parking lot for the car where the woman who had shrieked at Jon was waiting. It was gone.

Then she felt a hand on her elbow and looked into the face of a very serious man in a dark suit. "Ma'am, you'll need to come with me." He took her purse and led her around the side of the bank to a waiting police car. Her eyes were wide in horror and her panic skyrocketed.

"He tricked me! He's still in there. Go after him! Jon. Jake. Whatever his name is. *He's* the one you want. Not me! I'm innocent. I don't even know what he's up to. I thought I was just doing him a small favor."

"Relax, ma'am. We're just waiting for him to finish emptying the box."

Not a moment later, Jon strolled out of the bank, calm as could be, unaware that two undercover police officers were closing in on him. When he spotted them, he dropped his messenger bag and tried to run, but they cornered him against the wall and handcuffed him. "Jake Hertzler," she heard the man in the dark suit say. "I'm with the Securities Exchange

Commission. You're under arrest. These officers will read you your rights."

Jon—or Jake? or *whoever* he was—looked angry and defeated as he was led to another police car under the efficient armlock of an officer. Jon was a sham, she thought angrily, he was a fraud. His con man's eyes were as innocent as an altar boy's. How could she have been so naive? So stupid?!

Brooke felt as if she had stepped outside herself and was watching this whole terrible scene without being a part of it. She heard the police officer read Miranda rights to Jon/Jake. He repeated them to her as he told her to put her hands behind her back and slipped handcuffs around her wrists. "You have the right to remain silent . . ." Everything had turned out in the worst possible way. A terrible emptiness took hold of her.

What have I done? she thought. *What have I just gotten myself into?*

21

Allen Turner called Rose and said he was on his way to Eagle Hill, to expect him around half past eight. He asked if she could gather the entire family together to hear some important news about Jake Hertzler. "I'll pick up Geena and bring her along, if that's all right with you."

Rose assured him that would be fine.

She sent Sammy to bed early, but Luke was invited to be part of the meeting and it pleased him to be singled out. Naomi and Tobe, Bethany, Mim, Rose, Vera, and Luke all sat at the kitchen table, waiting for Allen Turner to arrive.

The clock was ticking and there was a little whir between each tick. Rose had never noticed that before. The clock ticked on with its new whir, and none of them said anything at all.

Allen Turner arrived at 8:30 on the dot with Geena by his side. He sat down in the chair at the kitchen table where he had first interrogated Tobe, months ago. Rose wasn't sure what had happened today at the bank, but she had a feeling that this night, finally, there would be closure. A revealing. *The* revealing.

"We seized the contents of the safety deposit box," Allen Turner said. "There was over one hundred thousand dollars in cash. Jake Hertzler admitted he had been skimming off the top of Schrock Investments during the two years he worked there. Not enough to be noticed, just enough to feather a nest." Allen let out a sigh. "That money will be divided up and returned to investors as part of their claims."

"I'm amazed he confessed to all that," Rose said.

"There's a reason," Tobe said, eyes fixed on Allen Turner. "He wanted to deflect other charges."

"Yes, Tobe's right," Allen said, nodding. "What I wanted to tell you in person was that Jake Hertzler plea-bargained with the state to reduce the charge of homicide to accidental manslaughter."

"Homicide?" Rose was confused. "I don't understand."

"According to Jake's confession, your husband found him fishing at the lake early one morning. Your husband had figured out the whole picture of what Jake had been doing to Schrock Investments—skimming money from the company, keeping a set of cooked books, faking bank statements. Dean Schrock went to confront him.

"They argued, pushed each other, and Dean Schrock slipped off the dock and fell into the lake. Jake said he thought he would come back to the surface, but he didn't."

Tobe leaned forward and jammed a finger on the tabletop. "But what if Jake was lying? What if he pushed Dad in the water? He couldn't swim well. Jake knew that!"

Allen Turner remained utterly calm. "There's a large rock near the dock—a diver confirmed as much this afternoon. Because there was no autopsy, we'll never be able to determine the exact cause of death."

"So Jake just left him?" Bethany said, eyes glistening with tears. "He just left?"

"He pulled him out of the water and onto the dock."

"But," Bethany said, her voice breaking, "how do you know that? How do you know he didn't push Dad in and leave? Are you just taking his word for it? Because he's a liar!"

Allen fixed his gaze on Tobe. "Because there was an eyewitness. Wasn't there, Tobe?"

The entire family snapped their heads in Tobe's direction, staring at him with wide eyes and dropped jaws.

"Tobe, were you there?" Horror sent Rose's heart clubbing at the thought of him watching his father drown.

Tobe gave a solemn nod. "I'm the one who found Dad on the dock. I ran to a cottage and asked them to call 911. I stayed with Dad, I tried to do CPR on him, but he never responded." He rubbed a hand through his hair.

"You did what you could," Rose said softly. She simply could not speak anymore, didn't know how he could. She put her hand on his shoulder.

"And I knew it was hopeless," Tobe continued. "Finally, I ran down the street and called 911 at a phone outside of a convenience store. I waited at the lake until I heard the sirens. But then I slipped away."

"Why were you there that morning? Did Dad take you with him to talk to Jake?"

"I knew about the cooked books Jake had given to the SEC—knew he was trying to pin those on me—and I wanted to find the real books." He swallowed and cleared his throat. "I had a hunch they were in his car trunk and knew Jake liked to fish on summer mornings. I parked down the road from the lake, out of sight, planning to get into his car and get out with the ledgers and key. I didn't realize Dad was with him until I heard them arguing, loudly—you know how sound travels early in the morning on a quiet lake—so I went as close as I could to them without being seen.

"I heard Dad demand the real ledgers—the accurate books—from Jake. He wanted the safety deposit key. Jake denied any wrongdoing and blamed me for the missing money. While they were arguing, I went through Jake's car. I found the ledgers in the trunk and the safety deposit key in the cup holder. I grabbed them and went back to my car. I was going to show them to Dad later . . . but . . . ," he tried to finish but his voice was choked, "there was . . ." He had to clear his throat and start again. "There was no later."

Naomi reached over and put her hand on his forearm, giving him the strength he needed to finish. "During Dad's funeral, I came back to Eagle Hill, hid the ledgers in the basement, kept the key with me, and took off. I knew it wouldn't take Jake long to figure out I'd taken the ledgers and the key. I wanted to try to get back to Eagle Hill but not with Jake on my trail. One day, I realized he was following me. I couldn't think of where else to go, so I ended up at my mother's nursing home. I panicked . . . and hid the safety deposit key in her room."

Bethany clapped her cheeks with her hands. "Tobe, did it ever occur to you that hiding something in the room of a schizophrenic woman who believed people were after her might make her even more paranoid?"

He bit his lip. "I didn't think she had noticed I was hiding something."

Rose felt something in herself uncoil. "Then . . . Dean didn't take his own life."

"No, Mrs. Schrock," Allen Turner said. "He didn't. You can rest assured about that."

"He didn't take his own life. Thank God," Rose whispered. "Thank God." Her vision blurred beneath a wash of unexpected tears and her chest was suddenly choked with feelings—feelings of love and relief and sorrow for Dean. A sob broke from her throat and she covered her face with her hands to gain control. She breathed deeply, wiped tears away from her face, and looked around the table at those she loved so much: Tobe, Bethany, Mim, Luke, resting on Vera. "Did you hear?"

Vera nodded, her eyes shiny with tears. She reached out and grabbed Rose's hands. "I heard. I always knew, deep down." She squeezed her eyes shut. "Was em aagebore is verliert mer net." *What is bred in the bone is never lost.*

"How long?" Tobe whispered in a gruff voice. "How long will Jake be in jail?"

"A long, long time," Allen Turner said. "Brooke Snyder, by the way, was also arrested."

Vera jerked her head up. "The tall lady in the guest flat? How is she involved?"

"She forged a signature at the bank—yours, in fact, Rose." Out of his pocket, Allen Turner pulled Rose's Social Security card and handed it to her. "This Paisley woman was in on it too. She lifted things from Eagle Hill and got them to Jake."

"What's going to happen to Brooke Snyder?" Mim said quietly.

"She said she's willing to testify against Jake, so she'll probably just get her hands slapped. My guess is she'll be put on probation, but her career in art is over."

Naomi cleared her throat. "What about Paisley? Are you going to find her?"

Allen Turner shook his head. "No. We don't need her. She was just a minor player. An opportunist."

"Do you think she'll turn up again?"

He shrugged. "I can't imagine why."

Naomi and Tobe exchanged a glance, then their eyes traveled to the baby, sound asleep in the Moses basket in the corner of the room.

"If you don't have any more questions, that's all I wanted to tell you," Allen Turner said. "It's over. It's finally over."

"There's one more thing," Rose said. "Would you tell Jake something for us? Tell him we forgive him."

The room went still. Even baby Sarah, who had been starting to stir and make noises, grew quiet.

Allen Turner's face went blank. "*What?* You want me to tell him you forgive him? After all that?"

Rose nodded.

"Charges have been filed. That's not going to change." Allen pressed his thumbs against his forehead. "I spent twenty months tracking this guy down. It's not going to stop the due process of the law just because you forgive him."

"I realize that. I'm not asking for him to be released from the consequences of his actions. But as for our family, we are not harboring any ill will toward him." She turned to Tobe, but he wouldn't lift his head to look at her.

Allen Turner tilted his head. "Did you decide that right now? How can you forget what he did? How can you forgive, just like that?" He snapped his fingers to prove his point.

"It wasn't just like that," Rose said. "I decided to forgive

Jake Hertzler a very long time ago. Forgiving and forgetting are two completely different things."

"I wish I felt the same way." Allen Turner glanced at Geena, seated next to him. His arms were crossed tightly over his chest.

"Go ahead and tell them, Allen," Geena said gently. "They should know."

Allen shifted uneasily in his chair. "Four years ago, my wife was a professor of accounting at a local college. Jake Hertzler was her student, the most intelligent and capable student she had ever had. Gifted, she called him. Brilliant." He had to stop and compose himself before going on. His voice got even quieter. "And he was the one who broke up my marriage."

Hours later, after Naomi, Geena, and Allen had left and the family had gone to bed, Rose took a hot bath, then read for a while in bed, hoping to fall asleep. An hour passed, then another. Still restless, she went downstairs. So much to sift through! Her mind was reeling with the day's revelations. She lit a kerosene lamp in the living room and sat down to mend a tear in a shirt of Tobe's, grateful for small, simple acts that were like balm to her soul.

Minutes later, she heard a noise and looked up to see Tobe leaning against the doorjamb, Sarah tucked in his arms with a bottle in her mouth. "Can't sleep?"

"No. I could take Sarah if you want to get to bed." No sense in both of them losing sleep.

But he didn't make any move to pass Sarah to him. "Rose, did you mean it when you said you forgave Jake Hertzler?"

"I meant it. I wanted Jake to know, though I doubt he cares. And it certainly doesn't mean it's easy to forget all he did." She knotted the thread and cut it off with her teeth. "I could tell you weren't happy with me for asking Allen Turner to let Jake know we forgive him."

Tobe crossed the room to sit in a chair, unfolded his long legs, and held Sarah up against his shoulder, the way she liked best. "I know you shouldn't pray for something bad to happen to another human, but I have prayed that Jake Hertzler would get a dose of his own medicine."

"Don't be trying to give back pain for pain," Rose said. "You can't get even measures in business like that."

"Don't you see?" He stared down at his hands. "I'm glad he'll be in prison for a long time. I want that for him. I want even worse for him. I even feel a little cheated that I wasn't the one who caught him. I tried. I tried so hard, but he was always two steps ahead of me."

"But you didn't cause it. The evil within Jake caused it all. He can't hurt anyone else. That's what you need to keep in your mind. He can't hurt anyone else." She put the shirt in the basket. "Tobe, you have a new life to live. A wife, a baby to care for. Spending another minute dwelling on the past would be like letting Jake continue to keep hurting you. It's over, Tobe. It's all over. Allen Turner said those very words."

They sat there quietly for a long time, the only sound coming from the hiss of the lamp. Finally, he rose and crossed the room to Rose's chair. He picked up the shirt she had repaired and examined her tiny stitches. "You're good at mending things. Shirts. Families too." He set down the shirt. "I don't say it enough, Rose, but thank you." He went upstairs with the baby asleep, her head tucked under his chin, and soon Rose turned out the light and went to bed.

While she was settling into bed, thoughts ran around and around in her head. All the same, she had a sweet, full feeling inside that warmed her, and soon she too slept, and all was silent in the farmhouse at Eagle Hill.

22

Brooke Snyder couldn't even look her aunt Lois in the eye when she arrived at the jail to bail her out. She sat in her aunt's car and stared out the window, sullen, sulky, guilty. Aunt Lois didn't say a word, an anomaly that grew increasingly distressing to Brooke.

"There are two sides to every story," Brooke finally said.

Aunt Lois sighed. "Yes, we know. His and hers. But then there's a third side; the truth. And who is to discover it?" She glanced at her. "Why did you do it?" Her eyes were hard and her voice was cold. "How could you do something so . . . deceitful? So obviously illegal?"

"I didn't mean to do anything wrong."

Her aunt gave her a look of disdain. "Just like you didn't mean to sell a forged painting as an original."

"But I didn't! I just painted a picture. And yesterday, I just signed a signature. I'm the victim here!"

"Brooke Snyder—you are many things, but you are *not* a victim."

Her aunt turned off the freeway and onto the Philadelphia Pike toward Amish country.

Brooke felt a hitch of alarm. "Where are you going?"

"Look in the backseat."

Brooke turned around to see her oil paints, brushes, canvas, and easel. "Where did you get those?"

"From your apartment." Aunt Lois turned off the Pike and onto a back road that led to the rolling hills of Amish farms. "It's time you start seeing yourself through the eyes of God. He didn't give you the gifts you have for copies and forgeries."

Brooke sighed. "I am useless."

"Pish. You're far from useless. You must use the tools God gave you. Find your tools and put them to use. Good use." She pulled the car to the side of the road. "Pick a spot. Any place. You choose your subject. It's high time you become an original."

Brooke looked at her aunt, with her spiky red hair and determined chin, then at her easel and paints, which she hadn't touched since she had reproduced the Corot, then out at the soft, gentle hills, dotted with cows. "Could you head toward Stoney Ridge? There's someone I need to see first."

For the first time all morning, her aunt cracked a smile.

Mim had finished putting fresh sheets on the beds in the guest flat. Two women were coming this afternoon, all the way from Georgia. She thought that might be the farthest distance a guest had traveled to stay at the Inn at Eagle Hill.

She heard a door open and walked into the living room, a pillow tucked under her chin as she struggled to get the case onto it. There, at the door, was Brooke Snyder, the woman who had taken away her newspaper column, merely because she was an ambitious woman.

Mim put the pillow on the small kitchen table. "Is there something you forgot? Or something else you want to take?" She was not rude, but she was very, very cool.

Brooke took a step inside. "I owe you an apology. I stole something from you."

"Yes, you did . . ." Mim stopped and shook her head. No. She didn't, she thought. And once thought, it had to be said. "You didn't steal it. I'm giving it to you." She picked up the pillow to finish stuffing it in the case. "I hope Mrs. Miracle will help you find what you're looking for, just like she did for me."

She turned and went back to the bedroom to fluff the pillow and set it on the bed, ready for the new guests. When she returned to the living room, Brooke Snyder was gone.

The potatoes spattered as they hit the melted butter in the pan and Rose hardly noticed. Her mind was on those new guests who had arrived at the inn this afternoon, stayed ten minutes, and promptly departed. Such an odd pair! They were two cousins, from Georgia, who were going to research their family ancestry.

"Do you have Amish relatives?" Rose asked them.

"No," the taller one said. "Quakers."

Rose looked at them, tilting her head. "You realize, of course, that Quakers came from England, started by George Fox. The Amish came from Europe. Their history is completely separate."

The cousins looked at each other, astounded by that information. "But the Quakers dress like you do."

Rose looked down at her plum-colored dress and black

apron. "Not really." Her hand went to her head. "I suppose they do wear bonnets. The Quakers and the Amish share some beliefs, like pacifism, but very little else."

The two cousins were astounded. "Where should we go to learn about the Quakers? Our great-great-great-grandfather was a whaling captain. Ebenezer Folger was his name."

"Then . . . Nantucket Island, I suppose."

And so the two lady cousins left. The guest flat was, once again, empty.

Tomorrow, Rose would need to go talk to the deacon about the pile of unpaid bills that were stacking up on her desk. More bills than money.

She had hoped that she might have that pigpen plowed and extra vegetables already planted to sell at a roadside stand this summer, but David Stoltzfus hadn't gotten back to it after he was interrupted on the day the nearly-falling-down barn had fallen down, and she didn't feel comfortable asking him after their awkward conversation earlier today.

Rose and David happened to be picking up their mail from the mailbox at the same time and he walked across the road. She could tell at once that he had something on his mind to say to her.

"Jesse is going to go stay with my sister, Peter's mother, and her husband for the summer. They need a little extra help on the farm and Jesse, well, he's been . . . missing his mother quite a lot. More than I realized. Seems he needs more than I can give him right now. It's hard, you know . . ." David took his hat off, turning it in his hands. "Rose, we don't know each other well, but I can see that you love God and you love children. It seems like we are both in a similar situation, needing a spouse, needing a parent for our children."

She looked at him, puzzled.

"The problem is, I don't quite know . . . where I stand."

She still couldn't understand what he was trying to say.

"I'm aware, you see, that you are very friendly with Galen King . . . but I don't know how . . ."

Now she had a sense of where he was going.

"You see, I don't want to be foolish and hope that you might be interested in me, if there's something . . . so I hoped you might tell me what you think. I've grown very fond of you, Anna, and I hoped you might be growing fond of me too."

"I am." And she was. But her name wasn't Anna.

"Would you consider me?" He looked so hopeful and eager, and almost dreading her reply.

"David," she said gently, "how long ago did your wife pass?"

"It'll be a year on July 9th."

"You must have loved her very much."

"Yes. Yes, I did." He looked at his hat in his hands.

"Do you have any idea how many times you have called me Anna?"

He looked at her, horrified. "I'm so sorry. I . . . didn't realize."

"Don't be. You're still grieving for her. You need time." She looked across Eagle Hill's front yard to see Galen working a new horse in the round training pen near his barn. She was flooded with a vague sense of loss. "Yes," she said softly, "there is something between Galen and me."

David nodded silently, fingering the brim of his hat as if anxious to put it back on. His glance lifted. "Thank you, Rose, for not making me feel like a fool. You're a very special woman." He turned and walked back up the driveway.

That night, Rose tossed and turned, thinking over that

conversation with David. She dangled her hand over the edge of the bed to touch the dog's head and stared out the windows at the stars. Suddenly there was a streak across the sky in a flash of light. Seeing a shooting star always made her feel honored, as if God had staged a show just for her. "O the mighty works of the heavens," she whispered. Galen always said that whenever they were outside at night.

Uninvited thoughts of Galen came to Rose at the oddest moments. She'd be pinning up her long hair and would remember him in his barn, running his fingers through a horse's mane to draw out the tangles. She'd be sitting in church, watching the women take turns holding baby Sarah, and she'd remember the tender way he'd held the baby on the porch swing. She'd fill her coffee cup in the morning and remember the way he'd worked so patiently with Luke and Sammy despite how exasperating those two could be.

She sorely missed him.

It had become a schoolhouse tradition, started years ago by Jimmy Fisher. On the last day of school, before the families arrived for the end-of-year program, the eighth graders carved their names in the oak tree that sheltered the schoolhouse with its canopy. The younger students, who would have to return to school after the summer, looked on enviously. The boys had brought pocketknives and were busy digging into the wood of the old tree.

Jesse Stoltzfus had been planning for weeks where he would put his name. Mim wished she could enjoy this moment the way the eighth grade boys did. They acted as if they were being set free from jail. She wasn't sure what it would feel like to not go to school, ever again. She borrowed Luke's knife and scratched out "M. S. was here." She felt there was more to say, but she didn't know what it was.

Danny told the class that he'd accepted the school board's offer to teach another term, so he was no longer the permanent substitute teacher. Instead, he was the permanent teacher. But she wouldn't be there next year. And Jesse was being sent off for the summer. Exiled, he told her, for being a bad influence on younger boys. He said it with that devilish grin of his, not looking at all sorry for his misdeeds, and she thought whoever decided to banish him—probably the deacon—was pretty smart. She wouldn't miss Jesse Stoltzfus and his sticky-up hair and torrent of nonsense. Not one bit. All of Stoney Ridge could breathe a sigh of relief that he would be gone this summer.

She wondered if he'd be back in August or September.

After the barbecue lunch had been eaten, the softball game between the eighth graders and the sixth and seventh graders started off. Jesse didn't want Mim to pitch to the sixth graders because they were too athletic, but he did let her pitch to the seventh graders because they were unusually uncoordinated. Then a boy tripped over his feet on the way to bat and twisted his ankle, so Danny stepped in to take his place at bat.

That was unfortunate, and Jesse Stoltzfus was beside himself at the unfairness of it all, but Mim was ready. She thought of all the crummy B- grades Danny Riehl had given her on her excellent essays this year, just to be mean and spiteful, and how often he treated her like she was just another student. She tried to remember the exact details of how to release the knuckleball. She wound her arm, flicked her wrist, released. The ball flew slow and Danny was ready for it—except it dropped unexpectedly at the last instant, and his bat met nothing but air.

Everyone looked at Mim, stunned. Why, she had thrown a strike at Danny Riehl! She would always be known as the girl who threw a knuckleball! She tried, without success, not to grin with delight.

An hour or so later, everyone packed up to head home. Luke and Sammy had started down the road when Mim remembered she had left her sweater in the schoolhouse and hurried back to get it. As she pulled open the door, she realized, with a heavy heart, this was the last time she would walk into the school.

Starting on Monday, she was going to take over Bethany's two-days-a-week job at the Sisters' House—organizing the rooms—because the deacon kept urging the sisters to prepare to host church one day. She would also be Ella's companion when the sisters had to leave the house on their many errands. Ella had declined enough that the sisters needed someone to shadow her. What the old sisters didn't know was, on Ella's good days, she was dictating the story of her life to Mim. Ella might not remember what she had for breakfast that day, but she did recall every detail of her childhood in Stoney Ridge, nearly a century ago.

It was all Bethany's handiwork—all except the dictation of Ella's life part. That was Mim's brainchild. But the job switch—Bethany said she was tired of trying to keep those sisters organized and she wanted to work someplace where she'd meet more people. She applied for an opening at the Bent N' Dent, available because Jesse wouldn't be working there this summer. Privately—something Mim would never dare voice aloud—she wondered if her sister might have an interest in working at the Bent N' Dent because Peter Stoltzfus worked there. For weeks now, Bethany had been very quick to offer to go on errands to the grocery store, when once she would have avoided it.

Danny was wiping down the chalkboard and turned when he heard the door open. The schoolhouse was empty. She yanked her sweater off the wall hook and started toward the door.

"Mim?"

She stopped and turned toward him. "Miriam. I want everyone to call me Miriam now."

He walked down the aisle of the schoolhouse toward her. "You threw quite a pitch, Miriam. A perfect knuckleball."

"But not the next pitch. You hit a double."

He took a step toward her. "Miriam, the reason I gave you B's instead of A's on your English essays was because I believe you could have done better."

She lowered her glance.

"Anyone who could write such fine prose, posing as Mrs. Miracle, should be writing dynamic essays."

Her jaw dropped open. He *knew* about *Mrs. Miracle*? Did everybody know? Did the whole town? "Jesse told you."

"Jesse? No. It seemed, well, sort of obvious. I guess I recognized your choice of words." His eyes were troubled as he peered at her. "Mim . . . Miriam . . . is there something between you and Jesse Stoltzfus?"

"How do you mean?"

"I don't know." Two red streaks started to crawl up his cheeks. "What about it?"

"What about what?"

"Do you have something going on with Jesse?"

She looked down at her feet. "You took Katrina Stoltzfus home in your buggy."

"She asked me to. She wasn't feeling well and wanted to go home. I was leaving early because . . . well, because it was a clear night and at nine, Venus would be low in the west and Jupiter would be about halfway down to the west and Mars could be seen coming up in the east."

Oh. "You act as if you don't even see me. All year, that's how you've acted."

"I've always seen you." His voice went from tenor to soprano in one crack and, visibly nervous, he poked his glasses up on the bridge of his nose. "I wrote your name on the tree."

Her chin jerked up. "You what?"

"I wrote DR + MS, very low down, near a root. I wrote it last year."

"You never did!" She could feel her cheeks grow blotchy pink. Soon, she knew, they would deepen to an all-over heliotrope.

"Let's go and see it," he said. "As proof."

And there it was, just as he had said.

Standing at the base of the tree, Mim and Danny looked at each other and looked away. A lot had been admitted.

Later that night, Mim tossed and turned as she lay in bed. Her sheets felt sticky. She tossed over, once, then twice, flipped her pillow to the cool side and shut her eyes. But she couldn't sleep. And she couldn't stop thinking of Jesse Stoltzfus.

In the middle of the night, Bethany woke to the sound of pebbles hitting her window. Groggily, she pulled herself out of bed and looked down at the yard. Jimmy Fisher was there, sending beams from a flashlight up to her bedroom.

She changed from her nightgown into a dress, wishing she could ignore him and crawl back into bed. "I'm just not sure if I'm in love with Jimmy Fisher anymore," she said aloud, pinning her dress together. Her voice echoed in her head. It was true. She might not love Jimmy. She might, but she might not. It had happened without her knowing, for the love she carried around for him had gone and she hadn't noticed it disappearing. It was only now that she became aware that it was missing. In fact, she hadn't thought about Jimmy for two full days.

He greeted her with arms stretched out to engulf her, his eyes eager and bright.

Why was he here, in the middle of the night? Bethany wanted to know. "You'd better have a good reason."

"Because I missed you," he said simply. "I wanted to see you again." He slipped his arms around her. "I don't want you to feel I'm rushing you or demanding you give me an answer, but I was hoping by now you would be ready to say yes."

Her heart didn't race anymore, she didn't try to find the right phrase, the best approach. She wasn't eyeing him nervously in case his expression might change. She pressed him away by the arms. "No, Jimmy. I don't have an answer for you. But if you insist on one now, I'd have to say no."

His face went blank. "But . . . but . . . but why? You've been dropping hints to get married for months now. You've talked of nothing else."

She stepped back. "I know, but I think I got tired of waiting and I slipped out of love with you."

A pair of creases appeared between his eyebrows. "It's that Peter Stoltzfus character, isn't it? He's been buzzing around you like a fly around honey."

"What? My feelings for you have nothing to do with Peter Stoltzfus."

He reached out to take her hand and laid it over his palm and ran his other hand over it, as if smoothing a curled page. "Is it possible that you might in time love me again?" He sounded hesitant, unsure. His face was an open book; he looked miserable and hopeful all at once.

Her resolve melted at the desperate look in his eyes. "I suppose anything is possible." Then she turned quickly away from him, feeling unexpectedly sad. She slipped back into the house and was startled to find Rose in the rocking chair, feeding a bottle to Sarah.

"A starlight tryst?" Rose asked with a smile.

"Not really. More like a starlight sayonara. I told Jimmy Fisher things were over between us."

Rose looked up in surprise. "And are they?"

"I think so. He doesn't seem to agree." She sighed. "It seems as if our timing is always off. When he's interested in me, I'm interested in someone else. When I'm finally interested in him, he's distracted with his horse. Now I'm not interested in him anymore and he seems to think he'll perish without me. I'm not sure we'll ever both be on the same page at the same time. I just . . . I want someone who loves me, unreservedly. I don't want to chase someone to the altar." She took off her prayer cap and held the pins in her hands. "Do you think God concerns himself with love?"

"Of course. Of course he does. Look at the love story of Isaac and Rebekah in the Old Testament."

"So . . . if it's meant to be, it will happen?" She let the sentence hang there.

"In God's timing. I'm confident of that." Rose tucked Sarah into the Moses basket and covered her with the pink quilt that Naomi had made for her.

Bethany wished she had those kinds of certainties.

"Don't give up on Jimmy Fisher quite yet. He's making great strides in maturity. Think of where he was a year ago, when his chief delight in life was to set firecrackers off in Amos Lapp's winter wheat to shoo the geese away."

Bethany shrugged. "I hope you're right." She turned to head up the stairs.

"Bethany . . . sometime . . . I'd like to go with you to visit your mother."

Bethany leaned against the doorjamb. "Are you sure, Rose? It's not an easy visit."

Rose nodded. "I'm sure. I'd like to meet the woman who gave life to you and Tobe. I'd like to thank her."

Bethany smiled at her stepmother, and Rose smiled back.

There was a pain in Jimmy Fisher's heart, although hearts were not supposed to hurt. Every day hearts went about their steady beat and no one gave them a second thought, until one day you felt a pain there. Standing next to Lodestar in the middle of the barn, brushing down his coat and mane like he did every afternoon, Jimmy pondered these deep thoughts.

His heart used to sing at the thought of seeing Bethany. She was his Number One. She was his darling. Now, his heart had sunk to his shoes. Peter Stoltzfus was aiming to take his place in Bethany's heart.

Jimmy felt weak, as if his legs didn't want to move. He had never felt weak like this in all his life. He unhooked Lodestar from the ties and led him to his stall. In just a few weeks, the horse was making great gains. His ribs didn't protrude as they had, his eyes were bright and lively, stubbles of hair were starting to grow in the bald spots on his rump. Best of all, he held his head high and pointed his ears forward.

The vet had told Jimmy there was no reason he couldn't be a stud. "You have to remember," Galen reminded Jimmy, "that you have no paperwork, no proof of pedigree, no evidence of Lodestar's lineage, no stud registration."

Jimmy, a born optimist, felt certain that Lodestar's future offspring would test his mettle. "We're back on track, Lodestar," he told the horse as he latched his stall in four places, just in case he did get the notion to escape.

He stopped. Against all possibilities, Lodestar had been found. Against another impossibility, Jimmy was soon to retire from the chicken business. And Bethany had said there was a possibility that she might fall in love with him again. Jimmy *loved* possibilities.

He was going to win Bethany back. Oh yes he was.

23

Rose was taking fresh towels down to the guest flat when she noticed Galen and Luke in the empty pigpen, holding the reins to a horse that was pulling a plow to turn the sod. She stopped and watched. Galen was patiently teaching Luke how to plow in a straight line. If the horse veered off, Galen showed Luke how to bring it back into alignment with the other row. Their backs were to her, they didn't see her standing there.

Tears stung her eyes. Despite how busy Galen was preparing his own farm for his sister's wedding, despite how she had hurt him, he hadn't changed. He still made time to help her.

She was struck by how deeply attached she felt to Galen. It was a different love than the heady, exciting feelings she'd had when she fell in love with Dean, and she would have thought younger love was the stronger force. But the feelings she had for Galen were like the deep roots of a sturdy willow tree, whose depth she was only beginning to sense.

She suddenly realized she wanted to grow old with him.

"Talk to him," Naomi said.

"What?" Rose startled in alarm. She hadn't realized that Naomi had come up behind her. Sarah was nestled in her arms.

"You're wondering whether you made a mistake with Galen. Talk to him. It can't do any harm. Talk to him, Rose."

She looked at Naomi, whose clear eyes seemed to see everything and know what was going on in every heart. "Do you always know what people are thinking?"

Naomi laughed. "No. I just try to be a good listener."

"Anyone can be a good listener," Rose said. "That's easy. It's hard to be a wise listener."

After the pigpen had been plowed under and Luke had shown her, proudly, the blisters on his hands that needed tending to, Rose put on a fresh apron and prayer cap and walked through the privet to find Galen. She found him in the barn. He had a gelding's right rear hoof up on his thigh and was scraping caked dirt out of it with a hoof pick. He straightened up as soon as he saw her.

For a moment, she could say nothing at all, only look at him. Her throat tightened, thick with the things she wanted to say to him.

"It's cold today, you'll catch a chill," he said, when he noticed that she was barefoot.

She shrugged, head down, trying to hide the tears that were streaming down her cheeks.

"Why, now, what's the matter?" he asked, concerned.

He put down the hoof pick and walked over to her. He cautiously put his arm around her, as if that might not still be proper—Rose not only accepted it, she moved closer.

"Is something wrong, Rose? Is Vera all right? The baby?"

"Everybody's fine. It's me."

His eyes were filled with worry. "What's the matter with you?"

"Nothing. Everything. I need to ask you something." She stepped back to face him and clasped his hands, tight. "Would you like to marry me?"

There was quiet—complete quiet. And on and on it went, not a word, not a sound. Rose waited, then went on undisturbed, her voice steady. "I'm in love with you, and I can't imagine life without you."

A slow smile, homey and unhurried and sweet, like syrup over hot flapjacks, spread across his face.

"Well, I can imagine it, actually," Rose said, "and it's awful."

That made her grin, and Galen's smile grew bigger, and then he opened his arms and she fell into them. It felt like home to be in his embrace, familiar and safe, but at the same time, exciting and new. They stood there for a long moment. Suddenly the silence was thick and heavy, and he pulled away but held on to her elbows. "Are you sure, Rose? No changing your mind this time? No postponements. We set a date and stick to it. Because I couldn't bear it if—"

She pressed her fingers against his mouth. She leaned into him, melted into the circling of his arms, and lifted her face, a shy invitation. His lips were so soft, so very soft on hers. No kiss had ever been like this. No kiss ever would be.

At Tobe's request, Mim waited by the mailbox every day to intercept the DNA results. She examined every envelope that arrived, but day after day, there was nothing.

"How long can it take to match up bits of tissue?" Tobe complained.

Mim had no idea about laboratories or DNA or bits of tissue, but she had promised to watch the mail for him.

And then, just a few days before Tobe and Naomi's wedding, the letter arrived. Mim had just been in the kitchen with Tobe, who was feeding a bottle of vile-smelling formula to Sarah, when she saw the mailman and ran to the mailbox. She ran back inside, waving the letter. "It's here, Tobe! The DNA results are here!"

In the kitchen, Naomi sat rocking Sarah. Mim froze. Tobe was nowhere in sight.

"The what?" Naomi asked.

Oh, boy. "Um, where is Tobe?"

"He went upstairs to change his clothes because Sarah spit up on his shirt." Naomi put Sarah in the Moses basket. "Did I hear you right, Mim? Did you say that envelope has DNA results?"

Mim didn't know what to say. Tobe walked into the kitchen and saw the envelope in her hand. He and Naomi exchanged a look, telling each other something, the way married people could do without talking, but she didn't know what it was.

Tobe turned to Mim. "Would you mind giving Naomi and me a moment alone?"

Mim put the envelope on the table and backed out of the room. "Sorry," she whispered to her brother as she passed by the doorjamb.

He gave her a gentle squeeze on her shoulder.

It was strange how perfectly normal a day could seem, and yet, Naomi thought, the most important secret of her and Tobe's life was resting in an envelope on the kitchen table. His hand hovered over it, too shaky to pick it up, which suited Naomi just fine. She had never felt so disappointed in anyone. "You weren't going to tell me that you had taken Sarah for a DNA test?"

"When I knew the results, I was going to tell you."

"What difference would the results make, Tobe?"

"It would make everything simpler."

"How so?"

"Sarah is someone else's child. Someone else fathered her, walked away, and got away with it."

"And if that were true?"

"Well . . . then, there's a place for children like her. Somewhere. I'm not sure exactly where, but I could find out. Make sure it's reputable . . ."

His voice drizzled off as the look in her eyes changed from disappointment to fury.

Heart pounding, Naomi tried to keep her voice calm and steady, but she was livid. Had he learned *nothing* in the last year? "And what sort of man would you be if you abandoned her now? What sort of woman would I be? Her mother doesn't want her. Sarah would be taken away to live in foster homes. She's a special child. Her chance of getting adopted is slim. Here, she has so many people who love her and are concerned about her. She's become a part of everyone's life in Stoney Ridge. She's part of our new life together."

Tobe looked surprised. Naomi didn't usually make speeches. He seemed startled at such strong words from her. "Naomi . . . I've been over and over it in my mind. I've thought of little else. But I always come back to this question: How can I bring up another man's child as my own?"

"You're only thinking of yourself. What sort of start in

life would Sarah have if you washed your hands of her now? She's a tiny, defenseless baby, who is missing an essential chromosome to have a normal life. Have you thought about her, Tobe? What kind of childhood would she have?"

Tobe jerked his head up, as if surprised by the line of questioning and the bite in her voice.

"Naomi, please listen to me. You asked me what difference it would make if I knew Sarah weren't mine, and I told you the truth. It's just not as simple as you're making it out to be."

"We can be the baby's parents in every way that matters. We loved this child yesterday, we still love her today. We will always love her. It's as simple as that."

After a full minute of silence she said, "Well? Aren't you going to open it?"

But he didn't, only stood rubbing his thumb over the writing, staring at it. Finally, he dropped his arms by his side. In a voice strangled with emotion, he said, "Naomi, what if Sarah happens to be the daughter of Jake Hertzler? I know Paisley and Jake had been . . . together."

"Is that what's been troubling you?" Such a thought had never occurred to her. Not once. She held out her hands to Tobe. He made an uncertain step toward her, taking her hands in his. "If that could be true . . . then it's all the more reason for us to raise her and love her as our own. To bring some good out of this whole sordid situation. You have two very simple roads to go down. To take the baby as she is. Or to walk away from her. Two clear roads."

He didn't move for a long while. He looked at Sarah, asleep in the basket. He looked at Naomi. Then he reached out and tore the letter with the DNA results into tiny pieces. He went over to Sarah and picked her up. "Love," he said quietly, "does extraordinary things to people."

Oh yes, Naomi thought. It does. It has a way of bringing out the very best in people. Her heart was full as she watched Tobe hold the baby close against his chest, tears streaming down his cheeks. In that moment, he had become the man she knew he could be. Little Sarah had done that.

And here Naomi was, getting ready to marry this wonderful man. About to become a mother to a beautiful little girl whom they needed as much as she needed them. The vista of Naomi's life had changed, and she marveled at what lay ahead.

Love did extraordinary things to people. Oh yes, it did.

Discussion Questions

1. If there's one overriding theme in this novel, it would be this: becoming your best self. Isn't that a hope we all have? For ourselves, for our loved ones. In your opinion, which character—Tobe or Naomi—grew the most and became his or her best self?

2. Some, perhaps most, of the couples in this story seem to be unlikely pairs: Naomi and Tobe, Rose and Galen, Mim and Jesse, Brooke and Jon. Consider Tobe and Naomi. Tobe is impulsive, on a quest to find himself, pulled to the outside world, and is uncertain of what his calling is. Naomi is thoroughly Amish. She leads a very sheltered, quiet life and relies heavily on her intuition and thought life. In many ways, they're complete opposites. Yet why are they drawn to each other?

3. Let's talk about Rose and Galen. Rose is older than Galen in both years and life experience. Galen has a rather narrow view of the world. He loves his sister, he loves his horses. And he loves Rose. Why does their relationship, which has its share of friction, actually work well for each other? They felt differently about

important family issues, but in what way were they both right?

4. The novel touches on many themes (love, family, forgiveness, second chances). Which do you think are the most important?

5. Brooke Snyder is a talented but hopelessly insecure young woman. Her aunt Lois said she was always copying because she had never found her "original." Her original self, she meant. How did Brooke's crippling insecurities about herself make her vulnerable to taking the wrong path? With work? With men? What a message for those of us who struggle with insecurity! And don't we all . . .

6. The importance of family is seen throughout this novel. It's so important to Naomi, for example, that she insists to Tobe that they remain in the Amish church to stay connected to their families. How did family impact Tobe and Naomi, in both positive and negative ways? How has your own family influenced your decisions for good or bad?

7. What do you think Brooke Snyder will end up doing with the Mrs. Miracle column?

8. Paisley is a mess. She's manipulative, selfish, and woefully unprepared to become a mother, especially of a child with special needs. Do you think she did the right thing for the wrong reasons by leaving the baby at Eagle Hill? Or did she do the wrong thing for the right reasons?

9. Galen and Rose experience tension over Tobe's return. Galen is very objective about Tobe and feels Rose has hobbled him with empathy. Naturally, Rose finds herself defending Tobe. "Galen," Rose warned, "a man's past is his past. It's what he contributes to the present that matters." Do you agree or disagree with Rose's remark?

10. Rose and Galen's friction is common among blended families. How does Galen's point of view about Tobe hold merit? Was there any takeaway value in how they both adjusted their expectations of Tobe?

11. Did you guess ahead of time that Jon Hoeffner was Jake Hertzler? If not, what did you think was going to happen with Jon and Brooke Snyder?

12. At the end of the novel, Tobe Schrock tore up the envelope with the results of the paternity test he had taken to determine if he was Sarah's father. He would never know for sure. What did that action mean for Tobe, and why was it such a turning point for him?

13. Another theme in the book is the idea of forgiveness, of second chances. How did you feel when Rose Schrock sent a message to Jake Hertzler to tell him he was forgiven, even though she knew he probably wouldn't even care? Why was it important for her to let her children know that was the intention of their family?

14. What did you think was ultimately the book's lesson?

Blueberry Lemon Squares
from the Inn at Eagle Hill

2 ¼ cups	all-purpose flour
½ cup	powdered sugar
1 cup (½ lb.)	butter
4 large	eggs
1 cup	sugar
1 teaspoon	grated lemon peel
⅓ cup	lemon juice (use real lemons)
½ teaspoon	baking powder
⅛ teaspoon	salt
1½ cups	blueberries, fresh and rinsed or frozen

Preheat oven to 350 degrees.

In large bowl, stir flour and ½ cup powdered sugar until blended. Add butter and stir until dough holds together. Press evenly over the bottom of a 9" x 13" pan.

Bake until crust is golden brown, 20 to 25 minutes.

While the crust is baking, beat eggs in a bowl with a mixer on medium speed (or use a whisk). Blend in sugar, lemon peel, lemon juice, baking powder, and salt. After mixing, gently stir in blueberries.

Pour egg mixture into pan over warm crust. Return to oven and bake until filling no longer jiggles when pan is gently shaken, 20 to 25 minutes. Sprinkle lightly with powdered sugar and let cool at least 15 minutes. Cut into 2" squares and lift out with a spatula. Serve warm or cool. If making up to a day ahead, wrap airtight when cool and chill.

Makes 24 squares.

Acknowledgments

I would like to thank my family for their encouragement and support. In particular, my daughter, Lindsey, for her insights and guiding comments. To my sister, Wendy, too. Both of them read messy first drafts and helped find the good and bad in my work. To A.J. Salch, for answering odd questions about Thoroughbred stallions. To her parents, Kim and Clayton, for providing true stories of childhood mischief that make it so often into my books. Thanks to Mary Ann Kinsinger, who helped me create a baptism scene that rang true.

In terms of print and paper, much gratitude goes to the team at Revell, who transform a bulky Word document into a book. Thank you to Michele Misiak, for marketing brainstorming, to Barb Barnes, for her editorial precision and long-suffering patience. To my remarkable editor, Andrea Doering, for cracking open the world of publication to me and keeping that door open. A special shout-out to my steadfast agent, Joyce Hart of The Hartline Literary Agency, for the dozen

323

roses she sent to celebrate my twelfth contract with Revell. You're all such delightful people to work with.

Hands lifted up high in praise to God for granting me this author gig and giving me a deep love of the written word.

Last of all, but never least of all, my heartfelt gratitude to you readers, near and far, for reading my stories. I love hearing from you—the good, the bad, and the ugly. I can take it. Just don't stop reading!

Fondly,
Suzanne
www.suzannewoodsfisher.com

Suzanne Woods Fisher is the author of the bestselling Lancaster County Secrets and Stoney Ridge Seasons series. *The Search* received a 2012 Carol Award, *The Waiting* was a finalist for the 2011 Christy Award, and *The Choice* was a finalist for the 2011 Carol Award. Suzanne's grandfather was raised in the Old Order German Baptist Brethren Church in Franklin County, Pennsylvania. Her interest in living a simple, faith-filled life began with her Dunkard cousins. Suzanne is also the author of the bestselling *Amish Peace: Simple Wisdom for a Complicated World* and *Amish Proverbs: Words of Wisdom from the Simple Life*, both finalists for the ECPA Book of the Year award, and *Amish Values for Your Family: What We Can Learn from the Simple Life*. She has an app, Amish Wisdom, to deliver a proverb a day to your iPhone, iPad, or Android. Visit her at www.suzannewoodsfisher.com to find out more.

Suzanne lives with her family and big yellow dogs in the San Francisco Bay Area.

Meet Suzanne online at

 Suzanne Woods Fisher

🐦 suzannewfisher

www.SuzanneWoodsFisher.com

Download the
Free **Amish Wisdom** App

WELCOME TO A PLACE OF UNCONDITIONAL LOVE AND UNEXPECTED BLESSINGS

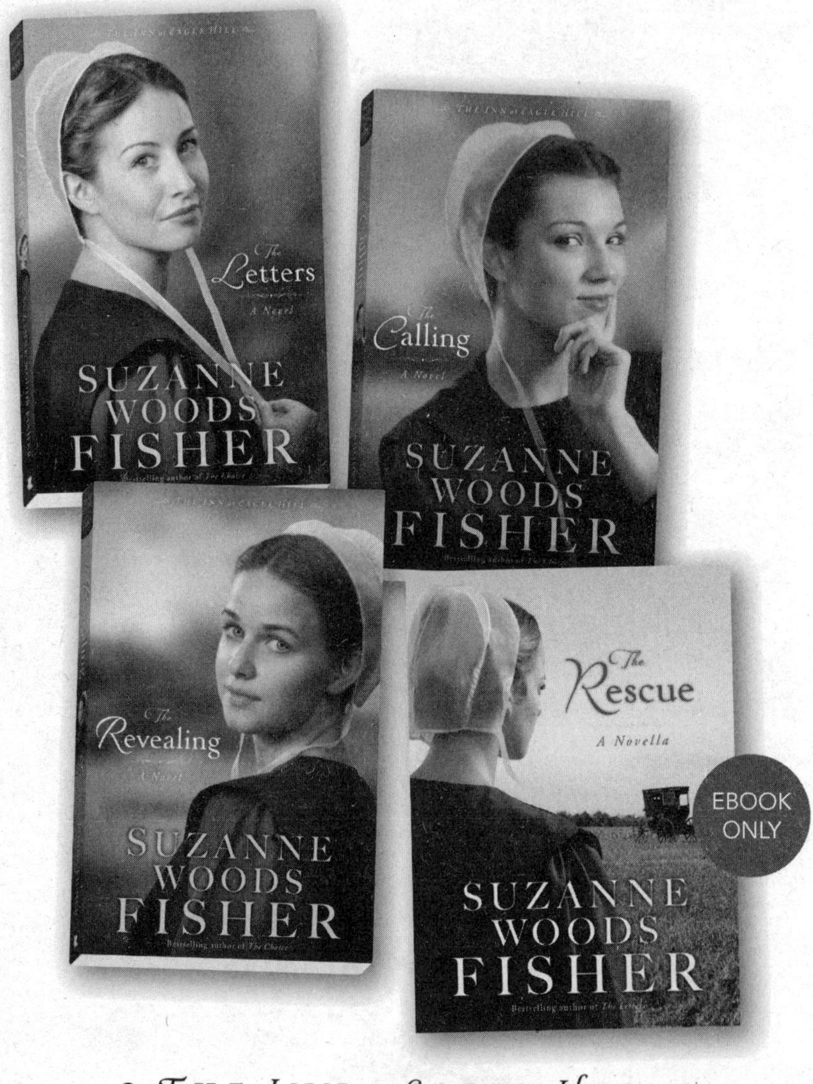

 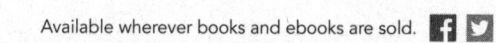

"Everything I love in a novel . . .
Fast paced, character driven, filled with
rich descriptions and enjoyable dialogue."
—SHELLEY SHEPARD GRAY,
New York Times and *USA Today* bestselling author

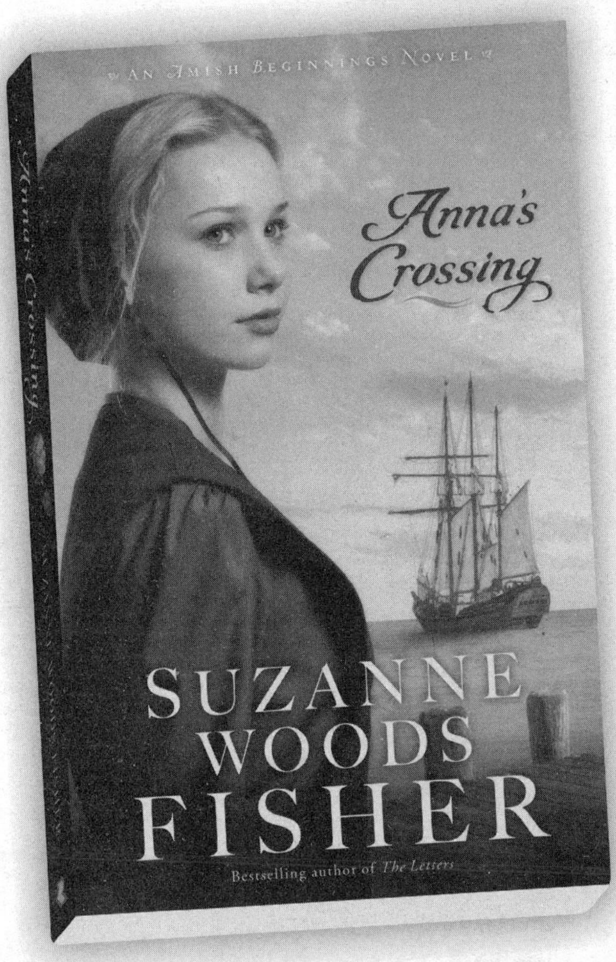

AN AMISH BEGINNINGS NOVEL

Anna's Crossing

SUZANNE
WOODS
FISHER

Bestselling author of *The Letters*

Suzanne Woods Fisher invites you back to the beginning of Amish life
in America with this fascinating glimpse into the first ocean crossing—
and the lives of two intrepid people who braved it.